SECRET KISSES

STERLING BROTHERS
BOOK 3

LAYLA HAGEN

Cover Design: Uplifting Designs

CHAPTER 1
GRIFFIN

"UNCLE GRIFFIN, YOUR HOUSE IS AWESOME," my nephew, Jeremy, said.

"Glad you think so."

He'd asked for another tour of my place after I'd already given one to the family. I was happy to spend the extra time with him as we walked together down the main hall.

"You can visit me anytime you want, even for a sleepover," I said.

I used to live in a bachelor condo before, which wasn't really suitable for sleepovers. It was basically one huge room with no privacy. Now, I had a luxury villa in the Wooded Area neighborhood within Point Loma.

Jeremy and my brother Duncan, along with his fiancée, Riley, lived closer to downtown. My brother was damn lucky. He'd done a great job as a single dad, but there was no denying that both he and Jeremy were happier now that Riley was part of their life.

We went downstairs to the living room, where the rest of my family was. The view through the floor-to-ceiling windows was amazing. There were many pine and fir trees surrounding the property, shielding my house from my neighbors. Everyone was milling around, conversing among themselves, while Mom inspected the fireplace. It was never warm enough to actually need a fire in San Diego, but I liked the optics of it.

Dad came over to me and put a hand on my shoulder. "Son, you've got a nice house. Congrats."

"Thanks," I said. Hearing that from him made me proud.

Mom, who was now looking at some photos above the fireplace, smiled at me. "I'm so happy you've still got this picture. I don't think I have a copy."

"I can make you one," I offered.

It was of all of us as kids before they divorced. We'd been on a trip with the tent. Most of us still had a camping bug, except Duncan. He hated it. Whenever Jeremy wanted to go, our youngest brothers Knox and Finn usually took him.

"Griffin, I'm jealous of this place," Hannah said. She was my brother Chase's fiancée and one of my favorite people in the world.

"You're welcome here anytime," I assured her. They lived nearby, so it was convenient for them to visit.

Glancing behind her, I noticed Chase and Wyatt helping themselves to my bar.

"How come you asked us to come over today instead of tomorrow?" Wyatt asked loudly as he poured himself a scotch. We'd originally planned my housewarming for tomorrow, but business calls.

"Because I've got a meeting later tonight for a potential business deal tomorrow, and I didn't want to have to cancel on you if need be. I'll throw another housewarming party some other time, though." Since I'd moved the get-together to today, Knox, Finn, and Riley couldn't join us, so I would definitely have another one soon.

"A business deal?" Duncan asked.

That got everyone's attention. My brothers and I had set up

Sterling Investments years ago. It was one of the biggest companies offering financial advice in the country, and it had made us very rich. But now only Chase and Duncan were running it full-time, while the rest of us worked on an as-needed basis. We had a weekly strategy meeting but didn't deal with the day-to-day operations. We'd each set up our own individual companies to run instead.

Wyatt raised a brow at me. "Is it with that Carson guy?" I'd mentioned it to him a while ago.

I nodded, focusing on the rest of the family. "Yes. Jude Carson owns a huge dating website, and I want to invest in it."

"That's interesting. What gave you the idea?" Chase asked.

"It's a booming market. People nowadays all seem to prefer meeting people online." That wasn't my thing, although I *had* signed up on Jude's website because I didn't want to invest in something I had no knowledge about.

"It's definitely a growing market," Duncan said.

I liked sharing business ideas with my brothers. They were among the smartest people I knew.

"They want to expand, and they're looking for investors. I have money." I shrugged. I also thought it might be fun too.

"Darling, you look concerned," Mom said. How did she pick up on that?

"The guy wasn't excited when I first set up the meeting," I admitted.

"Then maybe it's not the right move, son," Dad said.

"We'll see."

I didn't want to shut Dad down, but I wasn't the type who shied away when something was challenging. I was looking forward to meeting Jude Carson and finding out what made him tick. I liked working with people. It was one of the reasons why I essentially broke off from Sterling Investments. I needed more client contact, and my work at the company had been mostly strategic.

"I'm curious how this will turn out," Mom said. "By the way, and not to change the subject, but I've started offering cooking classes at the store, too, in addition to the yoga and pottery classes. If you know anyone who's interested, I'm offering a discount on the first class."

"I'll spread the word," I promised, and there was a murmur of agreement around the room. We all tried to support our parents as best as we could. Chase took the cake, though.

A year ago, he bought back the store they'd owned when we were kids. Our parents sold it after their divorce because they couldn't make the mortgage payments. They'd used the profit they made from the sale after paying what they owed to the bank to start over.

"So will I," Hannah said. "I'll share it with the guests who stay at the inn."

"Thank you," Mom replied, smiling at her.

"You can count on me, Grandma. I'll tell people at school." Jeremy nodded solemnly, looking like a carbon copy of Duncan.

Mom was over the moon. At first, I'd been skeptical about her and Dad being so close together for so many hours a day, considering they couldn't see eye to eye for years after the divorce. However, after Jeremy was born, they mellowed out a bit, and then to everyone's surprise, they were getting along fine. Hell, they were even semi-dating, although I didn't know all the details and didn't *want* to know them. Besides, they were each following their passion. Mom offered pottery, yoga, and now cooking classes, and Dad had a shop selling fishing equipment.

"All right, everyone. Let's order some dinner. I tried a nearby pizza restaurant earlier this week, and it was great," I said, looking straight at Jeremy.

He jumped up and down. "Yes! You're the best, Uncle Griffin."

Duncan chuckled. Yeah, I knew it was Jeremy's favorite. That's why I suggested it in the first place. Then again, it was usually a crowd pleaser. The rest of the family instantly agreed to the idea as well.

"While we wait, how about I make some cocktails for everyone?" I suggested.

"Yes!" Jeremy exclaimed. "Can I help you?"

"Sure, buddy. Why not?"

The combined kitchen and bar area was a huge space—perfect for entertaining. We all gathered around the counter.

"Hit me up with what you want, everyone. Search for the recipe online, too, so I can check if I have the ingredients."

"I'll go easy on you," Duncan said. "I want a mojito."

"That's real easy," I agreed, taking out the chopping board so I could cut up the lime.

Jeremy came next to me, looking up expectantly.

"Jeremy, you can crush the ice."

He nodded. "Okay."

I liked having the family here in my home. Buying this house was one of my best ideas. It was far larger than what I needed, but it accommodated us all nicely without being overly uncomfortable.

While I took out a pack of sugar, my mind drifted to the meeting I had tomorrow. It was a good sign that he'd agreed to see me on a Saturday. It meant there was real interest on his end. As a rule, I usually took time off on weekends, but I'd made an exception this time.

"Uncle Griffin, you're doing it wrong," Jeremy said. *Well, fuck.* I'd been about to make my brother's mojito with lemon instead of lime. "Are you thinking about work? Dad always says that thinking about the office in the kitchen is a bad idea."

Duncan smiled proudly.

"Guilty as charged," I replied.

Jeremy pointed at me. "That's no good."

"You're right. I promise to focus 100 percent on making drinks."

Jeremy grinned instantly. "Yes, yes, yes." The little guy liked to learn new things—and he'd probably make a great bartender when he grew up.

"All right, lesson learned," I said as I turned to take everyone else's orders.

Duncan was the only one who went easy on me. All the other cocktails required far more concentration. But that was fine. Tonight was for my family. Business could wait until tomorrow.

CHAPTER 2
PHOEBE

"OH GOD, THIS PLACE IS A DUMP," my best friend, Veronica, said.

I laughed. "Good morning to you too. And yes, it is. Do you need help?"

She'd accidentally stepped on a weak board on the front porch. Fortunately, she didn't hurt herself.

"No, I'm good," she said.

"Good thing I took the coffees from you beforehand. I'm going to mark that spot so we can sidestep it."

Veronica looked up at me with worried eyes. "You're sure this place doesn't have termites?"

I winced. "We had it inspected before buying it, so I hope not. I really can't deal with another financial blow right now."

"Okay."

"Come on, let's go inside. I made breakfast."

"Oh, it's *that* bad," Veronica muttered.

My friend knew me well. I usually skipped food in the morning, even on weekends, so whenever I made it, that meant I needed comfort food first thing in the morning. I'd made waffles. Yeah, that was a bad sign. I kept thinking my life couldn't get any worse, yet somehow it did with every passing week. I had some bad news to share with my best friend, and I'd told her as much on the phone.

Once inside, Veronica glanced around and pressed her lips together. She didn't have to say it. The place looked dreadful. I knew that. Honestly, it was practically a teardown. But City Heights was a decent neighborhood, and the house had two bedrooms and a tiny bathroom. The highlight was the small backyard. It looked dreamy, especially now in June, with the bougainvillea in bloom.

It was supposed to be mine and my boyfriend's starter home. We were going to renovate it together but never got the chance because he dumped me soon after we bought it. The same day I'd moved out of the apartment we shared and into this musty house.

The kitchen was furnished, and there was a bed and dresser in one bedroom, but I had to buy everything else, and nothing matched. This house had old-school wooden panels everywhere. I'd found a comfy gray couch on sale, but I didn't have any lighting fixtures at all, only naked light bulbs.

The dining room table and chairs were actually meant for outdoors, but they were a steal. Veronica didn't comment on them as we sat down. I'd already set the table so we could eat right away.

Everything was a mess—the house, the furniture, and my life. At least I'd started a part-time job as an accountant last week at H&R Block. It paid peanuts, but I needed something on my résumé other than "office assistant."

"Your waffles are amazing," she said after the first bite.

"I know, right? Thought I'd start the day by treating myself to something delicious."

Veronica gulped down her meal in silence. She was a breakfast person, and it was already nine o'clock. No wonder she was starving.

We finished the waffles in no time. Nodding at the coffee

cups, she said, "Want to go out in the backyard and sit in those comfy swings while we drink our coffee?"

I grinned, nodding. "Yes, let's go." I'd found the swings at Goodwill and was *so* proud of my purchase.

Grabbing our coffees, we headed to the back door. The wooden floor creaked like crazy on every step. I needed to get out of this place but knew that wasn't possible. I was stuck until my ex and I managed to sell it.

Veronica and I each sat on a swing. I closed my eyes, gently rocking back and forth. She wasn't saying anything, but I could feel that she was bursting at the seams.

A few minutes later, she said, "So… what do you need as a housewarming gift?"

"Oh, nothing, really."

"Are you certain?" She glanced over her shoulder, as if she could see through the walls. "Because you could use some things."

I nodded. "Like a life, huh? Yeah, I know."

"Phoebe," Veronica said with affection in her voice, "I shouldn't have mentioned it."

"It's kind of you to offer. Thanks for being in my corner."

"You can always count on me. I just wish you didn't have to go through this."

"Yeah, so do I."

Marshall and I had been together for six years. I met him in grad school, when he was just finishing his residency. Once he opened his own general practice office, he asked me to work as his office assistant. I was thrilled, although it was definitely not a good use for my accounting degree, but I'd wanted to build something together. But the years passed, and he didn't propose. Last week, we were supposed to go on our most romantic trip yet, to Maui. We were celebrating our anniversary. I'd hoped he was going to take the hint and propose. Three weeks before we were supposed to leave, he said that he couldn't be with me anymore.

I'd felt as if someone hit me in the face with a baseball bat. I left that very evening, packing all my clothes and fleeing from the apartment we'd shared. He didn't even try to stop me.

"So, what's the bad news?" Veronica asked with trepidation. "Is something wrong with the house?"

I shook my head. "Not exactly. Marshall is back in town."

"He come back rested and tanned from the trip?" Veronica asked with a snort.

The trip had been prepaid, and we had zero chance of getting the money back. I wasn't even mad that he still went on it. I didn't have any energy left to be mad. Besides, it wasn't as if I would have gone anyway.

That was the last thing on my mind. I'd been too busy figuring out a way to live and where to work.

"Something like that. He wants to meet with me," I said.

Veronica snapped her head up. "Oh hell no. I hope you told him no."

I sighed. "I didn't."

"Why not? Come on. You're going to take a look at that guy and cry your eyes out again for weeks."

"I don't think I can cry any longer." She scoffed, and I rolled my eyes at her. "Really! I have zero tears left. I promise. I've been trying to cry the past few evenings, and nothing comes out."

"Fuck him. Why does he want to meet?"

"I'm assuming he wants to discuss the sale of this place. We're both trapped making mortgage payments until we can get rid of it. And now he's paying rent by himself for his apartment and—"

"Please tell me you don't feel sorry for him."

I shook my head vehemently. "No. Honestly, not even one bit."

He'd hurt me too much for that.

"I don't love you anymore, Phoebe. I haven't in a while. I can't be with you anymore." It was a day I'd never forget.

In hindsight, I could see red flags everywhere. We'd grown

apart quite a bit. We were bickering more often, going to bed without touching each other. But I thought it might be just the stress of buying this place.

I'd been so damn wrong.

"Anyway, we haven't had any inquiries. I'm sure we'll have to lower the price."

"Even your realtor said the price was too high. Marshall was the one who set it anyway. Why the hell does he have to talk to you? He should talk to the realtor."

Veronica had lost her cool completely. I didn't have the energy to be angry anymore. I simply felt drained and overwhelmed at the prospect of having to start over, not only on a personal level but on a professional one.

"How about I come with you?" she offered.

I smiled nervously. "I was going to ask you to do that."

"Fantastic. I'm going to tell that guy to shove it."

"No, not to the actual meeting," I corrected before Veronica got all geared up. "I was hoping you could hang out at the bar while he and I talk."

"Where are you meeting him?"

"The Loft," I said.

Her eyes bulged. "Really? You're living in this dump, and he wants to splurge at The Loft? I hope he's buying."

I laughed. "If he doesn't, the joke's on him. I'm so broke, I can't even afford an olive at that place. But I didn't want to go back and forth with him when he suggested it. I just wanted to end the conversation."

"I don't blame you. When is it?"

"Tonight."

Her eyes widened. "Wow. Way to spring this on me, girl."

I sighed. "He called last night, but I didn't have any energy left to call you."

"All right. Let's do this," Veronica said.

I loved her so much. She was like the sister I never had. I was a single child. Mom and Dad suggested that they could move back here temporarily after Marshall and I broke up, but I assured them that I could do this on my own. They were in Montana, taking care of my grandparents, who were in their late nineties.

When I was growing up, they lived here, too, in the house next to ours. It had been a big dream of mine to have a child while they were still alive so they'd meet their great-grandchild. But that ship had obviously sailed. I was never becoming a mother. The thought punched a hole in my chest.

Veronica shifted her chair closer to mine. "You know what? Let's go to my place, spend the day there, and raid my closet for a hot dress for this evening."

"Thanks! I'd love that." Most of my stuff was still in bags. I didn't have the interest to put them in these musty old dressers, afraid they had bugs in them. Besides, it would do me good to wear something new. Well, new for me. I had zero budget for shopping, so Veronica's offer was amazing.

We used to do that a lot in our college years. We'd been so broke that we kept swapping clothes to keep our outfits "fresh." A day away from this dump with my best friend was exactly what I needed.

Veronica tilted her head. "You know what would be great? If we conjure up a hunk for you tonight. Just to rub it in Marshall's face."

I laughed. "Oh, Veronica. I trust that you have many skills, but even you can't pull that off."

She sighed wistfully. "I know I can't. But it's nice to dream, isn't it?"

I couldn't argue with that.

She snapped her fingers, as if she'd just had a brilliant idea. "I know exactly what dress you'll be wearing tonight. You'll look like a rock star."

I grinned. "I can't wait."

CHAPTER 3
GRIFFIN

JUDE CARSON and I were meeting at The Loft. I arrived five minutes before our meeting time. The server nodded when I told him my name.

"The rest of your party is already here at the table."

"Thank you."

I'd been in business long enough to know what that meant. By being the first one here, he'd established it as his territory. I wasn't worried, though. I was good at negotiating on anyone's turf. I preferred mine, of course, but I was adaptable.

The server led me to a table right in the center of the restaurant. The Loft was a very sought-after location in the city, although not one of my favorites. Many people wanted to be seen here, and that wasn't my MO. I preferred to be more discreet.

Jude was in his late fifties, slim with short gray hair. He rose to his feet, shaking my hand, and then we both sat at the table. He tapped his finger impatiently on the surface.

"Thank you for making the time to meet me," I said.

"Of course. May I call you Griffin?"

"I prefer it, actually." There were so many of us Sterlings that I was always confused when someone said "Mr. Sterling."

"Griffin, I'm very surprised that you're interested in my company."

That caught me off guard. "Why? You're in a growing market. You want to expand, and you need capital. I have that in spades."

"Yes, but I was under the impression that your family operates in the financial services area."

I waved my hand. "That's how we started, correct. But I've personally invested in multiple other businesses, and I act as an adviser. Most of my investments are in the digital world. It's what I know."

"Right." As he nodded, a waiter came to us with the drinks menu. I asked for a surprise aperitif. He did the same.

Once the waiter headed toward the bar, I went on with my pitch. "I have all the qualities you're searching for in an investor."

Jude frowned. Not good. I came on too strong.

"Why don't we do this another way?" I suggested. "You tell me what you're looking for."

"Ideally, someone who knows my market. Someone who's grown businesses before."

"I check both boxes," I replied with confidence.

He shook his head slightly. "I'm not so sure. I want someone who *understands* my market."

"I read extensively about the industry before I contacted you. From what I've researched, it's grown by leaps and bounds these past few years. Today, people generally spend less time in places where they could meet dating prospects. They tend to hang with the friends they already have. That's why they turn to apps like yours to find partners. It's quick and convenient. If a date doesn't work out, you waste no time finding another one."

He stared at me but didn't say anything as the waiter returned with our drinks.

As soon as we were alone again, he scoffed. "Quick and convenient? Griffin, that tells me you don't understand anything about *my* business. Frankly, it doesn't surprise me. Not many investors do."

I cleared my throat and fought to keep my tone polite. "What makes you say that?"

"I'm not in the business of facilitating hookups like other dating sites. Have you even read our mission statement?"

I blinked. "I did glance through it." In my opinion, mission statements were just pretty words intended to make a company look good. They rarely had anything to do with the truth.

"But did you pay close attention to it?"

Man, this guy was tough.

"No," I admitted. I thought it best not to say any more, as I could tell he was not thrilled with my answer.

"Right. Let me explain. Our goal is for people to find lifelong partners. We're not looking for repeat customers. In fact, we consider it a personal victory if they *don't* return to us and are happy with the partner they found."

I took a sip of my drink because I couldn't possibly keep a straight face. *He can't mean that. It's complete hogwash.* That was not how these sites made money.

"That's an admirable goal," I said. There, that sounded neutral.

"We survey our previous customers after the two-year mark and the five-year mark. Most of them are still with the partner they found through our platform. We rarely have repeat business." He was obviously very proud of their accomplishments.

"And yet you keep growing."

"That's through customer acquisition and word of mouth. When a customer is happy with something, they share with others." Jude sipped his drink, then nodded to me. "As you said, more and more people prefer to search for partners online. Our filters help them narrow down to people they have things in common with."

"Fantastic. I'm fluent in customer acquisition. The Sterling Investment Group has mastered obtaining clients in our business. Based on your analytics, I noticed that you could grow exponentially in the younger demographic, eighteen to twenty-five. I've reviewed your stats, and you're completely over-looking that age group. They're some of the heaviest users of dating apps."

"Yes, but see, they're not our target market at all. Young people are not looking to settle down, and we're not Tinder."

I nodded once. "Understood. I find your mission statement admirable, as I've said. But it's financially unwise to completely discard a group of potential customers."

He straightened up in his chair. "Griffin, you and I have very different visions for the company. I feared as much. I took the liberty of asking around about you." That didn't faze me at all. It was normal. "You have an interesting reputation."

I was extremely proud of it—I was known for being astute, smart, and hardworking. I couldn't think of a single person who'd say something negative about me.

"And you have a different woman on your arm every other month," he continued.

Whoa! I was stunned at first but recovered after a few seconds. *What the hell?*

"How is that relevant to the conversation at hand? And I don't appreciate the invasion of my privacy."

He scoffed. "Like you didn't have me looked up? Let's not quibble."

"Of course," I said. "But I asked people about your business acumen, not your personal life."

He held up his hands in self-defense. "That's fair, and I'm sorry. I didn't mean to intrude. But I want to work with people who understand the product. Who know what it's like to have a committed relationship, or at least want one. It's paramount to the success of the company. Otherwise, you can't support our marketing campaigns or our vision."

"So, everyone who's on your team is happily married?" I

sounded harsh, but I couldn't help myself. This was unbelievable. I was an excellent businessman. The rest shouldn't matter.

"Quite a few of them are. Look... investors usually want decision power."

"Yes, I'd want to be involved in all the processes. I don't just hand out money and become a silent investor. I want to help shape the company."

"And I want someone who shares my vision to shape it."

I had mad respect for him despite the fact that he was essentially turning down my offer. He was sticking to his guns. Still, the guy had a solid business, and I knew this hurdle wasn't insurmountable. But I also knew that pushing more tonight wouldn't help my cause—quite to the contrary. He'd made up his mind, and I wasn't going to persist.

"All right, well, I don't think there's a reason we should waste each other's Saturday evening," I said, summing up.

"No, there isn't," he agreed. "I've got the bill."

"No, don't worry about it. It's on me!"

"Thank you for your time, Griffin. Have a great weekend."

"And you."

I wasn't going to back down—I hadn't built a business empire with my brothers by giving up at the slightest inconvenience—but I'd completely underestimated his commitment to his mission statement. I was going to revise my pitch and approach him again, but one thing did bother me. How the hell did he know my dating habits? I was discreet, though apparently not enough so. My brothers sometimes teased me about it, but I'd brushed off their concerns.

Regardless, tonight was a bust. I wanted to stay for a drink, but I could do that at the bar. I preferred it to sitting by myself in the restaurant area, which just seemed awkward.

Getting up and heading that way, I saw there were plenty of seats at the counter. I zeroed in on a gorgeous blonde as I grabbed a stool. She wore a sparkling red dress and high heels with straps circling her ankles. There was a brunette next to her who was looking around the room furiously.

Fuck me, Jude was right. I was a manwhore. It wasn't a conscious thing. I just wasn't one for relationships. Then again, I'd never really tried having one. Dating was my thing. Relationships? Absolutely not.

"How dare he be late," the brunette exclaimed.

"He's not late," the blonde bombshell responded. "We just arrived a bit early. He's still got about ten minutes."

"Well, I stand by what I said. I can't even believe he's got the nerve to ask you to meet him after crapping on you after a six-year relationship."

The blonde's smile dropped. It was as if someone had snuffed the light out of her beautiful eyes. "Please don't say that again. It hurts me right here," she said, putting a hand to her chest.

Fuck that moron, whoever he is. I hated people like him. Why commit when you were obviously incapable of following through? My way was much better. I never made promises, never misled anyone.

I wasn't usually one to eavesdrop, but I couldn't block out the conversation next to me. Especially when the brunette said, "Oh, damn it, he's here. I'll wait for you at the bar. You tell me if you want me to intervene or something."

"I'm sure that's not going to be necessary, but I am grateful that you're here. Thanks."

I watched the blonde as she slid off her chair and walked to one of the tables. Then I focused my attention on the bartender and asked for a scotch on the rocks. It was my favorite drink.

The brunette kept her eyes on her friend and the guy who'd just arrived. She didn't order anything.

The bartender handed me the scotch, and while taking a few sips, I kept replaying the meeting with Jude over and over in my mind.

"Oh no," the brunette murmured a few minutes later. "I'm going to kill him."

"Want help?" I asked. I couldn't help myself. And besides, thinking about the issue with Jude was pointless right now. I needed a solid strategy, and I wasn't going to develop it while drinking scotch. I was still a bit pissed about him calling me out. Really, what did someone's dating record have to do with anything?

The brunette turned to look at me, narrowing her eyes, obviously annoyed that I'd been listening. "You've been sitting here a while, huh? I wasn't sure if you were eavesdropping or not."

"Hey, you weren't exactly keeping your voice down."

She nodded. "Yeah, that's true."

She turned to look at her friend and groaned. "Oh, that fucker. I always knew he wasn't good for her, you know. He jerked Phoebe around for years, and then he broke her heart. Crap! I should have hired someone to pretend to be her boyfriend this evening or something."

I looked at her incredulously, but she seemed completely serious.

Eh, why not?

"You know what? I'll do it. No need to pay me."

I had no idea what possessed me to do it. I was impulsive, but even for me, this was insane. The truth was, I was simply looking for an excuse to meet the blonde.

What a strange evening this was. It kept taking unexpected turns.

CHAPTER 4
PHOEBE

I WAS A MESS. I ordered a glass of pinot noir to calm my nerves and stupidly didn't even check the prices beforehand. God, I hoped Marshall picked up the tab. I couldn't afford twenty-eight bucks for a glass of wine. I didn't even know it could cost that much.

I sat straighter on my chair. Out of the corner of my eye, I noticed Veronica smiling at me from the bar.

Marshall hadn't seen her yet, but I didn't care if he did. I wouldn't apologize for needing the support of my best friend after what he put me through.

"You look great," he said once the waiter left with our drink orders. He was tan, and his hair had blond streaks from the sun, presumably from what was to have been our vacation.

I opened my mouth and realized I didn't even know how to start a conversation with him. I didn't know how to make small talk. What was I supposed to say? Ask him if he had fun on what was supposed to be *our* trip?

I rolled my shoulders back. "So, what was so important that you didn't want to tell me over the phone? Why did you need to meet me?"

He grimaced. "Look, I don't think there's any good way to

tell you this, so I'm just going to rip off the Band-Aid. I'm getting married."

I felt as if someone had just hit me with a ton of bricks. For a few seconds, my vision blurred, and my mouth went dry. I was about to fall out of my chair.

"I wanted you to find out from me, not from anyone else."

I grabbed my throat, but no words came out. Finally, I croaked, "How is that possible?"

He winced. "Do you really want details?"

Did I? I was trying not to scream or cry. But for some reason, I needed to know, even though I wasn't sure it would make me feel better.

"Yes, I fucking do. I deserve to know." I thought he might have gotten cold feet at the idea of proposing, and that's why he broke up with me. Ack, I felt ill.

"Listen, Adriana and I… Well, it's been going on for a while."

Oh my God! And I'd thought this couldn't get any more painful. I pushed back the tears as he continued.

"And then things became clear in Maui, and I proposed."

"Wait, you took her on *our* trip?" My voice was robotic. I felt like I was going to break out of my skin from so much pain. This simply couldn't be happening.

"Pheebs, it was a waste not to go with anyone since it was already prepaid. Anyway, I wanted you to know from me. And I'm sure that one day you're going to meet a guy—"

"Babe, here you are. Sorry I'm late," a male voice said.

What? I looked over my shoulder at the source of the voice. He was possibly the most handsome man alive. And had obviously mistaken me for someone else.

"I'm so—" I began, but he turned to Marshall and said, "And you must be Marshall, huh? I've heard a lot about you. Nothing good."

What is happening? Did Veronica pay someone to butt in and stop this nightmare?

"I'm sorry, you are…?" Marshall asked.

"Griffin Sterling. I'm with Phoebe."

I chanced a glance at Veronica, who was grinning. Clearly, this was her doing. I opened my mouth but then closed it again. I had no idea what to say.

"Wait, you've got a date?" Marshall said. He had the nerve to sound affronted. "And you let me talk all this time, making me feel guilty?"

Somehow, I got my voice back, along with my courage. "Oh sure, Marshall, because me showing up with a date is on the same level as you cheating on me, taking another woman on the trip I paid for, and then coming here to tell me to my face that you're going to get married."

The hot guy—Griffin, apparently—put an arm around my shoulders, and I immediately felt warm at the contact. He brushed my bare arm with his fingers, drawing small circles with them. My skin turned to goose bumps beneath his touch. *Goodness, this guy is electrifying my body.*

Marshall stared at exactly that spot. A sudden rush of satisfaction filled me. Maybe this guy was my guardian angel, come to save me from more humiliation. It certainly felt good watching Marshall's face. I mean, this stranger was about a hundred times more handsome than my ex. It was quite funny, actually.

"Well, Marshall," I said, because I couldn't stand being near him any longer, "thank you for meeting me and updating me on your personal life. Let's never do this again. If you want to communicate with me about the house or anything, just email me. There's no need to meet again."

"You heard my girl," Griffin said. "Time to take a hike so she and I can start our evening."

Marshall stared at him and then at me. "We still need to talk about the house."

I winced, and Griffin's grip on me tightened. Marshall had some nerve. He really thought he could come here, break my heart all over again, and then casually discuss the house?

"Email my realtor," I said.

Marshall opened his mouth, but Griffin cut him off. "No. Just get out. You're disturbing our romantic evening."

Marshall didn't reply, just pushed the chair backward and shot up to his feet. "Whatever," he said to me. "I'll be in touch."

He took one last look at Griffin before turning around and leaving, and I thought I heard my knight in shining armor mumble, "Asshole."

The second Marshall was out of sight, I let out a huge breath of relief, as if someone had just taken a weight off me. Then Griffin straightened up and removed his arm, and I felt cold.

I looked up at him. "Um, thanks. I hope my friend bought you a drink or something. I do appreciate your coming to my rescue."

He flashed me a smile. "You're welcome."

I opened my mouth to ask what in the ever-loving hell was happening, but I noticed Veronica hurrying to the table with an apologetic look. She sat on the chair that Marshall vacated.

"Don't kill me. Or Griffin. It was my idea."

"Well," Griffin said, "mine too."

"Will one of you explain what's going on?" I asked.

I turned to look at my best friend. For some reason, I couldn't maintain eye contact with Griffin. My cheeks heated up whenever he zeroed in on me.

"It looked like Marshall was accosting you, so I figured a date would help the matter."

"And I volunteered," Griffin said.

"That sounds a bit weird, but thanks again," I said honestly.

Veronica laughed. "Well, you know me. I'm weird and wild, and apparently so is Griffin." Then she asked, "So, what happened exactly? What the hell did he want?"

I took in a deep breath. "To tell me he's getting married to the woman he'd been seeing on the side."

She gasped. "Oh my God, I knew it. I was sure he had someone else. That jackass!"

"He proposed to her on the trip." *Oops, here come the tears.* I vehemently pushed them back.

Veronica jerked her head back. "He actually went on your trip with another woman?"

I nodded. "Never mind. I don't want to rehash it. I just can't believe he had the nerve to say he wanted to talk about the house after he dropped that bombshell."

It felt a bit bizarre to talk about my life with a stranger at the table. But Veronica didn't seem to have any problems.

She fixated on Griffin. "Just to fill you in, they bought a house together and were supposed to renovate it. Now she's stuck making mortgage payments while living in that dump."

Veronica really had a gift for synthesizing things. Was my life really as pathetic as it sounded?

"What the actual fuck?" Griffin asked. "Sorry, that's just fucked up."

"Right?" I said, pleased with his reaction, then turned to my friend. "How about we talk about something else?" I turned back and this time did manage to make eye contact with Griffin *and* held his gaze. "So, Griffin, do you usually chat up strange women in bars?"

His smile faltered for the first time. I had the feeling that I'd struck a nerve. But what kind of guy agreed to do what he just did?

"As a matter of fact, I do. Seems I even have a reputation of doing that. And it cost me a business deal tonight."

Goodness, that was raw. Obviously, I hit the nail on the head.

"Oh, I'm sorry to hear that. I wish we could help in some way. I mean, to return the favor," I said, realizing that there was no way we could help him. Still, it seemed the right thing to do considering he'd done me a solid.

"Unfortunately, no." He looked from me to Veronica. "It was great meeting you tonight, ladies."

"You were a great help," she replied. "Thanks again."

"Mission accomplished, then. Now, I'll leave the two of you

to enjoy the evening. Don't want to be a third wheel and all that." He tried to flag a waiter, but it was pointless. "I'll pay at the bar."

I took out my wallet. "No, let me pay for that," I said, even though I was absolutely broke. "It's the least I can do."

Griffin cocked a brow, clearly taken aback. "I won't hear of it. In fact, I'm going to leave my credit card on your tab. Tonight is on me."

"What? No, no, no. Why would you do that?"

"Because your night could possibly be worse than mine. There isn't much I can do about it, but I can offer you drinks. Grab some appetizers too. Go wild." He winked, and I melted.

I didn't protest this time, because Griffin's smile seemed genuine.

"All right, thanks," I said. I was just going to have the one drink, though.

Veronica was grinning from ear to ear. "Griffin, you are one hell of a guy. If you need anyone to vouch for you with your business partner, just let me know. I will gladly give you a reference."

Griffin started to laugh. "Somehow, I think that would work against me."

He nodded at us before leaving the table.

The second he was out of earshot, Veronica leaned in. "Do you hate me?"

"No, of course not. But this was a bit weird, even for you."

"I know, I know. But it was worth it to see that look on Marshall's face, wasn't it?"

A huge smile took over my own face as I admitted, "Hell yes."

CHAPTER 5
GRIFFIN

ON MONDAY MORNING, I met my brothers in the big meeting room at Sterling Investments as usual. The headquarters was on the corner of 4th Avenue and Market Street. We started the week by holding a strategic meeting, discussing the movements in the stock market from the past week. Once that was over, the team filtered out, leaving just us brothers. This was the fun part. We gave one another advice and also exchanged ideas about other potential markets we could get into. It was the highlight of my day.

"You're awfully quiet today," Chase said after we'd finished discussing marketing ideas for the other business we'd started together: a winery in Napa Valley. We'd decided on it after careful research, and I was enjoying setting up a new business with my brothers.

"How did your meeting about the dating app go?" Wyatt asked.

"Not well," I said. I wasn't used to admitting defeat. Although, I wasn't yet considering this a lost cause.

"He wasn't looking for an investor after all?" Duncan asked. "That sucks."

"No, he is. He just doesn't think I'm a good fit."

"That's insane," Wyatt said. I liked his confidence in me. "Did he give you a reason?"

"He feels that I'm not taking his mission statement seriously."

Wyatt stared at me. "Who takes any of those things seriously?"

"Apparently, he does. His dating platform is for people finding *soulmates*," I said. It truly felt like it was a foreign term for me.

Knox and Finn started to laugh at the same time. Knox stopped first. "Wait, you're serious."

I nodded.

Finn cocked a brow. "Dude, you know what? Maybe it's a good thing, and you dodged a bullet. I mean, you'd have a hard time getting him to push this on a younger generation."

"Exactly," I said. "But I'm not giving up. I just need better arguments."

"Or to start believing that mission statement is really how he feels. Who knows, maybe it'll help you find a... what was that? Soulmate," Finn teased.

"Ha ha," I replied, but I wasn't amused. I'd stalked Jude's website some more last night. From the outside, it was impossible to know if people joined it for a hookup or something more serious. But Jude didn't strike me as a liar. "He also said that he doesn't like that I'm constantly dating other women."

Chase groaned. "Man, I told you it would come back to bite you in the ass. You have to be more discreet."

I leaned back in my chair and shrugged. "I thought I was. I figured you only knew stuff because you're my brothers. I don't understand how he knows anything."

"Well...," Knox said.

I cocked a brow at him. "What?"

"We don't live in the Stone Age. There are plenty of pics with you and hotties online. And people talk."

"Yeah, I get your point. But he could have just told me he's not interested when I set up the meeting instead of wasting my time at The Loft."

What I did in my personal life didn't affect anyone. I couldn't understand how it could cost me a business deal. But I was determined not to let that happen. I just had to focus and find a better angle, then meet with Jude again.

"At least he chose a good spot for the meeting," Knox said.

Finn scoffed. "That's not a good spot. That's just where everyone wants to be seen these days. Though apparently they do have great food."

"I didn't eat anything," I said. "I just went to the bar, where I pretended to be someone's date."

The room went completely silent. Then, for the second time today, Knox started laughing. "That sounds like something *I* would do."

"Or me," Finn added. "Don't try to hog all the credit."

"Credit for what? Being the hothead in the family?" Knox asked.

Finn nodded. "Precisely."

"You can be a hothead," Wyatt said. "But this is too out there, even for you, Griffin."

"It is," I admitted. I had no idea what had gotten into me. It was just an impulse, an instinct, and I followed it. And then while I was at the table with her and her ex, all I'd wanted was to punch that idiot out of The Loft. I could feel her shrinking next to me every time he spoke. After he'd left, she'd completely relaxed. It had taken all of my self-restraint not to flirt with her. It was second nature to me, and I'd been so attracted to her that I could barely think straight. But that was the last thing she'd needed, so I'd left as soon as possible. If I'd stayed even one more minute, I would have asked her out. I was sure of it.

And asking her out would have been bad for both of us because she was obviously looking for marriage, and I was certainly not.

"What exactly happened?" Duncan asked.

I shook my head. "Doesn't matter. But I could use your help brainstorming ways to win over Jude."

"Come on, man. Throw us a bone," Finn said.

"Yeah. We never pictured that you could be as impulsive as us," Knox added, pointing at himself, then Finn. "But I see you've got potential."

They weren't going to let this go, so I told them everything.

Once I finished talking, Duncan and Chase exchanged a glance but said nothing, which was worrisome.

"Now, can we go back to brainstorming about the best way to tackle Jude?" I asked.

"Hey, I've got an idea. You said this Phoebe woman was game for faking things, right?" Knox asked.

"I think she was just blindsided but went along with it. According to her friend, she'd suggested it to her earlier in the day, and it just worked out that I was there."

"Why don't you ask her to pretend to be *your* date for a change?"

I just stared at him.

"That's the shittiest idea I've ever heard," Chase said.

"Well, that's what I would do," Knox replied.

"Yeah, hence why it's not the best idea," Wyatt said in a warning tone. Between the two of us, Wyatt was more rational. But even though I could be impulsive, this was insane.

Still, it was taking root in my mind.

Damn. No. It's a crazy idea.

"I'm getting under your skin," Knox continued. "I can't believe it."

Finn laughed. "Nah, he's far too… what was the word? *Cerebral* to do this."

"He'd better be," Duncan said.

I groaned. "Brother, please don't warn me off."

Chase set his jaw. "Maybe you should take us more seriously. We did tell you that your womanizing reputation might get in your way when doing business. This could bite you in the ass too. Pretty badly."

"I haven't even said two words."

"No, but you look like you don't hate the idea," Wyatt said. "No offense, but I don't think you could pull it off. I certainly could, and so could these two." He pointed at Knox and Finn. "But *you* are like these two." He jerked his thumb at Chase and Duncan. "You couldn't keep up a farce to save your life."

Chase cleared his throat. "I'll remind you that I did manage, sort of."

A while ago, he'd set up a shell company to be an investor because his then-girlfriend and now-fiancée, Hannah, needed funds for her inn, but she didn't want to take money from him.

"As I recall, it backfired spectacularly," I said. "Luckily, Hannah was quick to forgive you."

"Yeah, if anything, that's a cautionary tale," Finn said. "So maybe don't bring it up."

"Anyone else have ideas? Something I can actually use?" I asked.

Duncan narrowed his eyes. "His concern is that you don't have the same vision for the business. I'd focus on understanding his point of view… and that mission statement."

Even though I'd ridiculed it, I knew Duncan was right.

"That's a good starting point, brother. Thanks." I looked around at the rest of them. "Anyone else want to add something?"

"Nah, I'm still stuck on you pretending to be someone's date," Wyatt said.

Knox and Finn just laughed. Chase shook his head, but he was smiling.

Yeah, these bozos weren't going to be of any more help today.

The meeting ended a few minutes later, and I headed to my office. I'd rented floor space three blocks away. My team was small—only ten people—and they were in charge of keeping me up to date with the latest goings-on in my portfolio of companies. They also did the bulk of the research for any new investments.

My mind was on Jude Carson, however.

My instincts told me that this would be a great venture, and I never ignored my gut. Some of the most profitable deals in my career were because I'd followed my instincts when others pulled back because the numbers weren't spectacular. Sometimes, a business deal was more than just numbers and projections.

I liked to say that I invested in people, but that wasn't the case here. Jude and I hadn't clicked at all. For now, though, I had other business to tend to. I pushed the issue to the back of my mind and checked the agenda for today, then dove right in.

I spent the better part of the day in back-to-back meetings. I liked my job, but Mondays could be draining.

Toward the end of the day, my mind circled back to Jude. What had he heard or seen about me that made him so adamant that I wasn't a good fit?

I rarely looked myself up online, although I did have an alert to notify me if my name ever popped up in articles.

Come to think of it, I hadn't seen any of those notifications in a while, which could only mean one thing—they'd landed in spam. I opened my email and checked the spam folder. It was empty, but that didn't mean much; spam emails were deleted after a set period of time.

Next, I opened the website for the notification tracker. Sure enough, there were plenty of entries with my name—most regarding business, but some from the places I frequented. I'd even been tagged the evening before on Instagram. It was a benign pic of me at the bar.

The caption said **The Loft: a place where everything happens, from business meetings to pleasure and everything in between. What do you think this hunk was doing here? Let us know in the comments.**

Whoever was running their social media was an amateur.

I was about to close the app when a comment caught my attention. The user was @PhoebePointT.

Maybe he was looking for a social media manager.

I burst out laughing.

Damn, I liked her sense of humor. Clearly, she was as unimpressed with the post as I was.

I clicked on her profile. She only had a picture of a glass of wine and what looked like a complete teardown of a home in the background.

Was that the house she'd mentioned? No, she couldn't possibly live there. I wasn't even sure it could classify as a house. It seemed to be under construction. But still, the coincidence was too big. Phoebe wasn't that common of a name. My instincts nudged me to contact her, and I direct messaged her before I could second-guess myself.

Griffin: Is this Veronica's friend Phoebe?

She answered right away.

Phoebe: Yes, it is. And if this isn't the infamous Griffin, whom The Loft doesn't know whether he went there looking for business or pleasure.

I laughed. The woman definitely had a great sense of humor.

Griffin: What do you think? Should I call them out on it?

Phoebe: No, I don't think they're actually open to feedback. I just needed to get my frustration out, and I guess I took it out on them. The night didn't end well.

Griffin: Fuck. How come?

Phoebe: Long story.

Griffin: Do you have a phone number? I'd love to hear it.

Dots appeared and then disappeared before reappearing once more. Obviously, she was contemplating what to write.

Phoebe: Why?

That was a good question. And I didn't have an answer. She just seemed vulnerable, and I hated the idea of that moron hurting her.

I didn't reply, but she did, typing her phone number. I called her the next second.

"Hey, this is Griffin," I said as soon as she picked up.

"I figured." Her voice was so incredibly shy and different from her sassy messages that for a split second, I figured maybe I was talking to someone else. But no, I recognized her voice. She'd been shy at the bar too. It hadn't kept me from drinking her in, though. Even now, I could picture her perfectly in my mind. The image of her in that tight dress was permanently marked in my mind.

Don't flirt with her, Griffin. Don't flirt. She's in it for the long haul.

"Did anything happen when you went home?" I asked.

"Yeah, he called me."

"Why the hell would he call?" Anger pumped through my veins.

"About this damn house. It's gonna come crashing down on me soon."

Fuck. So she really lived in that run-down thing from her profile pic.

"He wanted to discuss the asking price. I want to lower it so that we can finally get rid of it. But if we lower our price, then we're going to make very little profit, and God knows that I could use it right now. So, hello, rock, and hello, hard place. I'm right between the two."

"I'm sorry to hear that."

"Oh my gosh, I can't believe I just told you that!"

I couldn't imagine the nightmare she was in. "Want to talk about something else?"

"Yes, please. What happened to your business deal? Did you manage to turn it around?"

I'd almost forgotten that I even told her about it. "No. I even shared everything with my brothers this morning in our business meeting."

"You work with your brothers?"

"Sort of. We own Sterling Investments."

"Oh, I think I've heard of it." She didn't sound stunned, or in awe, like people usually were when they made the connection. It was refreshing.

"We each own separate businesses, but on Mondays, we meet to brainstorm. None of them had any ideas I could actually use. They just fooled around, talking bullshit."

"Meaning?" she asked.

I hesitated, but why not tell her? We could laugh about it. She certainly seemed to need that distraction.

I couldn't believe I'd just called this stranger out of nowhere and that I was willing to share things with her.

"When I told them that one of the reasons he shot me down was because I had a reputation as a womanizer—"

"Oh. That would explain a few things," she muttered.

"What things?" I asked.

"Never mind. Go on."

Hmm... "Anyway, one thing led to another, and I told them that I ran into you."

"Wow, I feel so good now. Worthy of being mentioned in a business meeting."

"One of them suggested that I could present you to Jude as my girlfriend."

She started laughing. "Your brothers have a fantastic imagination. It wouldn't be such a bad idea," she said, then rushed to add, "For business reasons, of course."

For a second, I was certain that I'd misheard her. My intention was just to make her laugh, but now she had me thinking.

"Wait, what? Are you serious?"

"You did save my butt. I guess it could be a 'you scratch my back, I scratch yours' situation."

I rose from my chair, adrenaline coursing through my body the way it did when I was on the verge of sealing a very important deal.

"I haven't seriously considered this until now," I confessed. Though that wasn't strictly true, because from the second my brothers mentioned it, the idea had percolated in my mind. But Phoebe didn't need to know that. "Are you sure?" I double-checked. It was a dangerous idea, and not at all my style. I hated lying and pretending. And yet, pretending to date Phoebe didn't feel wrong.

This is insane.

"Honestly, no. I'm just figuring things out. But you would just need me to go with you to a dinner or something, right?"

"Yes."

She laughed. "I can't believe you'd put a deal in the hands of a stranger."

That was the insane thing. She didn't really feel like a stranger, though I couldn't explain why.

"The way I see it, as things stand right now, I wouldn't have a chance in hell to make the deal otherwise. I could probably find some arguments to convince him, but somehow I prefer showing up with a smoking-hot date on my arm, pretending she's my girlfriend."

I heard her suck in a breath at that. But it was 100 percent true.

"Sure, why not?"

"Listen, Phoebe," I said, because the hesitation in her voice was obvious, "if you don't feel comfortable with this, let's just drop it."

"It sounds like fun. And God knows I could use some fun in my life. It's pretty depressing right now."

"Why?"

"You mean beyond the obvious?"

"Well, yes." Because I had an inkling there was more to it—beyond the failed relationship and living in that decrepit house.

She sighed. "It's just that for the past few years, I worked with him. Marshall. I ran his doctor's office. And now—"

"You're out of a job," I realized. "Fuck, that's a shitty situation. How do you even make the mortgage payment?"

"From my savings," she said in a small voice. "But I'm on the right track with that. I found a part-time job as an accountant. It doesn't pay a lot, but it's better than nothing."

She was a fighter. I admired that.

"So..." Her voice sounded awkward now. "How exactly are we going to play this?"

I looked off into the distance, narrowing my eyes. "I'll ask Stella, my assistant, to send Jude an invitation to dinner for him and his wife. And she'll inform him that my girlfriend will also be attending. If he takes the bait, I'll let you know."

"That sounds like a good plan."

"Is your ex likely to bother you again?" I asked.

She swallowed audibly. "It's not like I can avoid him. Both of our names are on the deed for the house. Eventually, I'll have to see him again."

"Well, if you need someone to murder the hell out of him, let me know. And I'm your man for anything. A smoking-hot kiss, a love declaration right in front of the prick, whatever," I said in a teasing tone.

"You do tempt me," she said. I was pleased that her voice was light again. "But why would you bother?"

"Because as you said, you scratch my back, I'll scratch yours."

"Oh, Griffin, I think you're the most interesting person I've ever met."

It was my turn to laugh. "You say that now because you don't know me too well. You might change your mind."

"I don't think I will. Let me know if your potential business partner takes the bait. And if not, well... then I don't know. I'll see you around?"

"Sure."

She definitely would, because as I hung up, I'd made up my mind. Regardless of what Jude replied, I was going to see Phoebe again.

CHAPTER 6
PHOEBE

"THIS CAN'T BE RIGHT," I muttered as I rode the bus from work back home on Wednesday. I dutifully filled out all my expenses in the app I used to track everything. After everything was paid, I would have $5 in my account.

I closed my eyes, resting my forehead against the cool window. I needed to find a second job—right away. I'd sent a ton of applications but mostly got standard rejections saying my profile didn't fit their requirements.

No wonder. I'd spent five years managing a doctor's office. Still, I was hopeful that if I did a good job as a part-timer, they'd increase my hours at H&R Block. One could dream. I didn't love the job, but at this point, I just wanted to pay my bills.

When the bus stopped at the station closest to my house, I stepped out of it, shuddering. I loved AC, but I never understood why it was set so cold.

I had a tiny Toyota in front of the house, but I didn't want to waste any money on gas. Instead, I used public transportation and a bicycle I'd gotten for next to nothing on Craigslist.

As I walked home with quick steps, my phone rang in my purse. I immediately took it out, wondering if Mom was calling again. We'd spoken this morning, but only for a few minutes. I loved my parents to bits, and I usually talked to them for hours on end, but ever since Marshall and I broke up, I tried to keep our conversations short. I didn't want to worry them.

My heart somersaulted when I saw the caller ID. It was Griffin!

I hesitated for a split second, remembering the insane turn our last conversation took. Honestly, after hanging up, I was convinced that I'd imagined it. But I hadn't. Griffin Sterling was larger than life, plain and simple. I'd realized that the second we met.

Taking a deep breath, I answered and put the phone to my ear. "Hi."

"Phoebe, I have news."

Holy shit, his voice had my entire body on edge.

"I'm listening."

"As I told you, I invited Jude and his wife to dinner with both of us. And he accepted."

"Wow. Okay." I laughed nervously as I reached my house and sat down on the front steps.

"Did you change your mind? It's no problem if you did."

As if I'd leave him in the lurch like that. I wasn't a fool; I knew backing out now would put him in an even worse position. "No, of course not. Tell me more."

"The dinner is tomorrow evening."

"What?" My voice was high-pitched.

"If you have plans, we can work around them."

"I have no plans for the foreseeable year, Griffin. Really, I'm yours whenever you want."

There was a pause before he said, "Good to know." His voice was playful. Wait, no, it was more than that. It was… flirty?

I replayed my words in my mind and blushed. *Why did I have to phrase it like that?*

I cleared my throat. "So, where exactly are we going?"

"I don't have the location yet, but I'll tell you as soon as I book something. I'll pick you up and then drop you off."

"Thanks," I said.

"And we'll keep things simple. We'll say that we've been dating for the past six months, but you're a very private person. That's why there are no pictures of us together."

I played with the pendant at my neck, biting the inside of my cheek.

"You disagree?"

"Ha, you can tell that from silence? You've got skills."

"In my experience, when someone doesn't reply, it's because they think I'm wrong."

"I'm just thinking. By the way, are there pictures of you and other women?"

"Yes...that's what got me in this mess in the first place. But it's all circumstantial. I can argue that they were business meetings."

"Right. My past month has kind of been a shit show, so now I'm going to have to sort of invent a whole new persona."

"No, that's not what we're going to do. No lying. We should keep everything vague," he went on. "You say you worked at a doctor's office, and then I'll try to steer the conversation to business."

I bit my lip this time. This was a business dinner. The other guy wasn't going to pry and ask for details about my personal life, but *I* needed more details about Griffin.

"If we're going to pretend that we've been dating for six months, I need to know more about you."

"Sure. Like what?"

"Ummm... not even sure where to begin, honestly."

"I can stop by your place early tomorrow, and we can talk for a while."

"Yeah, that sounds good. That way everything you tell me will be fresh in my mind."

"I look forward to seeing you, Phoebe."

"I do have a question," I said. "What kind of outfit will I

need?" Most of my stuff was still packed. I'd have to find something.

"Just a dress, something you'd wear to a restaurant."

I wondered if it was a fancy restaurant. Then I realized that Griffin Sterling would never go to a cheap one, and his business partner wouldn't either.

"All right, I'll dig something up and knock their socks off."

"I know you will."

After hanging up, I stood from the porch, smiling for no reason as I went into the house. I was going to a fancy-ass dinner with the hottest guy on the planet tomorrow. I took it as a sign that my life was slowly turning around.

After changing into some comfy clothes, I cooked a paella, humming along to my favorite Spotify list. I was a bit on edge, waiting for Griffin to send me the details. I checked the phone a few times while I was eating, but he didn't message me until later that evening.

Griffin: It's all set. We're meeting tomorrow at seven o'clock. Should I come by your place at five?

Phoebe: Make it four. I have LOTS of questions.

Griffin: You can start firing away now.

Phoebe: Nah. If I start, we'll be up all night.

Griffin: I don't mind.

Goose bumps erupted across my skin for some reason. I imagined him saying it in that low, seductive voice of his.

Phoebe: I'll see you tomorrow, Griffin.

The next day, I was on pins and needles. I'd woken up to a few more job rejections in my inbox and also an email from Marshall.

I've thought more about the price. Let's lower it by 10K.

I broke out in a sweat at the words. That would still leave us a margin of a few thousand bucks as profit. I couldn't believe that I'd once looked at this house with dreamy eyes, thinking it was where we'd spend the early days of our marriage. I envisioned myself cooking a few times a week, maybe even having a small vegetable garden in the back. We'd save as much as possible. Then in a few years—

I shook my head. Why was I playing that scenario in my mind over and over again?

Because I still couldn't pinpoint the moment when our visions of the future started diverging. When did he start dreaming about a future without me? And why didn't I see it?

Since I had to find a dress for the evening, I bit the bullet and unpacked all of my bags. I was starting to accept that my situation was semipermanent. Even if we did manage by some miracle to get an offer right away, it would take time before the bank cleared it.

Another wave of sadness overtook me. That big red suitcase was the one I'd prepped for our trip. I'd bought special outfits for the occasion, including a few sexy beach dresses.

My eyes watered. *Damn it.* I wanted to close that suitcase and donate everything to Goodwill. But I couldn't afford to.

I knew the dress I needed for tonight was in there. I'd bought it especially for the trip, figuring I could wear it the evening Marshall proposed. In my mind, I'd been certain that I could guess when it would happen. It was a gold Stella McCartney dress that was high around my neck and reached the floor.

I'd hesitated when buying it. Even with the slashed price, it was an extravagance. Even though Marshall made bank from the practice, I rarely splurged or even asked for gifts. I'd been determined that we save for our next home. To find out that he'd spent all those savings with someone else was excruciatingly painful to say the least.

I held the dress in front of the ancient mirror in the living room. It looked like something out of a scary movie—like a ghost may walk out of it any second. But I didn't have another one, so I couldn't get rid of it. The dress was truly exquisite, and I had some beautiful heels to pair it with.

I set it on the couch and got to work. I didn't have to go into the office every day, which was a relief. The commute was grueling, and my assigned seat once I got to the office was far from any windows. I preferred the comfort of my own home.

The day passed by insanely quickly. Good thing, as I was getting more nervous with every hour.

At three o'clock, I realized I had to start getting ready. I got up from the couch and checked my phone. I had a missed call from Veronica, so I dialed her number.

"Hey, bestie," she said instead of hello. "What are you doing tonight? Want to hang out together?"

"I can't," I replied.

"You've got plans? Oh thank God."

I winced. I'd been a bit clingy lately, calling her every day.

"What are you doing?" she asked. "Actually, you know what? You don't even have to tell me. Oh, who am I kidding? I do want to know. Are you going to have fun?"

"Now that you're asking, something funny happened the other day. Griffin Sterling called."

"The Greek god from the bar? Hallelujah! Some good things *can* happen on this planet. I kept beating myself up that I didn't get his number for you or something."

"He tracked me down on Instagram. One thing led to another, and tonight I'm going with him to a dinner with a potential business partner. I'm pretending to be his girlfriend."

There was a pause, and then Veronica asked, "You're pulling my leg, aren't you? You're just going to stay home and curl up with a book."

"No. I'm so serious. I dug out the gold dress from my red bag."

"Holy shit, you *are* serious. I need details."

"Apparently, the business partner who walked out on him at the bar didn't like his womanizer reputation. And, as I said, one thing led to another."

"I still need more details. You have to fill in the blanks."

I summarized my conversations with Griffin, and she went silent again.

"Veronica, stop doing that. You're freaking me out."

"I'm sorry, but who are you, and what have you done with my best friend? This is the funniest thing you've done in a long time. Probably ever."

"I don't know. You had to be there to hear that conversation unfold. Griffin can be very charming."

"Wait, he coerced you into this?"

"No, no. God, no. That's not what I meant. It's just the way he talks. Everything seems so easy when he says it. Like 'Huh, what's the big deal? We can just pretend we've been dating for six months. No one is going to ask questions.' Then the second we finished the conversation, I realized how far off he was. Like, hello? *Of course* someone is going to ask questions. We can't just ignore them."

"You sound happy," Veronica said.

I couldn't help my grin. "I know. It's insane, but I am."

"I'm glad. You deserve the distraction."

"I think it's going to be fun." I might be nervous as hell, but I didn't have any doubt that the evening would take Marshall and the rest of this mess off my mind.

"Oh, by the way, please wear the lucky underwear I gifted you for the trip."

My face turned beet red in an instant. "Wh-Why would I do that?" I stammered.

"You don't want any panty lines showing through the dress, do you?"

I cleared my throat. "Really, Veronica?"

"What other reason would I possibly have?"

"I don't know. Your mind works in unique ways."

"Oh, that it does. And yet not in a million years would I have imagined that you'd play Griffin's fake girlfriend to help him secure a business deal."

I winced. "Wow. When you put it like that..."

"No, no, no. Don't let my rambling talk you out of it, okay? Have fun. That's all that matters."

"Yep. I'm going to have to hang up now. I need to make myself presentable. Griffin will be here in an hour."

"Early dinner?"

"No, that's at seven o'clock. I asked him to come earlier so we could get the story straight and stuff like that."

"Mm, uh-huh. I see."

Her voice was a bit off, but I didn't have time to overthink things right now. I had lots to do.

After hanging up, I took out some accessories, putting them on the dining room table. Then I grabbed my portable steamer and removed all the wrinkles in the dress before jumping into the shower. My hair was my favorite part of me, so I took extra time and care with it. After applying a conditioner and two sets of masks, I started styling it with the curling iron to make very defined curls, then brushed them out to create beach waves.

It was my favorite look, though Marshall had hated it. But now I was free of him, so I could do whatever I wanted.

I was about to start with my makeup when the doorbell rang. I gasped, checking the time. *Holy shit! How is it four o'clock already?* I could have sworn I just got in the shower. Damn it, being on time was definitely not my forte.

I dashed to the front door, checking the peephole to make sure it was him. Yep, it was Griffin. I swung the door open wide.

"Phoebe—" He stopped talking abruptly, looking straight at me and then down my body.

Then I remembered I was wearing a pretty revealing beach dress. *Shit!* I'd put on a camisole that reached down just past my ass after the shower, but I'd planned to change before he arrived.

I felt my cheeks heat up.

Well, this is a great *start.*

CHAPTER 7
PHOEBE

GRIFFIN STEPPED INSIDE and carefully closed the door. Then he inspected the handle as well as the hinges, almost as if he was afraid that it might crumble. For all I knew, it was possible.

He looked around the place slowly before focusing on me, and I instantly became very self-conscious about the house. I'd gotten used to the fact that it was a dump. But this was the first time I was having someone over besides Veronica.

"Where do you want me to wait for you until you finish getting ready?"

I fiddled with my thumbs, biting the inside of my cheek. "We'll talk while I'm applying my makeup in front of the huge-ass mirror here. You can sit on the couch. If you wait for me to get ready first, we might not have too much time for anything."

Nodding, he glanced around the room again.

Why was he making a concerted effort to look anywhere but at me? My heart rate accelerated. I didn't have any makeup on, but I felt fresh-faced and didn't think I looked that bad.

"I'll be right back."

I hurried to the bathroom, grabbing my mascara, eyeshadow, and foundation, then dashed back to the living room, putting them on the small round table next to the mirror. Griffin was sitting on the couch. I could see his reflection while I applied my mascara.

"Griffin, can you tell me a bit about tonight so I know what to expect? Maybe a bit about Jude's business."

He looked straight at my reflection. Our eye contact through the mirror made me shudder—in a good way. Then my entire body felt hot.

Oh boy.

"Sure. It's a dating platform," he answered.

"Is it worth it?" I asked, then muttered to myself, "I might have to join, the way things are going."

"It's surprisingly successful," Griffin said, "and now he's looking to expand. I want to be an investor."

I added mascara to my other lashes. "I don't understand what the problem is."

"He and I have different views of what a dating platform is and the type of audience it should attract."

I frowned. "But it's *his* platform, right? So what he says goes."

Griffin laughed. "It's not that easy. When you take on an outside investor, you give them decision power as well."

"Hmm," I said, now applying my foundation. I felt oddly at ease doing this in front of Griffin. In all honesty, I probably wouldn't see him again after tonight, so what did it matter?

"He says that his platform is for people 'looking to find soulmates.'" Griffin uttered the last word with complete disbelief, as if he were talking about mythical creatures.

"Damn, then I *really* have to join."

"He insists that because I'm not a relationship type of guy, I can't possibly understand his customers." Again, he had that look of disdain, but it disappeared quickly. "Now, what exactly do you want to know about me?"

"Everything. What do you do on a daily basis? What do you

like? Where do you live? Would I have met your family by now?"

He grinned, lacing his fingers together and putting them on top of his head as he relaxed back on the couch. He looked very out of place in this shithole with his cuff links and tailored shirt. I was certain he had his initials embroidered somewhere. He obviously had money.

"Trust me, if I've been dating you for six months, my family would be all over you."

"You see them often?" I asked.

"Hell yeah. Very often."

"Tell me a bit about them."

"I have five brothers."

"That must be epic." I couldn't even begin to imagine what it had to be like to grow up with five siblings.

I sighed. I used to want three kids, but who knew if that would happen now?

"So, my older brothers are Chase and Duncan."

"Are they married?" I asked.

"They're both engaged. Duncan also has a son."

"How old is he? I love babies and toddlers."

"No, my nephew's older. He's ten."

"Your brother is much older than you, then?"

"No, he had Jeremy when he was young."

"And you're close to your nephew?"

His grin grew even wider, and my heart somersaulted in my chest. I could tell the boy was important to him.

"Yeah, though Knox and Finn are his favorite uncles, probably because they're the youngest in the family. And then there's also Wyatt. I'd say that he's in the same spot on the scale as I am when it comes to Jeremy's favorites. Although now that I've bought a new house, I have to have him over more often."

"Oh my God, you've got a new house? See, that's something a girlfriend would know."

Griffin frowned. "True! It slipped my mind."

I turned around slowly because this question required direct eye contact, not eye-to-mirror-to-eye. "Griffin, have you *ever* had a long-term relationship?"

He shook his head. "No. I date often—too often, as Jude pointed out. But I haven't had a relationship since starting Sterling Investments. Relationships need time, and that's a luxury I don't have."

I was fighting to keep my face neutral. I mean, the man was smoking hot. If he wanted to be a serial dater—a term I much preferred to *womanizer*—then why not?

He rose to his feet, walking toward me with a wry smile. "You're judging me."

I cleared my throat. "I'm trying very hard not to."

"But you are." A smile played on his lips.

"And you're not mad about it."

"I don't care what people think about me. It's what got me into this situation in the first place. My brothers kept advising me to be more discreet. I told them it was no one's business what I did with my private life."

He cast a hot-as-hell glance at me. I couldn't maintain eye contact when he was this close. He seemed even larger than life than back at the bar.

I turned around, focusing on the mirror. He stood behind me. His presence was dominating the space, and it unnerved me.

"So, tell me about your house."

"It's in Point Loma. It's a very modern construction. Wait, I have some pictures." He took his phone out of his pocket, swiped a few times, then held it so I could see.

"Oh, wow. Griffin, this is wonderful." His house was like something out of a magazine.

Our worlds were on separate levels entirely. If it weren't for this freak coincidence of going to The Loft at the same time, we would *never* have met, I was sure of it. But all that didn't matter now. This was a favor. After tonight, I'd never see him again.

"I'll say that I've been to your house a few times. Oh, right, where did you live before? Not sure it'll come up, but it'll look bad if Jude asks and I don't know."

"I had a bachelor's pad in the Gaslamp Quarter."

"I love the Quarter," I said.

Griffin nodded. "So do I, but I wanted more space. I was a bit crammed in there."

I listened intently as I finished applying my foundation.

"So, what exactly do you do for a living? Would you talk about work with a real girlfriend?"

Griffin tilted his head as if considering my words. "If she was interested, why not? I'd share everything with her. So, I do several things. The first thing you have to know about me, what most people know, is that I founded Sterling Investments with my brothers."

"You mentioned that on the phone, but I don't know much about it. Is it a bank?"

He looked incredulous. "I think you're one of the first people I've met who doesn't know Sterling Investments."

I winced. "The financial world isn't really my scene."

"It's not a criticism." He put a hand on my arm. Goose bumps broke out on my skin, and it turned hot at the point of contact as he brushed his thumb up and down. "It's refreshing, honestly."

He removed his hand, pushing it into his pocket.

"We have a platform where people make transactions on the stock market. For bigger investors, we make investments for them. Chase and Duncan are co-CEOs. The rest of my brothers and I own shares and are involved in strategic decisions but don't do day-to-day operations anymore. Each of us has a few companies we manage by ourselves. I, for one, invest a lot in all sorts of digital companies. I'm on their boards as an adviser, investor, and co-owner."

"That sounds very interesting. I bet you never get bored."

"Never," he said without missing a beat. "I love what I do."

"All right," I said. "I'll just go change into my dress, and then we can chat more." I looked around, then groaned. "Oh my God, I didn't offer you anything to drink."

He flashed me a charming smile. "Don't worry about it. Go change."

I hurried to the bathroom, taking off my camisole and putting on my golden dress, carefully tucking my hair so I didn't mess it up. I didn't want to get dressed before applying makeup, mainly because I often ended up making a mess. After zipping and checking myself in the mirror, I sauntered to the living room, where I found Griffin pacing.

"This is my outfit. What do you think?"

He was completely silent as I twirled. When I stopped, he still said nothing. I chanced a glance at him. His eyes had darkened a bit, and he was pinning me with his gaze.

"Uh, Griffin? I'm going to need a reaction here. Is it too much, not enough? Should I change?"

"You look fucking perfect," he said. "Like a million bucks."

That filled me with pride. "Thank you," I murmured.

Why was I so nervous around him? Why did I care so much if he liked my appearance?

This isn't a real date, Phoebe. Somehow, I was starting to forget that, and I wasn't sure why.

"About the drinks. I can give you a glass of white wine. I opened a bottle yesterday. Or we can open a bottle of red."

"Just some water, please."

"Okay." I lifted the hem of my dress to keep from stepping on it because it was far too long without heels.

While I poured water into two glasses, I felt Griffin move behind me.

"Tell me about your parents," I said. "You've spoken a lot about your brothers, but are your parents around? Would I know them?"

"That's also a hell yes," Griffin said as I handed him one of the glasses. He narrowed his eyes. "My parents have an interesting story."

"I'm all ears," I said, taking a swig of water. I should have put even more ice in it. I was burning inside and needed to cool down.

We walked back to the couch. He sat at one end, and I ended up sitting on the other.

"They divorced when we were kids. And now they're actually getting along."

"That's great. And not something that happens often."

"The birth of my nephew started bringing them closer. And now… I've heard them *flirting* a few times. My brothers don't believe me, but I actually think my parents might be dating."

"I was *not* expecting that."

He laughed, undoing one cuff link and then the other, then pushing his sleeves to the elbows rather than rolling them. The rumpled appearance fit Griffin well.

"Mom has a pottery and yoga studio. And my father runs a fishing store in the same building."

I widened my eyes at that. "They are truly friendly, then."

"That's a complicated story in itself. They used to own the store back when we were kids. They had to sell it in the divorce. Then some time ago, my brother Chase bought it back and gifted it to them."

I was starting to understand that the Sterling brothers were something special.

"I think that covered everything. Your turn. Are your parents in San Diego?" he asked.

"No. I was born and raised here. And my parents lived here for years along with my grandparents." I smiled, remembering those happy days. "They had a house next to ours, and they often watched over me. But my grandparents now live in Montana. They moved there when they retired. And now that my parents have retired, they moved there as well, mainly to look after my grandparents. Old age isn't being very kind to them. I always hoped that I'd have kids really soon, and we'd get to do one of those cute pictures with four generations and—"

I pressed my lips together. "I'm not sure why I said that. That's not something you need to know."

Griffin's gaze was soft. "I'm sorry things didn't work out with your ex."

I looked at the glass I was resting on my lap. "Maybe it was for the best. That's what I'm trying to tell myself, anyway, so I don't wallow too much."

"You still care about him?" he asked.

I blinked, glancing up at him. "We were together for a long time," I replied. "That might sound strange, but I'm not used to just being on my own, you know? But he hurt me so damn much that I don't want to feel anything for him."

"But you do?" His voice was tight. "If he wanted to get back with you—"

"No!" I said categorically. "I'd never get back with him." I smiled, feeling relieved, and put a hand on my chest. "See, that's a good, spontaneous response. I think that means that I don't love him anymore."

"Well, you shouldn't. He sure as fuck doesn't deserve you. Right? So, it's obviously best to avoid the topic of him."

"Unless…," I began.

"Unless?" Griffin questioned.

"Well, we don't have to act as if he doesn't exist. But in case anyone asks, I can just say that all this happened six months ago, before you and I met."

His entire face lit up. "You're really good at this."

"Ha. I find out something new about myself every day. I wasn't even aware that I was good at improv, but you've brought out that side in me," I said playfully.

"My pleasure."

Oh my. Those two words sounded way more sensual than they had the right to. But I was certain he hadn't meant it that way. My mind was just playing tricks on me.

Wasn't it?

CHAPTER 8
PHOEBE

GRIFFIN CHECKED HIS PHONE. "It's getting late. Are you ready to go?"

Holy shit, time had slipped away from me. "Yep, I just want to put on some accessories."

I hurried to the dining room table where I'd laid out my jewelry. I was wearing a simple set of earrings and a matching pendant in the shape of a leaf. I went back to the mirror and started putting on the right earring.

"I always forget that these are so damn difficult to clasp," I muttered.

In an instant, Griffin was right behind me. "I'll do it."

"Thank you."

The second his fingers brushed my earlobe, I wondered if it was such a good idea. My body kept reacting in the most bizarre way around him. His cologne was delicious. I sucked in a breath, holding it while he fastened one earring and then the other. His knuckles brushed my cheek, and I felt warm all over.

What am I doing? Nah, this has to just be the typical reaction to a hot-as-sin man. If anything, it was proof that certain parts of me were still alive.

"While you're at it, could you please also clasp my pendant? That's always a hassle because the chain isn't very long."

"Sure," Griffin said.

Was my mind playing tricks again, or was his voice a bit rougher?

He stepped behind me and then pushed my hair to one side.

"Your hair is gorgeous," he said.

And just like that, I had an impulse I'd never had before in my life. I wanted to turn around and kiss him for no reason at all. I managed to stay put and just smile in the mirror.

"Thanks. I like it too."

Afterward, I put on my heels and grabbed a clutch from the small table where I'd deposited my makeup. "Okay, I'm ready for the evening."

He nodded, looking me up and down. "You truly look magnificent."

"Thank you," I said quietly. "I bought this dress at a super-clearance price. I wanted to wear it on the night I thought my ex would have proposed."

Griffin walked to me and tilted my chin up. "I promise you one thing tonight. You are going to have fun. Much more than you would have with that moron you were with. I'm sure he was a dead bore. I, on the other hand, am fantastic company. Anyway, once the dinner with Jude and his wife is over, I'll think of something else."

"What do you mean?"

"To keep you entertained for the rest of the evening."

I licked my lips. "Game on, Griffin."

We walked side by side out of the house and I locked the door behind us. Griffin was driving a Range Rover. I climbed into the passenger seat, arranging my dress because it had a slit on the left thigh that went almost all the way up. It was fine when I was walking, but I had to be careful when I was sitting. Griffin got in just as I finished arranging my dress.

I kept touching the leather seat and the inside of the door. It was plush and luxurious. "I feel like I'm flying first class. I imagine they have fancy seats like this. My car is old as dirt."

Griffin didn't say anything, but his eyebrows were almost up to his hairline.

I winced. "I promise I'll have a better filter around Jude and his wife. Do you know her name?"

"No, I don't. Listen, you don't have to pretend or anything. You're damn amazing just the way you are."

My heart soared in my chest. I realized that I hadn't been paid compliments in a long while, and that was fucked up.

"Just be yourself. I'm sure they'll like you."

"How can you be so sure?" I teased.

He looked straight at me before focusing on the road again. "I like you."

I blushed—there was no denying it. At least he couldn't see because he was driving.

Nope, he chanced a glance in my direction and zeroed in on my cheeks. He totally knew I was blushing.

There was no way for me to hide. Then again, why should I?

We spoke a bit about San Diego and our favorite spots in the city as he drove to the restaurant. We arrived twenty minutes later. Even before I stepped inside, I realized it was the fanciest place I'd ever been—even more so than The Loft. For one, they had a valet. He took the car fob and then drove Griffin's car off to a parking spot. The staff inside were dressed so elegantly that I almost felt out of place.

No, I corrected myself. Most of the things I owned would have been out of place, but not this dress.

"Our reservation is under Griffin Sterling," he told the hostess.

"Ah, yes. Mr. and Mrs. Carson are already here."

"Damn it," Griffin muttered.

"Are we late?" I asked.

"No, the guy just insists on coming early."

As we followed the hostess, Griffin put a hand at the small of my back. I instantly straightened up, and then he tucked me into his body.

Oh, right. We were supposed to be pretending to be crazy about each other. Being touchy-feely was part of the deal. Why didn't we discuss that before? Then again, what was there to discuss? It wasn't something you could choreograph. It had to be natural.

I leaned into him as if I couldn't get enough. I felt him suck in a breath when the side of my boob brushed his chest.

When we reached the table, a man rose to his feet. "Griffin, nice to see you."

"You as well. This is my girlfriend, Phoebe. She was kind enough to join us."

"Nice to meet you, Phoebe," Jude said, shaking my hand. "This is my wife, Emma."

"Hi, Mrs. Carson."

"Oh, please, just call me Emma. And call this grump here Jude."

"My darling," Jude said, "Griffin is a potential business partner."

"So, that means I should act like you're super important and I'm afraid of you?"

Jude looked stunned. "Not afraid, no." He glanced at Griffin, who was clearly biting back laughter.

I had a hunch that he didn't expect this sort of dynamic either. It was unfair, but I'd imagined a slightly snobbish and uptight couple.

Jude looked straight at me. "You know, I have to say, I was very surprised when Griffin told me that he was in a long-term relationship. I didn't hear anything of the sort when I asked around about him."

I laughed nervously, putting my hands on my lap. Griffin covered them with his under the table.

I startled and smiled at him, hoping I looked doe-eyed with appreciation and not that his touch was a surprise.

"That's because Phoebe doesn't like to attend many events. They make her nervous."

He was very good at this. I nodded, looking from him to Jude and Emma. "I really am, so excuse me if I seem a bit like a fish out of water." And then I decided to be myself, just as Griffin said. "If I'm honest, fancy restaurants make me a bit uneasy. It's not my scene, so to speak."

Emma put a hand on her chest. "Darling, we are two peas in a pod, then. Honestly, it's not ours either. We don't come from money, you know. For the first twenty years of our marriage, we really struggled financially. For me, coming to places like this is almost a waste."

Jude looked at her with affection. "You do enjoy the food."

"True," she said, "just not the price tag."

I felt as if a weight had lifted off my shoulders. At least I didn't have to pretend that I knew my way around a fancy restaurant. I could focus all my faking efforts on pretending that I had the hots for Griffin instead.

Somehow, I knew that wasn't going to be too hard.

I tilted my head, looking in his direction. "And Griffin's very kind to me. He knows that I'm a homebody, so he doesn't pressure me into joining him."

"I don't know how the two of you managed to keep this under wraps," Jude said. "People I've spoken to are convinced that Griffin is *very* single. They've told me a lot of stories."

"Jude," Griffin said, covering my hand again and squeezing it lightly. "Please don't believe everything you hear. Most of the stuff is made up or exaggerated."

Jude nodded. "You know, I'm starting to think you're right."

A waiter came and recited the special of the day while handing out the menus. Jude ordered a bottle of white wine and another of red right off the bat.

Once the waiter left, the focus shifted away from me, as everyone was trying to decide what to order.

"I'll take the sea bass and glazed honey with steamed vegetables," I said.

"Anyone want an appetizer?" Jude asked.

"Yes, please. The beef tartar sounds delicious," Emma said. "And so does the fried squid. Want to order both and share?"

I smiled to myself. She sounded a bit like a foodie.

Griffin turned to look at me. "What do you think about sharing a starter too? I'm starving."

"Sure. You pick one."

"If you're having fish as the main course, why don't we order the smoked trout for an appetizer?" he suggested.

It was oddly thoughtful of him to pair it to my main course instead of his. Then again, I had an inkling that Griffin was simply a thoughtful person.

I nodded. "All right."

The waiter returned as soon as we set the menus on the table. The service was impeccable. After we ordered, another waiter came with slices of bread and various spreads.

"That's on the house," he said before leaving.

I reached for the bread right away, putting a green spread on it. I was pretty hungry too. I just hadn't realized it.

"So, tell me," Jude said, "where did you two meet?"

I froze in the act of biting into my slice. *Crap!* Why didn't we think about coming up with a detailed story for that? It was one of the first things people wanted to know about a new couple.

CHAPTER 9
PHOEBE

"ON THE BEACH," Griffin answered smoothly.

I took a bite of my slice of bread to hide my surprise. The green spread was a delicious olive paste.

"I was jogging, and she was just strolling through the water. She caught my attention, and I immediately flirted with her. She told me off."

My face opened up in a huge smile. Well, I could actually see that happening in my mind's eye: the water lapping at my feet and Griffin jogging. Was he one of those guys who only wore shorts and nothing on top? Oh, I hoped he was. Then I thought of something to add to his story. "But I was just playing hard to get. He looked very attractive. In fact, so attractive that I'd been convinced he'd just come to jog shirtless to pick someone up. Like that was his motive."

Jude laughed. "That sounds like the Griffin I've heard about."

"He can be very cocky sometimes. But I adore it," I continued, deciding to tease him.

Griffin smiled, bringing his chair closer to mine and putting an arm around my shoulders. "I like to call it persuasive."

"That too," I agreed, licking my lips and shimmying slightly in my seat. I didn't even have to pretend this part. The man had an uncanny effect on me. My body temperature seemed to rise a few degrees whenever he was close.

Goodness, this was so unlike me! I'd never felt like this with Marshall, even in the beginning.

"What do you do for work, Phoebe?" Emma asked me, effectively slicing through the tension.

Griffin looked briefly at my lips before returning his attention to the table.

"I used to work in a doctor's office, managing the day-to-day business. Now I'm looking for something else."

I kept my fingers crossed that they wouldn't prod too much.

"I'm sure you'll find something great," Emma said.

My shoulders sank with relief. Just then, our appetizers arrived. My hunger had subsided a little bit from the bread with olive paste, and the conversation picked up once again.

"Phoebe," Jude said once our starter plates were empty, "did Griffin tell you about my business?"

"Yes, he did." I was grateful that the conversation wasn't about me or about us this time. I was starting to feel guilty for lying to Jude and Emma, as they seemed really nice. "I think it would complement his portfolio very well. I mean, he's a whiz with digital companies." I might not know a lot about Griffin, but I was 100 percent sure that I was right.

"Hmm," Jude said, clearly sounding unconvinced.

I chanced a glance at Griffin. I'd expected him to go into business mode, but he seemed remarkably relaxed, leaning back in his chair.

"Thank you, love, for singing my praises." He took my hand, kissing the back of it. Goose bumps broke out on my skin, and he looked at my arm, seemingly perplexed for a few seconds. No one could fake goose bumps. "But Jude is right. Our visions have to align for this to work out."

Out of the corner of my eye, I saw Jude straightening up. Was this some sort of reverse psychology that Griffin was employing?

"And you think they don't?" Jude asked. His voice was tighter than it had been all evening.

"Not sure." Griffin was goading him. Genius. He shrugged and then took another slice of bread, putting sundried tomato paste on it. "You said yourself that the mission statement is something you care deeply about, and you figured I didn't quite understand it."

Jude put one hand on the table, drumming his fingers on the surface. "I might have jumped to conclusions. I believed all the rumors circulating about you, but now I realize that might have been a mistake."

Yes. God, yes. I wanted to chant, "Victory!" Could it really be this easy?

"But we can meet again and discuss the business. I don't know why I brought it up. It's not a good subject for dinner," Jude finished.

"Oh, good," Emma said. "I respect your work, darling, but you know I don't like to spend my meals talking about it."

"Of course, dear," Jude replied, and my heart all but melted.

"How long have you two been together?" I blurted.

"We got married twenty-nine years ago, but this September, we'll celebrate our thirty-second anniversary since our first date. Let me tell you," Emma said in a conspiratorial tone, "it was quite a challenge to keep this one hidden and then to get my dad's blessing."

"And why is that?" Griffin asked, sounding thoroughly amused.

Jude glowered at his wife, but it was all pretense. "Her dad thought I wasn't going to amount to much. That I couldn't take care of his precious daughter."

"But then Dad completely fell for you," she said with a dreamy expression, "just like I did."

As the main course arrived, Emma and Jude regaled us with stories regarding their grown children. I was thoroughly relaxed, and so was Griffin. We'd gotten past the hard part. Besides, if

Jude's previous reaction was any indication, Griffin's deal was safe too.

"Emma, I agree with you," I said as I gobbled down my fish. "I think it's the best thing I've ever had. Pity it's so overpriced."

I caught Griffin watching me with a strange smile before he shook his head lightly as he focused on his steak.

"Penny for your thoughts," I whispered, leaning into him.

He brought his mouth to my ear. "Later."

His breath tickled me, and I giggled. When I looked up, I realized that Jude was looking at us intently. This was going well!

After we cleaned our plates, we ordered a mix of desserts and split them. I was about to burst at the seams, but dessert was even more delicious than either the appetizer or the main course.

Just as Emma was eating the last of the tiramisu, Jude leaned into her, asking something in a whisper. Griffin frowned. Emma nodded, and then Jude looked at us with a huge grin.

"I have an invitation for you two," he said.

Griffin turned rigid but casually replied, "Okay."

"Two Saturdays from now, Emma and I are going to our weekend home overnight. We'd love for you to join us if you don't have other plans."

Crap. Of course this couldn't be so easy.

"We wouldn't want to intrude on your personal time away," I hedged.

"Nonsense, we'd love to have you over," Emma said. "Phoebe, I would love to get to know you better."

Come on, Griffin. Come up with something smart to get us out of this.

"Thank you for the invitation," he said in a measured tone. "Love." *Oh my God, he has to stop calling me that. Here I go again with the goose bumps.* I couldn't understand why that one word affected me like this. "Didn't you say you had that birthday party the weekend after next?"

"We can push it to another weekend," Emma said quickly.

My shoulders slumped. I realized that even if we found an excuse for the next five weekends, they'd just invite us for another time.

Griffin caught my gaze, and I suspected that he'd reached the exact same conclusion. I pushed a strand of hair behind my ear, buying myself time.

"Let me check my calendar," I said. "And maybe you should do the same."

I wanted to send him a text so we were on the same page. I took out my phone and went directly to type a message.

Phoebe: I don't think we can get out of it.

He replied right away.

Griffin: I know.

"All right, let's see my calendar," he said slowly, pretending to be reviewing his commitments.

We were both holding our phones in our laps so no one could see if we were typing or not.

Phoebe: Then let's go.

Griffin: Are you sure?

Phoebe: Yes.

"No, the party's this week," I said, looking up.

"Excellent!" Emma exclaimed. "Then that's settled. It's going to be wonderful."

"Just the four of us?" Griffin asked.

"Yes," Jude replied. "Maybe we'll talk some more about the deal during that time."

"Nonsense," Emma said, playfully pushing him away. "They're our guests."

"I'll have my assistant arrange everything, and I'll drop you an email with the details," Jude added.

"I look forward to it," Griffin said.

"All right. You youngsters probably want to continue your evening, but it's getting late for these two old birds, so we're going to head out. I already took care of the bill."

"Jude," Griffin protested.

"No, I won't hear of it. I'm the one who suggested this restaurant."

"I'll pick up the tab next time." Griffin stood, then pulled back my chair, taking my hand as I rose to my feet. He was constantly touching me, and I liked it more than I wanted to admit. Secretly, I was happy that we'd get to do this all over again. Then it dawned on me that we'd have to spend the night there too. In the same room, presumably.

Shit, this was going to be more involved than I'd thought.

I tensed, and Griffin splayed his palm on the bare part of my back. I instantly relaxed into his touch. We walked side by side, right behind Jude and Emma. Once we stepped out of the restaurant, I noticed that Griffin's car was already waiting for us, and Jude's was here as well.

"It was great meeting you, Phoebe," Emma said and kissed my cheek, giving me a half hug that I returned. Guilt slammed into me once more.

Jude shook my hand. "I can't wait to see the two of you again."

"Likewise," Griffin replied.

After they went to their car, we headed to the Range Rover.

Once inside, Griffin asked, "Are you okay?"

I put on my seat belt, shimmying in my seat. "Yes. It went better than I expected. Although, I didn't count on having to do it again."

"Don't worry about it."

I looked at him as he drove off. "What do you mean? We agreed to go to their house."

"There was no way to say no to their faces. They would have just kept insisting."

"Exactly," I said slowly.

"But sometime this week, I'll find an excuse. An urgent business matter or something else. And then when they invite us the next time, I'll find another excuse, and so on."

"How is that going to help your business deal?"

"It's not," Griffin said, now driving even faster. "But I really need to think this through. It's not fair to ask you to keep putting up with this charade. I thought it would be just a one-and-done thing."

"Me too," I admitted.

The idea of him leaving Emma and Jude high and dry didn't sit well with me, but what was the alternative? He was right, this didn't make any sense. If we tried to keep this up for two days, they were bound to catch on that something was off. That would surely hurt his deal more than simply being a no-show. At most, Jude would think Griffin was a busy man or someone who wouldn't keep his word.

We didn't talk much on the way home. I was too busy thinking about the pros and cons of getting out of the commitment.

Griffin groaned as we arrived in front of my house. Marshall was pacing in front of it.

"What is that douchebag doing here?" he asked.

"No clue. Look, thanks for bringing me home."

"Nonsense, I'm getting out with you."

"What? Why?" I asked.

"Because the second you realized he was here, you practically withdrew into yourself." I was surprised he'd noticed this. He was right, too, and I hadn't even realized it.

"That's because I don't want to talk to him."

"Then let's make sure he won't bother you again."

"What are you talking about?"

Before I realized what was going on, he got out of the car and came over to my side. I opened the door, but he grabbed the handle from outside, then took my hand as I stepped out of the Range Rover.

Marshall jumped down from the porch, looking straight at us as we came closer to the house. "What's he doing here?" he asked, pointing at Griffin.

"The question is, why the hell are you here?" Griffin asked. He put a possessive arm around my waist, tucking me into him.

"You're not serious," Marshall said. "You're really dating this braggart?"

"Shut your mouth," I said. "You've got no right coming here."

"My name is on the deed."

"Then talk to her through your fucking realtor," Griffin growled.

"You can't tell me what to do."

"You'll find that I can, actually, because I'll do anything to keep you from annoying her or hurting her again. You've done more than enough."

Marshall cocked a brow. "How long has this been going on? All this time you've been gouging my eyes out for breaking up when you've had someone on the side?"

Griffin stepped right in Marshall's face. "You're a lying piece of shit. Don't you ever *dare* talk to Phoebe like that again. You may have dated her for years, but you didn't know how to respect her, how to appreciate her, how to treat her like a real man does. She's mine now, so stay the fuck away."

Marshall looked shell-shocked, but the bastard recovered quickly.

"Oh, really?" he challenged.

"You say one bad thing about her, and I'll knock your teeth out. Get the fuck away from us, and don't bother her again. You have a realtor, communicate through them. Otherwise, if you want to reach Phoebe, you go through me."

Marshall looked at me. "You're going to let this controlling bastard take over?"

Those words snapped me out of my shock. "You don't get to ask anything about my life or say one bad word about Griffin. Get the hell away from me."

Marshall shook his head and then walked right past us to a brand-new Mercedes parked across the street. He looked at the

Range Rover, and even though I couldn't see his eyes, I knew they were full of rage. He was forever jealous of the things he didn't have. Now that he didn't have *me* anymore, he didn't want anyone else to either.

Tough luck, buddy.

"You're shaking," Griffin murmured once Marshall reached his car.

"I'm just… I can't believe he'd show up here."

He touched beneath my chin and brushed it with his thumb. "Do you trust me, Phoebe?"

"Yes. Why?"

He captured my mouth the next second.

I immediately opened up for him, letting him do with me whatever he wanted. He slipped his tongue into my mouth and gave me the hottest kiss I'd ever had. My entire body sprang to life. I wrapped my arms around his neck, pushing myself up onto my toes and leaning into him. He crushed my waist with both hands, pulling me tight to him, my breasts pushing against his chest.

Then he groaned, and the sound sent tendrils of heat through my body. It was impossible to fake a groan. This kiss was turning him on just as much as me. Adrenaline coursed through my veins at the thought. I didn't care if Marshall was looking. Frankly, I wouldn't care if an asteroid fell next to us. I just didn't want Griffin to stop kissing me.

I was shaking in earnest now, but not because I was mad or angry. My entire body was throbbing. Energy pulsed through me like never before.

When Griffin pulled back, his breathing was ragged. His eyes were darker than I'd seen them before now. "Better?"

"Yes." My smile stretched from ear to ear. "Yeah, much better."

He looked over his shoulder. Marshall was rooted in his spot, staring at us. But the second he saw that we were watching him, he got in his car and drove away.

Griffin turned his attention back to me. "The way he talked to you… Fuck, I don't even know how I kept from pounding his teeth in. He certainly deserves it."

I was speechless. I'd kind of thought everything he told Marshall was for show.

"Did he treat you that way when you were together?"

I ran a hand through my hair. My curls were already undone. "Sometimes. Especially when things didn't go his way. I thought that was normal, that I was supposed to lift him up. What does it say about me?"

"It tells me that you're a very kind person and can't always see when those around you don't deserve you." He pointed at the now-vacant parking spot. "But that moron, he definitely didn't deserve you. Find someone better, someone who can give you everything."

Why was I starting to want this "someone" to be a certain six-foot god with green eyes, like the man standing in front of me?

"Thanks, Griffin. That means a lot to me."

Still looking at my mouth, he took a step back, putting both hands in his pockets. "So, listen, I'll talk to Jude and get us out of it, okay? I'll be in touch."

"Sure," I said even though I really didn't want him to cancel.

CHAPTER 10
GRIFFIN

THE STOCK MARKET went completely haywire the next week, so I wasn't surprised when Chase and Duncan called a surprise meeting at the office on Friday evening. We were seeing each other later on anyway because Mom invited us to dinner, but we needed to gather with all the senior managers.

Plenty of clients were up in arms. This was always a frustrating development. Whenever the market was down, people insisted on selling their stocks, and that was the worst possible moment to do so. Most feared that the price would drop even more. But what they didn't understand was that panic selling was *creating* the spiral downward. I always told them that if they didn't absolutely need the money that very second, they should hold on. Some listened, some didn't.

As I went inside, there was already a lively debate going on. Then again, the meeting started an hour ago. Most of the senior management was here too.

"Listen," Chase said with that calm demeanor he always had during turbulent times, "there are no signs that this is a systemic problem. I believe there is a correlation with all the tech announcements that took place this week." Several tech companies fired thousands of people, and that sent shock waves throughout the markets, with people expecting more companies to follow suit.

"Whenever something like this happens, our clients inquire if we're going to change the structure of our portfolio," Duncan went on.

"I usually say no, but I'm starting to think that maybe it's time we invested in green energy more than tech companies," one of our most senior members of management suggested.

Chase didn't immediately reply, which meant he was actually considering this. "Then draft up a presentation about what that would entail. I don't see anything wrong with our current portfolios, but diversification can be good. We could add portfolios focusing on green energy."

Wyatt looked at me. "Nice of you to finally join us."

"Sorry I'm late," I said. "For what it's worth, I've been looking at the market movements intensely, and all the big culprits announced new products to be released later this year. As far as I see, it's just about greed and profits. Letting so many people go will actually boost their profits at the end of the year. The share price will skyrocket."

There was a murmur of agreement around the table.

Knox cleared his throat. "Finn and I have been thinking we could add another feature to the platform. That way, when people want to sell their stocks in a moment of downturn, we can instantly generate predictions of where we think the stock price will be in a few months."

"That's a great idea," Duncan said.

"Yeah, I like that," Wyatt agreed. "Just make sure it's very obvious that it's just a prediction, and we don't take any liability for how the market actually turns out."

I was about to say the same thing, but he'd beaten me to the punch. Wyatt might be a hothead in his personal life, but when it came to business, he was cold and calculated.

"Obviously. We're not amateurs!" Knox spoke in a tone that

implied that if the management team weren't here, he would have added "dickhead" at the end of the sentence.

Everyone brainstormed with Knox and Finn for another half hour, and then Duncan adjourned the meeting.

Once the team filtered out, Knox rolled his shoulders back and said, "Let it be known that Finn and I were on time, and he was late," he said, pointing at me.

I rolled my eyes. "Dude, it's a onetime thing. Being late is more of a problem when it's repetitive. I was in the middle of a negotiation when I read Chase's text, and I couldn't just get rid of my conversation partner."

"Was it about the dating app?" Duncan asked.

"No, that's... well, that's ongoing. Haven't really made progress, but I'm still in the running."

"Really? How so?" Knox asked.

I waved my hand. "Never mind."

"Wait a second. We need details." That came from Wyatt. Of course he'd picked up that I was trying to avoid the conversation.

I looked around the room and said, "I followed Knox's advice."

Knox's eyes bulged. "*My* advice? Dude, I was pulling your leg. Holy shit."

Finn held up a finger. "Wait, what do you mean, you followed it?"

I cleared my throat. "I asked Phoebe to come to dinner with me. We pretended that we were an item."

There was a long pause, and then Duncan said, "That is the stupidest thing I've ever heard."

"Yeah, I think I have to agree with him," Chase said.

I stared at him. "Chase, you set up a fake company to invest in your girlfriend's business. You've lost the right to say anything is wrong or stupid for eternity."

He nodded. "Fair enough."

Knox pushed his chest forward a bit theatrically. "I'm proud of you. I didn't think you had it in you."

"Let's continue the gossip session at Mom's house," Finn said. "I do want details, but I also don't want us to get there late. Last time, Mom said she might starve us if we didn't show up on time."

"I'm sure she meant you two." I pointed between him and Knox.

Finn laughed. "Well, I can't argue with that because you're right."

After we left the meeting room, Hannah joined us. She was one of our best employees. We were lucky she was on our team. I had no idea how she managed to run an inn and hold a full-time job, but I had mad respect for her. She first started working here because she needed money to repair the inn, and now she was somehow doing both.

"How did it go?" she asked Chase.

"Well, we'll consider adding more green companies to our portfolios of managed funds. How was your day?"

"Productive. Although, I've gotten a few cancellations at the inn for next month."

We all drove separately to Mom's house. I got there first, and my brothers arrived as I inspected her garden. We used to drop by more often, taking turns fixing whatever she needed around the house. Lately, Dad kept stopping by more often than we did. As I was about to head to the front door, I heard Mom's and Dad's voices filter around from the backyard. They were both laughing.

"Oh, come on. You know the kids will like this," he said.

They came around the corner, and Dad froze. He had an arm around Mom's waist that he immediately dropped. I wanted to wash my eyes instantly.

"Hi, Mom." That was from Chase.

"Hey, I didn't know you were here already."

"Clearly," Duncan said.

I chanced a glance at the other three. Wyatt was looking at me, nodding as if to say, *"Yep, you called it."* Knox and Finn were just perplexed. We were all glad that our parents were getting along. They hadn't officially announced that they were back together or dating, but I had a hunch that it wasn't going to take long. Still, it had taken us the better part of our adult lives to get used to the fact that they were divorced. Seeing them back together was… an adjustment. I figured it was probably weirdest for Knox and Finn. They'd been very young when our parents split; I wasn't even sure they remembered them being together.

"Jeremy's already inside, setting the table. Your dad was helping me with the irrigation system. I always manage to mess up the digital console," Mom said, but she was *blushing*.

Shoot me now. That was a lie. Mom wasn't good with stuff like repairing a sprinkler or something, but she aced digital systems. But we all pretended we believed them as we walked inside the house. As she'd said, Jeremy was already setting the table.

"I figured Riley would be here too," I said, looking at Duncan.

"Nah, she's going to join us later."

I shook my head. "Damn, they're running her ragged."

"I know," he replied. "But it's her career, and I respect that she wants to climb the ladder."

Riley was a hardworking woman. She'd been Jeremy's nanny for a few months in between graduating law school and starting at a law firm. She was working late into the evenings most of the time.

Jeremy looked at each of us as we entered, grinning at Knox and Finn in particular. I had to learn some tricks and tips from my brothers if I ever wanted to get that level of admiration.

"I already set the table the way Riley and I practiced, Dad," he said.

Duncan went to him, ruffling his hair. I remembered when I

found out my brother was going to have a kid. It seemed like such a strange concept. Over the years, I'd realized I wanted kids of my own, but somehow that had never worked out. The combination of work and my lifestyle just wasn't conducive to having kids. And as with all things in my life, I wanted to do it right. If I couldn't be a good parent, I'd rather not have children at all.

"I made a chicken casserole and my famous goat cheese salad," Mom exclaimed. The salad was already on the table. "I'll take out the casserole after we eat the salad."

Mom's house was rather small. After the divorce, we'd lived with her in a slightly bigger one three blocks away. But as soon as Knox and Finn were in college, she sold that one and downsized.

She insisted on having a big dining area, though, so we could all gather here. We didn't do it very often, unfortunately, but it was a treat whenever we all came over.

"Was everything okay at work? The stock market's been making headlines this week, and not good ones," Dad said.

"We've got it under control," Knox said. "But we have some more interesting news to share, or at least Griffin does."

I growled at him. *What a fucker. Why would he bring this up in front of Mom and Dad?*

"We can talk about it later," I said smoothly.

"No, we cannot," Finn said. "We cut you slack at the office, but come on now, spill it."

"What is it, Griffin darling?" Mom asked. "Is everything okay?"

"Really, Mom, it's nothing bad. Just not something we should discuss at the table," I said.

"He's asked a woman to pretend to be his girlfriend so he can secure a business deal because his potential business partner was worried about his manwhore reputation."

Hannah's eyes bulged. Mom gasped. Dad put down the forkful of salad he'd been about to eat. Then he looked at Jeremy, who was frowning, and glanced at Duncan. Duncan was furious with Knox. Good! At least I wasn't the only one, even though everyone else was beyond amused.

"Griffin, you didn't!" Mom exclaimed.

"Son, that is really beneath you," Dad added. "Disrespectful to this woman too."

"Let it be known that I suggested it," Knox said. "I didn't actually think he'd do it, though, but kudos for having the—" He stopped abruptly, like he'd suddenly read the room and realized not everyone was cool with this.

"Well, however it happened," Mom said, "it's not fair to deceive others."

"I know," I said. *Way to make me feel like crap.* Of course I knew that, but because of Phoebe, it seemed okay.

"We taught you better." Dad's voice was uncharacteristically harsh.

I looked at Knox. "You truly are enjoying this, aren't you?"

He grinned. "A lot."

"So am I," Finn said. "We're at the top of everyone's shit list all the time. Now, for once, you're behaving worse than we are."

I looked around the table once, especially at Jeremy. For fuck's sake, what kind of example was I setting for him?

"This wasn't one of my brightest ideas," I admitted. "It's not how I usually do things, but I won't move forward with the charade."

I was supposed to reach out to Jude this week and cancel the plans, but I didn't. I'd have to take care of that as soon as possible.

"Good," Mom said. "It's not fair, you know, to your business partners or that poor girl."

"She knows what's going on," I pointed out. "But I'll make things right. This was a bad idea from all angles."

Mom sighed. "Regardless, it's not a good situation overall."

"I agree," I said.

My brothers were relentless the rest of the evening. But then again, if any of them were in my shoes, I'd do the exact same thing. The more I talked about the situation, the more insane it seemed.

At eight o'clock, Duncan left with Jeremy because my nephew had a strict bedtime routine. Riley didn't make it to dinner after all; they took leftover casserole with them for her.

The rest of us filtered out soon after that. The only one who stayed behind was Dad.

I got in my car and intended to head home, but instead, I texted Phoebe. I hadn't gotten to talk to her this week, but I didn't want to postpone it any longer.

Griffin: Are you free for a call?

Phoebe: :)

Phoebe: Yes, you don't have to check before calling.

I pushed her number right away, then put the call on speakerphone.

"It's a force of habit," I said when she answered. "In business, most people just won't pick up if you don't give them a heads-up about a call."

She laughed. "Well, this isn't business, and my calendar is not nearly full enough to warrant scheduling a call."

She sounded out of breath.

"What are you doing?" I asked her.

"I just finished a Zumba routine. It feels so good. I haven't done one in a while. I've been so worked up, and it was good to get rid of some of that energy."

Her words traveled straight below my belt. Fucking hell. She hadn't even meant it in a sexual way. Or perhaps she had. She didn't specify what kind of pent-up energy she had, and I decided not to ask.

"Now I was thinking about ordering something for dinner," she continued.

"What do you want? I'll buy it and bring it to you."

"Why would you do that?"

Because I want to please you was the honest answer. I had no idea why, but that was how I felt.

"Why not?" I replied.

"Because you're probably busy and would like to relax in that amazing house of yours."

"I can relax with you," I assured her. "Besides, I was MIA the whole week. I kind of owe you."

"No, you don't. Really, Griffin, you don't owe me anything."

"We'll debate that some more once I bring dinner," I said.

I could swear she was smiling when she said, "I see. Well, there is a place with delicious bowls near the beach. I'll text you the exact address. It's going to be easier than explaining."

"Sure."

"Then I'll call and order so you just have to pick it up."

"Deal."

She texted me before we'd even finished speaking.

After checking the address, I said, "I'm not far at all. I'll be there as soon as possible."

"Thanks. I only have white or red wine."

"I'm good."

I didn't really care if I drank anything or not. I just wanted to spend time with her, I realized, without having to pretend for Jude's sake or for that ass of an ex of hers.

CHAPTER 11
GRIFFIN

I FOUND the restaurant quick enough. I wasn't a fan of these bowl things—I felt like it was just an excuse for them to put in a bunch of scraps, cover it in five different types of sauces, and call it a meal. But I had to admit that this place looked good. I'd have to remember it.

I wasn't hungry, so buying a bowl for myself was out of the question. And as promised, Phoebe had already ordered her meal, so all I had to do was pick it up.

Twenty minutes later, I parked in front of her house. Hurrying up the front steps, I noticed how they creaked under my weight. I hoped she got rid of this place. It was a death trap. I'd stayed in quite a few dumps as a student, when saving money was more important than comfort, but this place took the cake.

She opened the door before I even managed to knock. Once again, she was flustered. I expected her to be wearing sweats or something, but she was in a dress, and her hair was elegantly pulled to one side.

"Hey!" She sounded breathless. "I heard the car."

Had she dressed up for me? I loved the thought of that.

I held up her bowl. "Dinner is served."

"You didn't buy anything for you?"

"I was at my parents. Mom cooked, so I'm stuffed."

Her face fell. "Griffin, I thought…" She shook her head.

"What?"

"I thought you wanted to have dinner together to discuss how things were going with Jude or something."

"Phoebe, I just wanted to bring you dinner. Besides, look how happy you are."

She smiled, taking the bag from me and carefully pulling out the bowl as we approached the dining room. She'd already put forks and knives for two on the table.

"Thanks, it's my favorite. I haven't had it since I moved here because it's not exactly close."

"Where did you live before?" I asked.

"In the Encanto neighborhood."

"With him," I stated.

She nodded, lowering her eyes to the bowl. "We lived together in a one-bedroom apartment."

"I don't get it. He's a doctor, and you were working in his office. He must have made a lot of bank."

"He wanted to pay back his student debt as quickly as possible."

"There's more to that," I said firmly.

She looked up from her bowl. "How do you know?"

"You tensed up."

Her eyes turned misty. "I never really asked for anything. And… he used a lot of those savings to buy *her* a car. I saw it on Facebook today. He posted it with the comment 'Surprising my baby for no reason at all. Because she deserves it.'" She waved her hand in front of her face. "I don't even know why it upsets me so much."

"Phoebe, it's a normal reaction."

"I knew we were saving money, so whenever he asked me if I wanted something, I'd tell him I didn't need anything. It didn't matter if it was Christmas or my birthday. I think the most extravagant thing I ever asked for was a Kindle, and that was during a Prime Day, so it was already on sale." She swallowed hard, and her voice was rougher when she spoke again. "I just don't get why I wasn't worth anything to him."

I pulled my chair closer, fighting to keep my temper under control, which was insane because I usually had zero temper. Clearly, that didn't apply where Phoebe was concerned.

"Some people are the lowest of the low. They're so self-centered that they don't care about anyone else but themselves."

"You're right. I think he simply saw me as a painting or piece of furniture, someone who'd been part of his life for so long that he could completely neglect me."

If she were mine, I'd give her the world: everything I owned, everything money could buy. If money couldn't buy it, I'd somehow still find a way to get it for her. But she wasn't mine. And she was obviously still working on recovering from the relationship fiasco. The last thing she needed was me barreling into her life. Besides, relationships weren't my thing. I didn't want to hurt her.

"Phoebe, listen, I plan on calling Jude next week to tell him that we won't be able to make it at all. *Ever*. I'll think about a good excuse."

"No, don't do that. I was actually going to call and talk to you about that, but the week got away from me. Don't cancel it. We can do it," she said.

I frowned. "What?"

"One weekend won't be that hard. And I don't think he'll keep inviting us to things. Eventually, he'll just want to talk to you about the deal, and either it goes through or it doesn't."

"But this isn't fair to you. You have a lot on your plate. You don't need to deal with this complication." Plus, I was thinking how disappointed my family was in me for even doing it in the first place. My conscience was winning.

She smiled at me. "It's a delicious complication, and I could use some more of those."

I narrowed my eyes at her. If she started flirting, I wasn't responsible for where we ended up.

Probably with me sinking inside her and her legs wrapped around my waist.

"I thought about it. *Really* thought about it," she added. "I don't think it's going to be too much of an inconvenience. Besides, it might be fun! I'm sure their weekend getaway will be fabulous."

I wiggled my eyebrows. "It might involve kissing."

"I figured. I think we're very good at it."

My cock twitched. Fucking hell, this wasn't going the way I'd intended. Then again, I'd postponed canceling the weekend with Jude this week… because I didn't actually want to.

This was what I'd come here tonight for, I realized. To hear her tell me that she wanted to continue the ruse.

"Just so you know, I was kind of holding back."

She jerked her head back. "What? With the kiss? That's not possible."

I grinned at her. "I was putting on a very good show for that moron."

She smiled. "Well, it worked. He didn't contact me again."

"Thank fuck." I leaned back in my chair, happy that I'd managed to intimidate Marshall, but quicky sobered up. "Phoebe, are you sure?" I asked her again, because I wouldn't move forward with this unless she gave an absolutely resounding yes. My parents wouldn't look poorly on me if this was more than just me trying to convince someone into doing business.

She sat up straighter, rolling her shoulders back, and flashed me a very big grin. "Hell yes, we can do this. We'll get your stake in Jude's company. I do have a request, though."

"Sure." Why shouldn't she? It was an agreement, after all.

"If we do run into Marshall again at some point, give me another hot kiss."

I burst out laughing, throwing my head back. "You've got it. Let's celebrate sealing the deal."

She blushed for real this time, pressing her hand to her right cheek as if she couldn't quite believe it.

"I wasn't trying to suggest—" I began.

Phoebe laughed nervously, saying, "No worries, but I don't have champagne. I have white and red. Your pick."

"I don't need anything to drink. You go ahead. I'll have water to toast."

She pouted. "No. I don't want to drink by myself."

"Okay. I'll join you, then."

"I've got a bottle of white wine already open in the fridge."

I went there with her, pulling on the door, and a loud crack splintered through the air.

"Holy crap!" I exclaimed. "The handle just broke." I put it on the counter, inspecting the refrigerator door.

"Oh shit! Are you hurt?"

"No."

She ran a hand through her hair. "I'll buy superglue tomorrow and fix it. I've already done it three times."

"That would explain why it came off so easily."

"You can still open it like this." She put both her hands at the edge of the door and pulled with force, then took out the bottle of wine.

"Phoebe," I said slowly as we headed back to the table.

"Don't say it."

"You don't even know what I was about to say."

"That I should buy another fridge."

I moved up behind her, looking over her shoulder as she poured the wine. "You can't live like this."

She turned around so quickly that I nearly got whiplash. "This is my house, for better or for worse. At this point, I'm glad I have a place to live and don't have to beg my friends to take me in."

"One of my brothers invested in a block of condos. I'm sure he can put in a word for you."

She shook her head. "Griffin, don't ask, please. I know this house isn't what you're used to, but it's mine. Are you uncomfortable being here?"

I stepped closer. "It's not about me. It's uncomfortable for you. The front steps are a death trap, and the furniture is falling apart."

"It's just old."

"I'm not sure this house is safe for you."

"It doesn't have mold," she said proudly. "The inspector checked that before we bought it."

Mold. That was rock bottom when it came to requirements for a house as far as I was concerned. But Phoebe was clinging to that like it was her salvation.

"I know our lives are very different—"

"It's not about that, Phoebe," I countered.

"Yes, it is. You look around and see a fucking disaster," she said. I'd clearly pissed her off unintentionally. "I see it as a way for me to start over, okay? I don't need you to make me feel even worse about this place than I already do."

"I'm sorry. That was not my intention. I apologize. I didn't want to upset you."

"Apology accepted." She held up one glass. I took the other one. "As long as *you* don't bring it up again." She jabbed her finger at me for emphasis.

"Fine," I said. "I'll do my best, but I can't promise."

She gave me a strange look, licking her lips. "But there's one thing we should talk about." Her cheeks turned red.

"Anything."

"Sleeping arrangements."

I grinned. "That's got you blushing, huh?"

She pressed her lips together. "Griffin..."

"I'll think of something. We'll say that I'm a bad sleeper, so we usually use separate bedrooms. I'll ask to be in another guest room."

"You think they're going to be fine with that?"

"Sure."

"All right." She was still blushing, though. "Then let's toast to next weekend."

I grinned and clinked my glass against hers. I had the strangest feeling that it was going to be epic.

CHAPTER 12
PHOEBE

THE NEXT WEEK PASSED QUICKLY, and before I knew it, it was Saturday morning. Griffin texted me yesterday with the plan for the weekend, and I'd gotten into a bit of a frenzy. We were going to be spending a few hours on Jude's boat today, and I was to bring a bathing suit.

I only owned a tiny bikini that didn't cover much. I debated going out to buy another one, but I couldn't afford to spend money on anything. Having to pack for the weekend also forced me to go through all the clothes I'd planned to take on the trip with Marshall.

For some reason, it didn't hurt as much to look at everything. My heart felt lighter somehow. Griffin was right about Marshall. Yes, he was doing things for his fiancée that he'd never done for me (I'd stalked his social media some more—he bought her a Louis Vuitton bag and a pair of Louboutins all in one week!), but that didn't mean there was something wrong with me. He just wasn't the right one for me. I wish I'd had the guts to leave him years ago.

He'd turned into a bit of a douchebag when he started his practice. I'd been so silly that I accepted working for him at minimum wage. Marshall insisted that we'd save on taxes if I did.

I shrugged it off, not really wanting to think about it anymore. I had a fantastic weekend ahead of me, and I was certain that Griffin and I could pull this off. And I wasn't feeling as guilty for what we were doing as I had at the restaurant.

The more I thought about it, the more I wanted to help Griffin. Who cared what he did with his personal life as long as he would be an asset to Jude's business? Jude shouldn't have held Griffin's reputation against him in the first place.

Liar, liar, pants on fire. You're just looking for any excuse to spend some time with Griffin—maybe get one or two of those smoking-hot kisses again.

Yep, I wasn't even going to pretend otherwise. I was definitely looking forward to another lip-lock with this handsome man.

Because I wasn't sure what to expect at the house, I packed more outfits than necessary. I was so giddy that I even locked up and headed out with my suitcase five minutes before Griffin arrived.

As I trudged down the front steps, the wood finally gave in, and the lower step broke right in the middle. I managed to avoid sinking my foot through it, but only barely. I lost my balance, dropping the bag to one side, and falling on all fours.

Holy shit, Griffin wasn't wrong. The place truly was a death trap.

I quickly got up, brushing the dirt off my palms and knees before lifting my bag. Then I inspected the staircase. The hole looked nasty. Whatever, I'd deal with it on Monday. I was determined not to let it get me down.

This was going to be an amazing day and weekend. I didn't break my neck on the stairs, for starters, and the hottest guy on the planet was picking me up. What more could I want?

I sent a pic of my suitcase to Veronica, who replied instantly.

Veronica: Girl, I can't believe you're going through with this, but HAVE FUN.

Phoebe: Yes, ma'am.

Veronica: And if you get the chance to jump his bones for real, DO IT.

I laughed but didn't reply. She'd been shocked when I first told her we were going away for the weekend, then insisted that I could get another hot kiss or two out of it. I mean… she wasn't wrong. I was certain we'd have an opportunity to kiss. And I was going to grab it with both hands.

A few seconds later, I spotted Griffin's Range Rover at the corner and smiled for no reason at all. I rolled my suitcase right to the edge of the pavement.

He jumped out of the car the second he stopped and said, "Why did you trudge your bag out here? I would have helped you."

"I was excited," I admitted. "I've never been on a boat."

"You'll enjoy it. You did pack a bathing suit, right?" he double-checked.

"Yes." I debated telling him that it might not be entirely appropriate but decided not to. I was just trying to roll with the punches today. I needed some spontaneity in my life. For the past decade, everything had been set in stone, so I was relishing this little adventure with Griffin. It made me feel alive like nothing had before.

"You had breakfast?" he asked once we were in the car.

"Just coffee. I usually don't have breakfast. By the way, I think I packed far too many outfits."

"I was going to ask about that. That's a huge-ass bag."

"It's the biggest one I own," I said proudly.

He laughed, which was when I realized, "You don't have a bag."

He jerked his thumb toward the back seat, and I turned my head.

"That's… a gym bag."

"All my stuff fit in there."

"Oh, to be a man," I said. "Things are so easy. So, where are we going exactly?"

"To the harbor."

When Griffin said we'd spend a few hours on the water, I'd imagined a big boat. But this was most definitely a yacht. Griffin parked the car in the designated parking area, then grabbed my huge-ass bag, putting his tiny one on top. Jude and Emma were already on board, waving at us.

It had two levels. There was a deck on the upper level and a cabin, whereas there seemed to be an entire suite on the lower one. Through the windows, I could see that it looked a lot like a living room with a couch and a table. I was certain there was a bedroom somewhere too.

"Welcome, you two," Jude said once we'd joined them on the deck.

"Hi," I said, securing my hat on my head. The sun and I weren't great friends.

"I'm so glad this worked out."

"You've got yourself quite a boat here," Griffin told Jude.

"Thanks. I've spent a few months learning how to navigate it."

Griffin looked at him with appreciation. "Really? I assumed there'd be a captain with us."

"Nah, I got my certification. Took a while, but I managed it. I want to spend some time on the water with Emma. That's why I bought this baby, too, so I can give my wife all the comfort she wants."

Emma looked at him like he hung the moon. Was it weird that I just liked being around them? They had this bright energy surrounding them.

As I stepped into the suite, Griffin put a hand on my back.

My dress dipped right above my tailbone, and I swallowed hard at the contact.

Damn it, Phoebe. Get used to it.

For some reason, I didn't think I would.

"You can put your bags wherever," Emma said.

Griffin rolled my suitcase into a small nook by the door. Then he turned around, eyes trained on me. They flashed, and my cheeks heated violently.

Griffin

Fuck, how can she be so sexy?

She was wearing a white dress, and her back was exposed. It dipped into a V between her breasts and didn't look out of place here on a yacht. She was so damn cute with that hat on, and I wanted to kiss her senseless for no reason at all. Still, I had to get a grip on myself for now. I was certain the opportunity for kissing would present itself later, and I was going to take full advantage of it.

Jude gave us a tour of the yacht, and Emma explained the places they planned to explore while boating. The idea had merit. I hadn't thought about it until now, but being out on a boat gave you a lot of privacy as well as flexibility to explore the coast.

"We also want to sail the Mediterranean soon, but we're not taking this baby there," Emma shared. "We'll probably just rent a yacht."

"This looks great," I said when we reached the deck.

"We took the liberty of preparing some drinks."

They'd gone all out. Orange juice, waters, champagne. I looked at Phoebe, who seemed awed by everything.

"This is amazing," she gushed. "But you really didn't have to."

"Nonsense," Emma said. "It's our pleasure, and honestly, I didn't really have to do much. This one here decided to spoil all of us today and had a concierge arrange everything." She squeezed Jude's arm, and he smiled at her.

I had a good feeling about this. Jude was putting a lot of effort into accommodating us. I couldn't see him turning down my investment offer after this.

Jude clapped his hands together. "All right, I'll be going to the captain's cabin." He sounded extremely proud as he said it. "You three make yourselves comfortable."

"Actually, I'll come with you," Emma said. "I want us to be together when we sail out of the harbor."

"Sure, let's go, darling."

He took her hand, and they both disappeared into the captain's cabin.

Phoebe sighed. "I didn't even know a relationship could ever be like that, let alone after so many years."

"That makes two of us," I admitted. "But wait, I thought you said your parents are still together."

"They are, and they have a happy marriage. But they aren't *that* close." She laughed nervously before adding, "I'm going to change into my bathing suit."

"Sure."

Thank fuck she was taking off that sinful dress. It was completely appropriate for the occasion, yet it drove me crazy.

When she returned several minutes later, I realized I was in a world of trouble. She'd taken off the dress all right, but this wasn't any better. In fact, it was so much worse. Her bikini was black and tiny. In my mind, she was simply walking around in lingerie. It barely covered her breasts, and her ass cheeks were completely on display. And Phoebe wore it damn well.

Marshall was a stupid asshole.

She tiptoed toward me and said, "I feel a bit embarrassed about this bikini, but I didn't have another one."

"You look fucking gorgeous."

"Oh, okay. Thanks." Her cheeks turned red again.

"Your problem isn't going to be Emma and Jude. It's going to be fighting me off."

She grinned. "That's good. It'll give us more credibility. Aren't you going to change?"

"I've got my swimming trunks on underneath my shorts."

I took off my T-shirt and then pushed down my pants. Phoebe swallowed audibly. When I straightened up, she looked like she might drool any second.

"Seems I'm not the only who's got a huge problem, am I?" I questioned.

She looked up slowly, then shook herself as if realizing she was checking me out in plain sight. I held her gaze stubbornly until she looked away.

"Umm, I'm thirsty," she said.

I decided not to put her on the spot. "What do you want to drink?"

"Orange juice."

She licked her lips as I poured her a glass, which she downed right away. The yacht was moving ahead at a pleasant speed. I glanced in the captain's cabin. Emma and Jude were concentrating on the wheel, or perhaps the screen in front of them.

"I don't think we're going to have company anytime soon," I said.

"I agree," Phoebe said, then took a huge spray bottle of sunblock out of her purse. "I need to put this on or I'm going to get burned. The sun is already so damn hot."

"I never use sunscreen."

She stared at me. "Griffin, that can't possibly be true. Do you know how many risks you're incurring?"

I shrugged. "I've always had good skin. I never get burned."

"That's not the point," she said. "Sun damage is… Oh, you're not going to get away with that today. You're putting on sunscreen."

I grinned, leaning into her. "I accept on one condition."

"What's that?"

"You put it on me," I said, emphasizing the words.

"You and y-your b-bargains," she said, stuttering the words a bit.

This was something fun I hadn't anticipated. We stepped farther away from the snack table so we didn't risk any of the spray drifting over it. She put sunblock on herself and then rubbed her hands vigorously. Watching her was a form of torture, and yet I couldn't look away as she spread it on her arms and belly, then up her chest. She was very thorough, applying it along her bikini top and even dipping her hands slightly beneath it. Watching her fingertips disappear behind the fabric was almost too much. I had to look away.

Damn! It was eleven o'clock in the morning and I was already sporting a hard-on. How the hell was I going to survive the weekend?

When I looked at Phoebe again, she was spraying her legs, having put one foot up on a lounge chair and then carefully massaging her calf. When she touched her buttock, I nearly lost it. I wanted so damn badly to help her, but if I touched her right now, I'd make a spectacle of us, pretend relationship or not.

After she finished applying it on her face, she waved the bottle at me. "Your turn."

I grinned lazily.

She lowered the bottle. "You weren't serious earlier, were you?"

I shrugged. "Dead serious. I won't wear any if you don't spread it on me."

"You play dirty," she said but walked closer to me.

"Phoebe, you haven't even seen anything yet."

She sucked in a breath. I sat down on the chair as she sprayed a generous amount on my shoulders and started spreading it with her delicate hands.

Fuck my life. What was I thinking, asking her to do this? Feeling her hands on my back and arms was far too much. I was making a conscious effort to breathe in and out.

I needed to focus on anything else. On business, yes. Today was all about getting in Jude's good graces.

She was touching my chest now.

If I could convince him that I could apply my strategies to the age groups he wanted—

She was at my navel. I wasn't just sporting a semi at this point, I was completely hard.

Come on. You had a pitch, Griffin. Remember it. What was it?

She went down my lower abdomen and then brushed her fingers against the waistband of my trunks. I groaned, gripping her hand.

"No," I said in a dangerously low voice.

She looked at me with a sly smile. "You talk a big game, don't you? This is payback. Besides, you can easily get burned there."

"No," I repeated.

Something in my eyes must have tipped her off that I was losing control, because she didn't insist. Her smile widened, and she went behind me, spreading the lotion on my lower back.

"Thanks for doing that."

"It was my pleasure, darling," she said in a sassy voice I hadn't heard it before.

It was precisely at that moment that I realized she hadn't actually just done it for my benefit.

"You wanted to maul me," I concluded.

She laughed softly. "Took you long enough to catch on."

"Damn, and here I was thinking you were worried for my well-being."

"Well, I was. But I realized there were also benefits to giving in."

I smiled, satisfaction growing inside my chest. I'd felt a bit guilty about roping Phoebe into this weekend, but not anymore. She was enjoying herself, and she clearly loved spreading that sunblock over every ridge of my muscles. Wasn't that the whole point of this, to have some fun? Get her out of that funk she'd been in for months?

I thought she might be done after finishing with my back, but then she sprayed some more liquid on my legs. If I felt her hands anywhere on my inner thighs, I really was going to lose it.

"I'll do this part," I said. I barely recognized my voice.

"You really can't play at your own game, can you?" she said as I spread it on my thighs.

"I didn't realize you'd be so good at it," I admitted.

"Oh, I didn't think I was. But you're making me discover new things about myself, Griffin, and I like them."

Fuck me.

CHAPTER 13
PHOEBE

I WAS PUTTING on a good show, but I was on fire. Luckily, in case my cheeks turned beet red, I could blame it on the sun. Despite covering myself with sunblock, I always managed to get red in the face.

Griffin tilted his head, a smile playing on his lips. "I can see that. And I'm liking it too."

I practically felt myself melt beneath his intense gaze. I looked toward the captain's cabin again. Jude was showing Emma how to move the wheel.

Oh goodness, they really weren't going to come out anytime soon. I hadn't anticipated being alone with Griffin for so long. I could join them in the captain's cabin, but I'd be a bit of a third wheel.

I dreamed of having a love like that one day. Seeing those two together, I realized Marshall and I never had that. How could I ever fool myself into thinking otherwise?

To give myself something to do, I went to the buffet. The setup was very professional, with a cooling mechanism to keep things fresh. Plus, it helped that the table was shaded.

I grabbed a plate and put some canapés on it. I had no idea

what they were, but everything looked delicious. I'd just added some grapes when I felt Griffin behind me.

"Trying to get away from me already, Phoebe?"

I laughed nervously. "Is it that obvious?"

"Just to me." His tone was playful. He came even closer and said, "I don't want to make you nervous."

I looked at him over my shoulder. "I don't think you can help it, but it's not a bad nervous."

He narrowed his eyes. "That doesn't make any sense."

I licked my lips; he inhaled sharply.

Oh wow. My entire body reacted to that. My nipples tightened, and I barely resisted the urge to press my thighs together. I felt as if something had awoken inside me.

I focused on the table again. "To me it does." I desperately needed to change the subject. "I've been trying to think about what to drink."

"Champagne?" he tempted.

I shook my head. "I don't want anything with bubbles, but I'll have some white wine. It feels so decadent to drink at this time of the day."

He laughed. "It is, but why the hell not? It's Saturday. I have to give it to Emma and Jude: owning a boat is a brilliant idea. It never even occurred to me, but it gives you a lot of privacy and flexibility."

"That's true," I said. "And being out at sea gives you a sense of freedom."

"You know what I like most? That no one can see you. If Emma and Jude weren't here, I would—" He stopped abruptly, and I turned to look at him. His nostrils flared, and his eyes were fixed on me.

What was he about to say? What would he do if Emma and Jude weren't here? I was pathetically desperate to know. Because if they weren't here, we wouldn't even have to pretend we were an item.

I swallowed hard but didn't have the guts to ask him to

finish that thought. He poured a glass of white wine for himself and also one for me. We clinked them together and then went down to sit in the shade of an umbrella between the lounge chairs. I was amazed that it was holding steady despite the strong breeze.

I ate a handful of canapés before taking a sip of wine; otherwise, I'd be drunk as a skunk in no time, and that wouldn't do. I needed to be on my best behavior.

"This is so relaxing," I said, keeping the grapes in one hand and my glass in the other. "This is one of the best days I've had in a long time."

"I'm glad, Phoebe. You deserve good things," Griffin said. He was sitting on the chaise lounge right next to mine.

I smiled, eating another grape. "I am fully confident that good things are coming my way."

"I love your optimism."

"I try. That's what keeps me going. I can't let the bad things get me down. If I did, I don't think I'd ever get up."

"Most people in your position probably wouldn't have the strength to go on, at least not at the rate that you are," he said. "I admire you for that—a lot."

"Thank you." His words truly touched me.

I was proud of myself for pulling through these past few weeks, but hearing someone else say it was entirely different

The boat stopped after a while, and I knew Emma and Jude would be joining us soon. Sure enough, a few minutes later, they came over to where we were sitting.

"How are the canapés?" Jude asked. "Which are your favorites?"

Griffin spoke first. "I haven't even touched them. I went straight for the wine."

"Attaboy," Emma said with a wink.

"Oh, I've had one of each. The ones with cheese are my favorite, but all of them are delicious. Thank you for setting everything up," I gushed.

"Of course," Jude said, sounding distracted. "Emma took care of everything."

She beamed. I loved how he always praised her. He wasn't trying to claim credit, nor was he afraid to put the spotlight on his wife.

"Well, when I spoke to the cleaning company in charge of this, I mentioned that we were going out to sea, and they advised that we should always have food on board. They recommended this catering company, and I'm going to keep them in mind."

"How long are we staying here?" Griffin asked.

"Not long," Jude said. "Emma and I just wanted to grab a bite because we didn't have breakfast. Afterward, I'll keep driving for another hour and a half or so, and then we'll reach our destination."

"This day is shaping up to be lovely," Emma said. "We're so happy you could join us."

"So am I," I said truthfully.

Jude and Emma lingered for about an hour before they went back up to the captain's cabin to continue our journey. The conversation we had was lighthearted and fun. Too bad I'd never see them after this weekend.

After they left, Griffin and I relaxed on the lounge chairs. I closed my eyes and had almost drifted off when a phone beeped.

Opening my eyes, I looked around, searching for my bag, when Griffin said, "Oh, that's mine. My nephew responded to me." He checked the message and then barked out a laugh. "Ha, I knew it."

"What?" I was genuinely curious to know.

He turned the phone to me. There was a bit of glare from the sun, so I tilted closer.

Griffin: Buddy, do you think you'd like to go out on a boat at sea?

Jeremy: Yes! You are the best, Uncle Griffin. I've never been out at sea.

Griffin had a triumphant smile.

"Why do you look so full of yourself?" I asked.

"Because I'm finally getting the hang of how to convince my nephew to spend some time with me."

I barely bit back a laugh. "By bribing him?"

"No." He looked affronted. "I'm not saying I'm above that, but I'm simply choosing to expose him to new experiences."

I started laughing at that. Then several things happened at the same time. First, I realized that, despite the canapés, perhaps drinking alcohol in this heat wasn't my best idea. My balance wasn't as good as I'd assumed. I'd been leaning in too far to read the text message when I lost my balance. I attempted to catch myself, but somehow my hand slid from the edge of the chair and I went forward, headfirst into Griffin. I landed with my cheek on his abs, near his navel. He immediately put a hand on my torso, two fingers grazing the fabric of my bikini top.

My nipples turned rock hard, which shocked me. *From that mere touch? Damn.* I'd never been so responsive before. I blamed it on the alcohol and the hot-as-hell man next to me.

I finally straightened up, and Griffin looked at me carefully, immediately pulling his hand away.

"Are you okay?"

"Yep. Sorry. No more wine for me. I lost my balance."

"Yeah, I figured," he replied. "You sure you didn't hurt yourself? I heard something crack."

I twisted my neck to the left and the right, grinning. "That's my neck. It makes creepy sounds."

I lay back on my lounger and made a mental note not to lean over again too soon. I closed my eyes once more, and this time I actually did fall asleep. I only woke up when Griffin gently said, "We're here."

"Oh my God. You're all dressed," I exclaimed, jumping up from the chair. "I'm going to put on my dress."

Griffin nodded. "Don't stress out. Jude said we still have ten minutes or so."

I glanced at the captain's cabin. Both Jude and Emma were still there. I went inside, heading to the corner where I'd left my dress. I wasn't in the mood to take off my bikini, so I simply slid it back on over my suit. Then I went to the small bathroom to freshen up.

Ten minutes later, we headed off the boat.

Griffin rolled my suitcase, putting his gym bag over his shoulder. Jude was rolling two small carry-on suitcases. Emma and I were walking in front of the guys. We'd docked right in front of their place.

Once again, I was taken by complete surprise. Emma and Jude's weekend home was truly small. For some reason, I'd expected a huge mansion or something.

"This was where we lived *before* I managed to make money," Jude explained.

"Oh, that's so lovely," I said. "I like that you kept the house."

Emma sighed. "It's where our kids grew up. Jude tried to convince me to tear it down and build something bigger, but I just couldn't bring myself to do it."

"It's not big, but it's got all the comforts."

Looking over my shoulder, I noticed Griffin was frowning, but I couldn't understand why.

Once we entered the house, I completely forgot about him. Emma started explaining what was where. Seeing everything, I couldn't help thinking that this was exactly how I imagined my home would look one day. The kitchen and living room were one big space. The island wasn't very big, but I could picture little kids sitting around it, baking with Emma or just generally flouncing around her. The cabinets were painted white, and the countertops were a dark granite. The dining area was right next to it. The couch and the armchairs were at the far end of the room.

"All right," Emma said. "So, one bedroom is upstairs, and the other one is downstairs. When our boys were little, they bunked upstairs, and we kept the downstairs room."

It took several seconds for her words to register. *Oh my God. One bedroom.*

I glanced at Griffin, realizing why he'd frowned upon seeing the house. He could probably tell even before we'd stepped inside that there wouldn't be an extra bedroom.

CHAPTER 14
PHOEBE

I BREATHED in deeply through my nose and then out my mouth. Griffin said nothing as he took both our bags and hauled them upstairs.

"I'll go check out the bedroom," I said.

"Excellent," Emma said. "If you need anything, just holler and I'll come help with whatever. But everything should be there. I put towels on the bed. The bathroom is an en suite."

"Thank you." Panic rose in my throat as I hurried up the stairs.

Griffin had put the bags by the door and was looking around. The room was spacious enough, but there was no couch or anything.

He turned to face me. "I'll tell them that I'll sleep on the couch downstairs."

I grimaced. "That looks super uncomfortable."

"You don't know that," Griffin commented.

"It didn't look like a pullout."

"You're right."

Shit, shit, shit. Why didn't I even think about this scenario?

Griffin cleared his throat. "Look, it's no big deal if it's uncomfortable. It's just one night. I'll tell them I'm a very bad sleeper and have to sleep downstairs."

I bit my lower lip, running a hand through my hair. "But you'll kind of be in their way downstairs. The bathroom isn't close by."

He frowned. "I didn't think about that."

My heart was beating so damn fast that I wasn't even sure how to calm it down. I felt like I'd been racing around the house at top speed.

"Um, look, this can work," I said. "The bed is huge, and we're adults."

He opened his mouth, but only something resembling a growl came out. He cleared his throat again, a bit roughly this time.

"No."

"Huh?"

"We're not doing this," he said.

I swallowed hard. "I don't see any other solution."

"We can stay for a few hours, and then we'll tell them that you aren't feeling well and we need to head back."

I put a hand on my hip, considering this. "Do you think you can seal the deal with him before then?"

Griffin shook his head. "Not likely."

"That's what I thought too. So then this whole weekend will have been for nothing."

"I don't want you to do anything you're uncomfortable with, Phoebe."

I fiddled with my thumbs. The problem wasn't that I was uncomfortable, it was that I didn't know how to be so close to this handsome man and not cross a line.

Oh come on. Shake yourself off, Phoebe. This truly is a huge bed.

I pressed my palms together, crossing my fingers. "The bed is enormous, Griffin. I'm sure we won't even know the other one is in it."

He took in a sharp breath. "I'll know. I'll so fucking know you're there."

I didn't have any reply to that. My throat thickened as he stepped closer. Oh sweet Lord, this wasn't helping my case. My pulse was even faster. How on Earth was this possible?

"Phoebe, are you sure?"

I nodded. "Yes, of course. I wouldn't have suggested it otherwise."

He looked straight at me for a few seconds, then tilted his head, glancing at the bed. I had the distinct feeling that he was bracing himself somehow. His nostrils flared as he took in a deep breath.

"All right. But if at any point you change your mind, just tell me. I'll find an excuse, and we'll go back to the city."

"But it's not fair to you, your deal."

"Fuck the deal." His voice was so damn sexy. "I don't want you to be uncomfortable."

"I'm not, I promise. I'll tell you if I change my mind, but I don't think it's fair to ruin their weekend."

He shook his head. "It wouldn't ruin it. I'd ask for a car to be sent to pick us up. This isn't an island."

My eyes bulged. *What? That's something he could just do?* I'd never heard anyone say that except in the movies.

"Thanks." I was utterly happy that he was willing to go to any lengths to make me feel comfortable.

"How about we change and then join them downstairs?" Griffin asked.

"Good idea." I needed to get rid of my bikini.

"I'll change in the bathroom."

"Sure."

He put my suitcase and his gym bag on the desk under the window. There was no dresser here, so I assumed they never had a guest who stayed longer than a few days. Griffin took out some clothes and went into the bathroom. Before closing the door, he said, "I'll take a shower too. Actually, do you want to take one?"

"No, I'm good."

"Then I'll go ahead. Don't wait for me."

"All right."

I opened my suitcase, trying to decide what to wear. I hadn't packed the right dresses. Most were too fancy, but after our dinner in the city, I wanted to be prepared for anything.

I took out a white beach dress, smoothing some of the wrinkles. As quickly as possible, I removed my bikini, keeping my fingers crossed that Griffin wouldn't walk out right at that moment. I put on a white thong and bra before slipping the dress on.

Is this too casual?

Ugh, I had to stop overthinking.

A groan from the bathroom distracted me from my thoughts, and I hurried to the door. Shit, had Griffin hurt himself?

I stood in front of it for a few seconds, and then I heard another groan. I was about to knock and ask if he was okay when I heard a low sound. If I hadn't practically pegged my ear to the door, I would have missed it completely.

"Fuck, Phoebe!" And then another groan.

Heat pooled between my thighs. I barely bit back a groan myself as I realized what was happening.

Griffin was pleasuring himself.

Heat like I'd never known coursed through me. I fanned myself as I took deep breaths, then I swallowed hard. I was already slick between my thighs. *Holy shit.*

I looked at the bed, then back at the door to the bathroom. I wasn't going to survive the night. There was no way I could sleep next to this man and not give in to my feelings, knowing he'd touched himself while thinking about me.

I hurried out of the room before Griffin had the chance to come out. If I saw him with damp skin, I was going to maul him right there and then, there was no question about that.

Emma and Jude were both at the kitchen island chopping vegetables when I stepped in.

"Hey," I said. "Can I help in any way?"

This would be an excellent way to take my mind off all the sexy things happening upstairs.

"That would be great. We'd finish the preparation faster," Emma said.

"It's going to take a while for everything to be ready," Jude added.

"What are we making?" I asked.

"Skewers," Jude replied proudly, nodding toward the long metal rods on the table.

Emma was chopping up cucumbers. "We're also making a salad," she explained.

"This looks delicious."

"You want to start the fire, honey?" Emma asked Jude.

He nodded. "Yes, I'd better. The fire does take me a while." He looked at me. "We have a grill, but I prefer the fire pit."

"My parents had that too," I said as Emma handed me a cutting board and gave me tomatoes and cucumbers.

"Please chop those finely into small bites. They have more flavor like that."

"Got it," I said.

"You were saying about your parents?" Jude asked.

"Oh, we had a fire pit when I was growing up."

"You're from San Diego?" Emma asked.

"Yes. My parents lived here until a few years ago. My grandparents moved to Montana about eight years ago. That's where they're from, and now they need a bit of help, so my parents moved there as well."

"What am I missing?" Griffin asked, jogging down the stairs.

He came straight to me, putting a hand at my lower back. I hoped to God I wasn't blushing.

"You already put her to work?" Griffin teased.

"Nah, we were just hoping to get some insider info on you," Jude said with good humor.

Emma elbowed him lightly. "She's telling us about her parents."

Griffin kissed my shoulder, and shivers raced all over my body. His groan from earlier resounded in my mind. I wouldn't be able to forget that moment anytime soon, if at all.

"Phoebe?" Griffin asked, and I realized he'd been talking to me.

"I spaced out, I'm sorry."

"Emma asked you if you prefer chicken or beef." He was so close to me that his mouth was almost on mine.

"I eat everything," I said, looking straight at Emma.

She nodded. "Fair enough. Then we'll make half with chicken and half with beef."

I realized that they'd given Griffin a cutting board too. He was in charge of slicing the meat. I grimaced at that, and Emma laughed.

"Is that how you usually do things?" she asked us. "He chops the meat, and you do the veggies?"

I hadn't realized she was watching us so closely.

"We're a good team," Griffin said, and I simply nodded.

We all worked side by side to assemble the skewers. Half an hour later, Emma put them on a platter and took them outside for Jude to cook.

The second Griffin and I were alone in the kitchen, I became jittery. I tried focusing on taking out plates and cutlery. Emma had tried to fight me on it, but I truly needed to do something.

"Phoebe," Griffin said slowly, coming right next to me. I almost expected for him to touch my lower back again, but he didn't. "Are you okay?"

I licked my lips, pushing a strand of hair behind my ear before turning around and looking straight at him. "Um, yeah, sure. Why?"

"You seem uneasy."

Uneasy, huh? More like turned on and confused. There was no way to talk about what I'd heard without being even more awkward. And certainly not here in front of Jude and his wife.

"I'm just trying to find my footing," I told him, which was true.

"If you change your mind about spending the night here—"

I shook my head vehemently. "No, that's not it."

"So, there is something," he pressed.

Damnit, he was really good at reading me.

"I'm trying to gauge how to best play this. It's a bit different than at the restaurant."

His shoulders relaxed. "Yeah, it is. It's more intimate."

"Exactly." I averted my gaze because I was sure that if he made eye contact long enough, he'd realize I'd heard him.

"When did you come downstairs?" he asked me.

I turned around, taking out the plates from the overhead cabinet. "After you went into the bathroom. I didn't need much time to change."

"All right," he said.

His voice was a bit different. I wasn't sure if he was buying it. He grabbed the stacked plates and cutlery, I gathered four glasses, and we headed outside.

The outdoor dining area was in the back of the house. I hadn't even noticed it when we first got here. The fire pit was a few feet away. Jude had set the skewers on the bench next to it and was busy stoking the fire. The salad was already on the table.

Once Griffin and I put the glasses, plates, and cutlery down, Emma asked, "What does everyone want to drink? We have the same wine we drank on the boat."

I nodded. "Yeah, I'll have that. I don't want to mix drinks even though it's been a few hours."

"That's good for me too," Griffin said.

"We'll bring a bottle of red too. We always like to have both on hand," Emma said before hurrying inside.

Griffin and I headed to the fire pit.

"Jude, you need help with that?" Griffin asked.

"No, don't get close. This is my domain," Jude replied with a laugh.

"My dad is the same. He's very territorial with his grill," I said.

"You miss your parents," Griffin said with a soft voice.

"A lot."

"When's the last time you visited them?"

Jude narrowed his eyes, and I felt as if someone had dropped ice cubes on my back. Thank God Emma wasn't here; she would pick up that something wasn't right.

"I was there last month, remember? When you and your brothers went to…" My voice faded because I had no idea what to say. Once again, I felt utterly unprepared. Every time Griffin and I spoke alone, it was like I already knew him and didn't need to ask anything else. Yet when we were together with Emma and Jude, I realized how many things I actually didn't know and should have asked.

"Napa Valley," Griffin finished.

"That's right," I said.

"You're doing business in Napa?" Jude asked.

Crisis averted. Thank heavens.

Griffin looked at him, putting his hand in his pocket. "My brothers and I bought a winery, and we're going to rebrand it."

"I thought your businesses were separate from your brothers'."

"They are, but we decided on a whim to do this together. I'm enjoying it. It's been a while since we started something from the ground up together. I didn't even realize I missed working with them until we embarked on this project."

"Tell me more," Jude said.

Griffin held up a finger. "On one condition. I want to stoke the fire."

Jude looked at me. "He always drives a hard bargain, doesn't he?"

I laughed. "He truly does." He didn't even know the half of it.

Jude and Griffin fiddled with the fire for close to twenty minutes before Jude declared it hot enough to place the skewers.

After that, it took another forty minutes for the food to be ready.

"They're delicious," I exclaimed after the first bite. "I personally feel like food is more delicious when cooked on a fire pit."

We debated the pros and cons of an actual grill versus a pit, and then the conversation moved to comparing gas and wood grills.

As I helped myself to a second skewer, I decided to get a fire pit in my backyard too. I didn't want to splurge on anything, but I was certain I could find some cheap ones online. I didn't need anything fancy, just something where I could make a fire in the evening and roast something on it. Or honestly just look at it.

The flames had a calming effect on me. I smiled to myself as Emma and Jude went inside for more drinks.

Griffin brought his mouth to my ear. "You look cute. Remember to tell me later what you're smiling about."

Our hosts were nowhere around, so he hadn't said this for their benefit. The lines between us were blurring.

Before I had a chance to reply, they came back with yet another bottle of red and one of white wine.

"Do you have a favorite? If not, we'll just open both," Jude asked. They started to laugh for no reason. God, they were cute.

Griffin beamed widely, "Go ahead, open them both. Phoebe, want some red wine too?"

"No, I'm sticking with white. Who knows what will happen if I mix them."

"We don't want to get drunk, do we?" Griffin asked, and I blushed.

After Griffin refilled our glasses, Jude held his up. I did the same with mine.

"To a great weekend and making new friends," Jude said.

I felt Griffin tense next to me.

Friends. That could turn into a complication. But I was certain Griffin would solve it. Once he'd signed the deal, he could come up with an excuse about why I wasn't in the picture anymore. I had full confidence that he could get out of that.

But I wasn't nearly confident enough that we could spend the night together and not touch each other.

CHAPTER 15
GRIFFIN

THIS WEEKEND WAS nothing like I'd expected. For one, I'd assumed that Phoebe and I wouldn't be alone for too long. And I definitely assumed the house was much bigger.

"Which ones are your favorite?" Emma asked.

"The chicken," I replied. Whatever marinade she'd used was really good and gave the meat a sweeter taste that I quite liked.

"Mine too," Phoebe said.

I couldn't take my eyes off her. Even though I'd jacked off while thinking about her in the shower like a damn teenager, I was still on edge. I still wanted her.

I needed to find a solution for tonight. There was no way in hell I could sleep next to her. I could try the floor—actually, no. I'd be no good tomorrow with a stiff body. I'd wait until Emma and Jude went to sleep, then go downstairs to the living room. Tomorrow morning, I'd come up with an excuse.

"Want another drink?" Jude asked me.

I shook my head. "I'm fine." I definitely didn't want my judgment clouded around Phoebe.

She seemed far more relaxed than I was. I couldn't believe she'd taken everything in stride. Frankly, I was stunned that she'd agreed to it at all. But as her best friend had put it, she really needed something to take her mind off that asshole. And I'd volunteered for that job.

After we finished dinner, we stayed out for a while longer, as the weather was just perfect. Gradually, I began to relax as well. Emma and Jude were recounting the details of their latest trip to Egypt. Phoebe was listening with rapt attention, asking pertinent questions.

"You'd like to visit the pyramids," I concluded.

She batted her eyelashes. "Well, yeah. If this doesn't count as a hint, I don't know what will."

She smiled at me before focusing on Emma again. She was so good at playing her role.

That's right, Griffin. It's just a role. Get yourself together.

But my dick was definitely not getting the memo. It had been clouding my fucking judgment ever since I saw her in that bikini on the boat.

"Where did you last travel?" Emma asked Phoebe, who looked at me warily. I nodded, gesturing for her to speak.

Whenever an unexpected question popped up, the easiest way was to let one of us talk. The other could just agree to the story.

"We haven't had any time to travel," Phoebe said, which was smart because we didn't have to come up with fake details.

"Both of us have been pretty busy with work," I added.

"We wholeheartedly recommend traveling," Jude said. "I sometimes take weeks off so we can spend as much time as needed in a new destination. If there's anything I'd have done differently when I was younger, it would have been to travel more."

"Oh, honey! We're making up for it now in spades," Emma said. "We didn't really have that much money back then, and with the kids, it was easier to just visit local destinations for a quick getaway."

"True, true," Jude said, looking from Phoebe to me. "But Phoebe here looks like she'd enjoy traveling."

She turned to me, grinning. I straightened in my seat, leaning into her and kissing her temple. "Hint taken," I said.

I'd go with her on a world tour if she wanted to.

Oh wow. That was a dangerous thought. Relationships were not my thing. Never had been. All my life, my focus had been entirely on Sterling Investments, then growing my own portfolio of businesses.

Phoebe was made of something different. She wanted marriage and a lot of other things I couldn't give her. I had to make damn sure I remembered that later tonight.

She yawned after a while. "Goodness, it's very late."

To my astonishment, it was eleven o'clock. Their stories about Egypt had taken up most of the evening, but I'd enjoyed them.

"All right, we'll go to bed. You youngsters can stay out here for as long as you want," Emma said. "It's a good thing you insisted on us putting everything in the dishwasher after we finished eating." She winked at Phoebe, who laughed.

"I always do that. Marshall used to say—" She stopped midsentence, throwing me a panicked look.

Damn it.

"I had a roommate for a long time," she said slowly.

"And he was an asshole," I added. That was 100 percent true.

"Well, anyway, I always want to get the dishes out of the way before relaxing."

"It's a good strategy," Emma said, winking at her. "We're early risers. I get up at 5:00 a.m."

Fuck me. I'd planned to sleep on the couch and head upstairs before they woke up.

"Good night," Jude said as they went inside the house.

I waited for a bit before turning to Phoebe.

"You want to go up too?" She yawned again. "It's pretty late."

I glanced behind me. I didn't see anyone moving inside the house, but I knew they'd come out soon to use the bathroom.

"Let's go upstairs, and we can talk."

She nodded.

I stood up abruptly, pulling her chair back, and she stood as well.

She walked slightly in front of me. On instinct, I put a hand on the small of her back. There was no reason for it whatsoever. We were completely alone. She didn't pull away, though. If anything, she pressed herself into my fingers as if she couldn't get enough of my touch.

If she knew everything I wanted to do to her…

We went up the narrow staircase. "Be careful where you step," I warned. There was a night-light along each step, but it wasn't nearly enough for someone who wasn't familiar with the house.

Once we entered the bedroom, I closed the door. It was pitch-dark except for the sliver of moonlight coming through the window, but I didn't make any move to turn on the light.

"Phoebe, I have a plan."

"All right," she whispered.

"I'm going to stay here until I'm certain that they've gone to sleep. Then I'll go down to the couch. Tomorrow morning, I'll wake up before them."

"But Emma said she wakes up at five."

I cleared my throat. "I heard her. That's going to hurt like a bitch."

Phoebe laughed softly.

"I'm going to set my alarm clock before that and go for a run."

She furrowed her brow. "Wait, you've got running gear with you?"

"Yeah. I figured it'd be a good idea to bring it. That's my go-to when I need to release tension."

There was a brief pause, and then Phoebe murmured, "Griffin, that's insane. We agreed that the bed is big enough."

"Yes, but that was before—" I caught myself in time and

stopped talking. What the hell was I going to say? *"Before I jacked off"*?

"Before what?" she pressed.

I swallowed hard. "Before dinner."

She stepped closer. "What changed?"

I didn't say anything for a few beats, considering my words. "Things are blurring, Phoebe. For me."

With a heavy sigh, I decided to be completely honest. "I don't know how it is for you, but I can't be in the same room with you…" I couldn't finish my thought. It was one thing to open up, another thing altogether to be graphic about it.

"I heard you earlier," she said, "in the shower."

I took in a deep breath, stepping closer. I'd tried to be silent. I'd told myself there was no way she could hear.

"I apologize. I didn't want to make you uncomfortable."

"You didn't. It made me want to burst through that door and join you."

The full weight of her words didn't hit me right away, but when it did, my entire body became a live wire.

"Fuck, Phoebe." I brought my hands to her face, tilting her head back slightly. Her eyes glinted from the moonlight. "Do you mean that?"

"Yes. That's why I hurried downstairs." She laughed softly. "Didn't want to give in to temptation."

I took a deep breath and exhaled sharply. "I should go downstairs. Tell me to go."

"No," she whispered. "I don't want you to go. I want you here with me. I want you."

I stepped closer until there was maybe an inch between our bodies. "Are you sure?"

"Yes."

"What do you mean exactly? I need you to tell me in your own words. Sleeping next to you or—"

"With me." Even though her voice was breathy, it was also strong. There was no hesitation.

"Phoebe, you've had a few glasses of wine."

"Not too much," she said quickly. "I didn't want to risk forgetting our stories or getting things messed up."

She started to shake lightly. "Just this once."

And that gave me the permission I needed. Because it could only be this once. We were too different for more.

I brushed my hand over her lips, and she opened her mouth slowly. I pushed my thumb in, and when I felt her tongue on the tip, I nearly lost my composure. I pulled my thumb back out and kissed her, exploring her slowly, parting her lips and giving her my tongue. She whimpered against my mouth, and I moved my hands to the sides of her body, then her back, sliding them down to her ass. When I pushed her against me, she whimpered again. I loved that she was so damn wound up.

I wondered how many strokes of her clit it would take to make her come. She needed this release badly, I realized. I'd had mine earlier in the afternoon, but she'd been holding this tension in her body for much longer. I needed to know how long exactly.

I moved my mouth in a straight line to her earlobe. "Since when have you wanted me, Phoebe?"

"Since you kissed me the first time."

Oh fuck. That made my erection painfully hard. "Did the kiss make you wet?"

"Yes."

New plan: I was going to explore her slowly, but only after she came once.

Cupping the back of her head, I captured her mouth again. With my other hand, I bunched her dress until my fingertips brushed her inner thigh. Then I moved farther up to her panties.

She held her breath as the muscles in her thighs clenched. I slowly pushed her panties down just past her ass, then covered her pussy with my palm. She was so damn wet. She moaned, gripping my shoulders.

"Can you keep quiet?" I asked.

Phoebe trembled in my arms. "I don't think so."

I didn't think that either. But the guest room was on the opposite side of the house from the master bedroom, and on another level. There was no way in hell they were going to hear anything.

Still, I kissed her. I didn't want to risk anything. I wanted to feel the vibrations in her body, to take in all her sounds. I tangled our tongues and moved my palm over her clit.

She'd been wound up since the first time I kissed her. She was going to need more than one orgasm tonight to release all that tension.

I pressed two fingers on her clit and rubbed them down toward her entrance, then dipped in the tips before going back up. She liked that a lot; I felt it in the way she pushed herself into my fingers, the way she gripped my shoulders even tighter. She didn't even attempt to break the kiss. I swirled my tongue against hers even more fiercely as I repeatedly dipped my fingers inside her.

When Phoebe dug her nails into my shoulders, I knew she was close. I kept her hips in place, moving my hand at the pace she liked.

She came hard, and it filled me with so much damn pride. I slid my fingers inside her, thrusting them in while she was still orgasming. I alternated between applying pressure on her clit and massaging her G-spot until she all but crumbled in my arms. Tearing her mouth away from mine, she buried her face in my chest, muffling her sounds.

It didn't matter that I'd relieved all that tension before. It had built back up in no time. She rode out her orgasm far too fast, and I knew that only meant one thing: she needed another one soon because she still had built-up tension to release.

Phoebe straightened up slowly as I dropped my hand.

"Griffin," she murmured.

"You're exquisite," I said, but I was certain she didn't understand a thing. My voice was hoarse, like I'd been screaming right along with her. I cleared my throat. "I'm going to make you come again." My voice was stronger now as I kissed the corner of her mouth. "I know you need it."

"I do," she confessed. "So damn much."

I put a hand on her back, guiding her toward the bed. She was still wearing her dress. I was going to need that out of the way.

"Does your dress have a zipper?"

"No, it's very stretchy," she said.

That was all I needed to know. I yanked it over her head before throwing it in the room. I removed her bra, too, but then I couldn't help myself and also pushed my pants down. I wasn't going to withstand the pressure of the zipper on my cock for too long.

When I took off my T-shirt, she traced my muscles with her fingertips, starting on my chest and trailing down to my abs. She slowed down as her fingers traveled to my navel before moving sideways.

"I've fantasized about these V-lines."

"When?" I wanted to know every detail.

"On the boat," she replied without hesitation.

I touched her collarbone and then cupped one breast. While I kissed her shoulder, she grabbed my cock, squeezing it tightly.

"Fuuuuuck," I exclaimed, standing ramrod straight and sucking in a deep breath. I wanted my mouth on her. I needed to feel her come while my tongue was deep inside. So even though I desperately craved her touch, I took a step back and kneeled in front of her.

"Sit down. Don't lie down, just sit and spread your thighs for me."

I pressed a finger on her clit, and her body started to shake lightly. She lowered herself to the edge of the bed and opened her legs.

I licked up and down one side of her pussy, then the other. I didn't touch her clit yet; from the way she'd reacted just now, it was probably very sensitive.

"Griffin, I can't keep quiet." She reached over to the left, grabbing one of the big pillows and putting it over her chest.

"Not yet," I said. "I want to see you."

I dipped my tongue inside her, and she clenched around it.

She was close already. I'd assumed that her clit was still tender from the first orgasm, but no. Her body was already craving the second one. When she pressed her face into the pillow, lifting her ass a fraction of an inch from the mattress, I had my cue. She didn't need gentle exploration—she needed another wild orgasm.

And then she needed my cock.

I drew circles with my tongue over her clit faster and faster before sucking it into my mouth. Her ass shot up, and I moved my head at the same time, still keeping my mouth pressed on her. Her cry pierced the air, then became completely muffled as she bit into the pillow.

I could spend the rest of my life pleasuring Phoebe. Bringing her over the edge was fucking delicious. Her thighs gave in, and I still didn't take my tongue off her. I wanted to apply pressure while she was still thrashing around.

She was now holding the pillow on her face with both hands. This was just the beginning. I needed her again after tonight, in a space where she could scream the walls down.

When I felt her muscles loosen, I kissed up her pelvis before pushing her farther back on the bed. I climbed over her, sitting on my knees and hunching forward until my face was level with her breast, then licked around her nipple slowly.

She pushed the pillow away as I moved to her other nipple before kissing her sternum.

"How are you feeling?" I asked her.

"Great. Perfect." She put both arms around my neck before dragging her palms down my chest to my abs.

"That's your favorite spot, huh?"

"Sort of. Can't compete with this." She wrapped her hand around my cock.

"Fuck," I exclaimed. "Let me get a condom."

"Okay," she whispered.

I got up from the bed and went to the bathroom. Grabbing a condom from my toiletries bag, I tore it open and put it on immediately.

Turning around, I stopped in the doorway of the bathroom, watching her. She was sitting again on the bed, right in the center of it. Her knees were bent.

I walked toward the bed, climbing on it and quickly moving in front of her. I kissed her long and deep, relishing how she melted against my mouth. Then I pulled back, watching her intently.

"Turn around," I said.

She swallowed audibly. "On all fours?"

I nodded.

She smiled wickedly before turning around. Grabbing the pillow from before, she put it under her head and then shoved her ass up in the air, wiggling it—teasing me. I slapped it once playfully.

"Oh," she moaned.

"You like that?" I asked.

"Yes," she muttered.

I gave her other buttock a slap before positioning myself behind her. I didn't have it in me to tease her again; I knew she was on edge still, and I was far beyond that. I was wound up tight, so I slid inside her carefully. She was dripping wet, but I didn't want to risk her being uncomfortable.

A muffled sound filled the room even though she'd buried her head in the pillow while I slid in.

I dropped my head back, pushing in until I was buried inside her completely. For a few seconds, the room was completely silent. Then the mattress caved in as she moved her knees slightly. She squeezed her muscles once, and I didn't hold back any longer.

Jacking off in the shower was nothing compared to feeling

her around me. She needed me, and I was not ashamed to admit that I was desperate for her in a way I'd never been for anything in my entire life. I pulled my hips back and then thrust in. She moved to match my rhythm. The wilder I became, the wilder she was too.

She wanted everything I had to give her, and I wasn't going to hold back. I hunched my back so I could reach to touch her clit from the side. At first, I just drummed my fingertips on it slowly, but then I increased the pace. When her cries grew louder, I started pressing harder all the way. Thrusting in and out, in and out. Our bodies were perfectly in sync.

Then I slammed harder into her, and she moved forward. The new angle was delicious. Then her knees gave in, and she went flat on the mattress. I was fucking her so good that she couldn't even sustain her weight on her knees. The thought almost sent me over the edge.

I wasn't touching her clit anymore, but I knew she was already close to climaxing. I felt it in the way she squeezed me, and then I heard it as her cry resounded through the pillow. I gave in too. I no longer had the energy to hold back, and there was no need to do it anyway. She was riding out her orgasm, and so did I.

I stayed on top of her as she relaxed her hands, holding them just to the sides of the pillow. I covered them with mine, interlacing our fingers. Then she turned her head sideways, drawing in a deep breath. I liked hearing it. At first, it was uneven and erratic, but then it slowed down.

A few seconds later, we both moved until I was at the edge of the bed. I immediately got up, taking care of the condom in the bathroom and then washing at the sink. When I came out, she was still lying on her belly. She was a sight to behold. Ducking back into the bathroom, I grabbed one of the small towels, putting one corner under hot running water. Then I went next to her on the bed.

"Turn around, Phoebe. I brought a wet cloth."

"Oh," she whispered and moved. "Um, I can do that."

"I don't mind at all."

After cleaning her up, I scooted next to her.

"And you wanted to go downstairs on that uncomfortable couch," she murmured.

We both lay down, facing each other. "I knew it was the only way I could resist you."

"Hmm," she said playfully. "But why resist when this is so much more delicious?"

"Why indeed?" I replied.

She turned onto her other side.

"I'm a side sleeper," she informed me. "And I am so exhausted that I think I'm going to fall asleep in no time."

"That's fine by me."

I liked her sleeping position a lot. I could stay behind her and still have access to her breasts and stomach with one hand. As a bonus, she could even push her ass against me.

"Hmm. You like to spoon?"

"Do what?" I asked.

She looked over her shoulder. "Spoon. You've never heard that before?"

"No, but I'm liking it."

She grinned. "So do I."

She resumed her previous position and pushed her ass into me.

"Oh, someone's not ready to go to sleep," she said.

"No shit." My cock wasn't getting the memo.

But the next second, her breathing was completely even.

I stopped touching her and leaned over. Yeah, she was already asleep. I couldn't help but smile, working hard to bite down my laughter. I'd worn her out.

I brought my pillow close to hers, mirroring her position. Even though I didn't want to wake her up, I still felt the need to be close to her, so I put a hand on her stomach and shifted so there was little space between my chest and her back. She sighed softly in her sleep, putting her hand over mine and moving it farther up, nestling it between her breasts.

Hell yes!

I could die a happy man right now with her ass against my crotch and my hand between her breasts.

CHAPTER 16
PHOEBE

I YAWNED, hugging a pillow under my head, and then smiled even though I was still half asleep. The sound of water lapping onto the shore filled the room. The air smelled salty too. I heard footsteps and opened my eyes to see Griffin was already dressed.

"Sorry, I didn't want to wake you up," he said.

His morning voice was unexpectedly sexy.

"That's fine." I tilted my head. "And come to think of it, I wouldn't have minded if you'd woken me a few minutes earlier." I wiggled my eyebrows. "Such as when you were getting dressed."

He started to laugh. "You're funny this morning."

"The humorous side of my brain is the first one to come to life."

He came to my side of the bed, kissing my forehead.

"You look surprisingly fit."

"I went for a run," he said.

I blinked. "Wait, what? Today?"

He nodded. "Yeah. I did a good time too. Five miles. I beat my own record by twenty seconds."

"Last night gave you a good burst of energy, huh?"

He laughed. "You could say that. I even took a shower and didn't wake you. I'm going downstairs to get a coffee. I didn't have one before my run."

"All right," I said. "I'm going to need some time in the bathroom."

"Don't worry."

After he left, I was tempted to go back to sleep because this mattress was utter perfection. When I moved into my house, I'd bought the cheapest mattress at Home Depot. Let's just say it was cheap for a reason. I was pretty sure it had given me a permanent neck strain. But this had some sort of gel or something. It was amazing. But I knew if I put my head back down, I'd probably fall asleep again, so instead, I headed to the shower.

As the water poured over me, last night's memories became more vivid. My skin started to simmer just thinking about every delicious thing Griffin had done to me. I stepped out quickly and put on yet another beach dress before hurrying downstairs. I didn't want to make anyone wait too long to eat breakfast.

When I reached the lower floor, there was no one around. Then I realized they were already outside. They'd set the table, but they were all standing, pointing at something in the water.

Crap, crap, crap. I'd made them wait.

I hurried outside, exclaiming, "I'm here!"

Emma and Jude turned first. "Good morning," Emma said.

"I'm so sorry to keep you waiting," I said. "That bed is so comfortable that I didn't want to leave it." I inspected the table. It was bursting with food. "Oh, I didn't help set the table for breakfast."

"You're a guest," Emma said. "Let's dig in."

"Before we do that," Jude said, "we want to share some great news."

Griffin smiled widely.

"What's that?" I asked as we all sat down.

"I have decided that I'll consider Griffin's proposal to invest in my company. I was far too quick to shut him down."

"That's fantastic!" I exclaimed. *Mission accomplished.*

My heart was so happy. Griffin deserved this. I glanced his way, and he beamed at me.

"We'll get together to discuss this in more detail because I don't want to spoil the weekend talking shop," Jude continued. "But I have a feeling that we're going to get along just fine."

"So do I," Griffin said. "I promise you won't regret this. I've got—"

"Tut, tut," Emma interrupted. "No business talk."

Griffin laughed. "You're right."

I was ecstatic all the way through breakfast, but then a realization started to dawn on me. There was no use for our ruse anymore. Griffin could tell him that we broke up after this weekend, and that would be that. I might tell him to blame it on me so Jude wouldn't think less of him.

"All right. How about we spend the rest of the day doing nothing at all? I suggest we just lie in the sun, enjoying drinks," Emma said.

"Sounds like my kind of Sunday," I agreed.

We finished breakfast quickly, and then Emma and Jude asked us to help them take out some lounge chairs to put by the water.

I wasn't sure how to act around Griffin. At some point, I was certain we should talk about last night, but I blushed every time I even thought about it.

As we sat down on our respective chairs, I applied sunscreen, then held the bottle for him.

"Sunscreen?" I asked.

He tilted his head, a playful smile on his lips. If he was going to ask me to apply it on him, I'd spontaneously combust. But he probably suspected as much, because he simply nodded and took the bottle. "Yeah, thanks."

We didn't actually get the chance to talk at all, though, because either Emma or Jude was always around. But every time

I caught his eye, my stomach somersaulted and my pulse sped up.

Only after Emma and Jude decided that it was time to start packing did we have our first moment completely alone. We stayed behind, carrying our respective lounge chairs to the woodshed behind the house.

It was completely dark inside. After I dropped off my chair, I started to head out, but Griffin touched my forearm.

"Wait a second." He drew in a sharp breath. "Fuck, I've wanted a moment alone with you the whole day." He ran his fingers along my jaw, and I shuddered. There was no need to pretend, so why was he touching me? Then again, after last night, that wasn't really a valid question.

"Phoebe, last night was surreal," he said.

What a good opener. Why didn't I think of that? Every time I tried to play out in my mind how this conversation would go, I got tongue-tied.

"It was," I agreed.

"I don't regret it one bit."

I smiled in the darkness. "You don't?"

"No fucking way. You?"

"No, not at all. It's just that..." I paused, and Griffin swallowed hard. I couldn't see him, but my other senses were on hyperalert. His breath quickened. His cologne smelled even more delicious than I remembered.

"I'm not sure what it meant," I admitted.

"It can mean whatever we want it to. I'd like to see you again."

My heart was beating even faster now. "I don't think Jude will need—"

"This isn't about him. I want to see *you*."

"Oh, Griffin... I'm honestly still reeling from everything I've been through. It's not fair to pull you into all of this." I'd said all of this quickly, rambling nervously. I paused, taking a deep breath, before whispering, "I'm not ready."

"I understand."

"You do?"

"Of course."

"We could still be friends."

"I can't just be your friend, Phoebe. Not after I've tasted you. Not after I've had you. I could never do it. Not in a million years."

A pang of disappointment sliced through me.

"So, where does that leave us?" I asked. "After today, we won't see each other anymore?"

I realized that I couldn't bear the thought.

For a few seconds, neither of us spoke.

My God, that cologne was giving me wild ideas. What if I jumped him again, right here in this shed?

You can't do that, Phoebe. Behave.

"We'll see," Griffin said. And then I felt his arm by my side. For a fraction of a second, I thought he was going to pull me into a kiss. My entire body vibrated. I parted my lips, even rose on my toes to meet him halfway.

Oh, he just pushed the door open. Light filtered in, blinding me momentarily.

I lowered myself back to my heels, trying not to show how disappointed I was.

He stepped out first and gestured for me to walk in front of him. "For now, let's go upstairs and pack."

CHAPTER 17
GRIFFIN

"STELLA, we need to hit the ground running on this," I told my right hand and VP of business development on Monday.

She nodded. "I still can't believe you got that cantankerous old man to change his mind."

"It was just luck," I said.

"Uh-huh," Stella said, frowning. "You're never self-deprecating."

It was all Phoebe. She'd charmed both of them. If I was honest, she'd charmed me too. She'd been constantly on my mind since I dropped her off at her home last night.

Early this morning, Jude's team had sent several options for a meeting for next week, hence why I had my entire team working on the pitch. I needed this done today because I was heading to Napa tomorrow morning.

As luck would have it, my brothers and I cut our usual brainstorming session short—Chase had to jump on a call with a huge client who was getting cold feet because the Dow Jones had opened abysmally. So I'd suggested everyone stop by my house in the evening for dinner.

In the meantime, I could focus all my efforts on Jude. I had a good feeling about this. My team and I spent the entire morning discussing strategic options. Then they started working on the presentation, sending me the PowerPoint slides to review in the afternoon.

I revised them and was so damn proud of how everything turned out. I'd handpicked everyone on my team, as I knew how to hire the best people, and they'd done a great job. I'd gotten us the foot in the door with Jude, but it was a team effort to pull it all together.

I worked on the slides until five o'clock. Then I sent the team my feedback and called it a day.

My family was arriving at my house in one hour. I'd buy takeout for everyone, thinking immediately about Phoebe's bowl place.

As I got in the car, I quickly texted the family to ask if they were okay with it. No one protested, so I took that as a yes and placed an order right away.

I was feeling victorious even though I had a long way to go until I sealed the deal with Jude. But my company was in the running, and it felt damn good.

While I waited for the food to be ready, I couldn't help but remember the last time I was here. I was very tempted to text Phoebe, but I didn't. She wasn't ready for anything; she was clear about that, and I had to respect it.

After picking up the bowls, I headed straight home. I didn't have much time before my family arrived. The only ones who weren't coming tonight were Mom and Dad. Mom offered yoga classes late on Mondays, and now Dad claimed that he also wanted to stick around to make sure Mom didn't need anything. It was a clever excuse. Those two had become inseparable.

I was starting to be less reticent about them rekindling their relationship. My parents weren't the same people they'd been years ago. They didn't have as much pressure. This time around, they could make it work.

My brother Duncan called as I was approaching the house.

"Hey," I answered. "I'm almost home."

"Yeah, just one thing. Jeremy's not going to be a fan of the bowls."

"Shit. You're right. I didn't think about it."

"Do you have time to pick something up for him? If not, I'll do it."

"No, that's fine. I'm going to drive by his favorite pizza place, and I'll get the one he likes with extra cheese."

"Yes, Uncle Griffin!" I heard Jeremy exclaim in the background.

I laughed. "Consider it done." His favorite pizza place wasn't anywhere near the house, but it was worth a detour. He absolutely loved it.

I got home fifty minutes later. When I arrived, the gate to the house was open, which meant at least one of my brothers was already here. Chase was getting out of the car when I pulled up next to him.

"No Hannah?" I asked.

"Some clients just came to the inn. She'll join us later."

"All right."

The whole reason why my brother and Hannah lived in Point Loma was because she'd inherited an inn from her grandmother. It was the property next to their home.

"She's really burning the candle at both ends," I said.

Chase took the pizza from me and two of the bags with food. I was carrying three more. "Don't get me started on that. I'm trying to convince her to slow down, but the woman's stubborn."

"Takes one to know one. Maybe that's why she likes you so much," I teased. "But the reason she took the job at Sterling Investments in the first place was to have a nest egg that she could invest in the inn, right? Which she's already done. It looks incredible."

"Yes. But now she says that she likes the certainty of a steady paycheck and isn't ready to give it up again."

Frowning, I pressed the unlock feature on my phone, and the front door sprang open. I loved technology. "She does know you're loaded, right? We all are."

"I think she just needs to have a security blanket."

That reminded me of Phoebe. Fucking hell, everything reminded me of Phoebe today. I needed to talk to her. I'd postponed calling her all day because I didn't want to disturb her at work, but I should have called her when I left the office. Now I'd just obsess all evening.

She's not ready, Griffin.

Still, her idea of being friends was starting to take root. It was better than nothing.

The rest of the group arrived one after another. Jeremy didn't even look at the bowls, just went straight for his pizza.

Chase whistled appreciatively as he ate up. "This is actually good."

"You thought I'd buy shit for dinner?" I countered.

"No, but I was suspicious. It sounded… *healthy*."

Chase took out his phone and frowned. "Hannah says the new guests are a handful. She can't leave them. She asked if I could take her dinner with me."

"Anytime you need help convincing that woman of yours not to overwork herself, we're happy to help," Knox said.

"Yeah, clearly you can't do it by yourself," Finn added.

Chase looked at them. "Is there a reason you're particularly annoying this evening?"

"Can everyone just behave?" Duncan asked even though Jeremy was sitting in front of the TV, eating his pizza. There was no way he could hear us. Riley hadn't come with them, so I assumed she was stuck at the office.

Wyatt flashed a shit-eating grin. "Not tonight. Stop stirring shit up, you two. Chase knows how to convince people. He's just biding his time." He looked at Chase. "Aren't you?"

"Exactly."

Wyatt fist-bumped the air. "See, I knew it."

"Yeah, stop butting in," Duncan added, looking pointedly at Finn and Knox.

Finn narrowed his eyes at Duncan. "Rumor has it, you asked Riley to be a lawyer at Sterling Investments, and she turned you down."

"You did? Good for you, man," I said.

"Where's the good part?" Knox asked. "She turned him down."

I couldn't help but laugh.

"News flash, Knox. People have their own free will," Wyatt countered.

"It's just a matter of using the right arguments," Finn said. He had a point.

Duncan shook his head. "Riley wants a career in a law firm. She doesn't want to be a corporate lawyer for one company."

I cleared my throat. "Speaking of using the right arguments, I'm happy to inform all of you that Jude changed his mind. I'm now in the running as an investor."

"Congrats," Chase said.

"Well done," Duncan added.

Wyatt narrowed his eyes. "So, wait, your winning argument was having a girlfriend?"

I laughed, stopping in the act of eating another forkful of my bowl. "I'm sure that helped tremendously. He wouldn't have given me a second shot if I didn't go to the dinner with Phoebe."

"I'll have to remember that as a business tactic," Knox said.

"It wasn't just a dinner," I said quickly, then immediately stopped, but it was too late. My brothers were eerily silent.

"What do you mean?" Finn asked.

"He invited us for the weekend at his home."

"You said you'd turn it down," Knox replied.

"I didn't. We went, and now the deal is moving forward."

My brothers all started talking at the same time.

"Holy shit! If Mom were here...," Finn said above everyone else.

I zeroed in on him. "Is there any particular reason why you're riding my ass so hard lately?"

Finn wiggled his eyebrows. "Because Mom's been riding my ass for years. It's good to finally see her focus all her efforts on someone else."

Duncan and Chase were silent. I pointed at the two of them. "I can feel the judgment coming off you."

"We can't help that," Duncan said. "I think we deserve prizes for withholding any comment."

"You do," I admitted. "I appreciate it."

"What the actual fuck?" Chase said.

Duncan elbowed him. "Chase, come on. Loosen up a bit."

"We all do crazy things sometimes, don't we?" Wyatt asked.

"There are crazy things, and there are stupid things," Chase countered. "This could bite you in the ass anytime."

"I'm aware of that," I said coolly, "and I'll manage that if the situation arises. But for now, I'm going to take it as a win."

"It is one," Finn concluded. "Even I wouldn't have had the balls to go about it like that, but I'll take it."

It was a strange day indeed when all the Sterling brothers turned on one of their own.

"What's gotten into all of you? When Chase had that outlandish idea with the shell company, only Duncan was completely against it. The rest of us grudgingly agreed. Now you've somehow all decided that this is completely insane."

"There's a difference," Duncan said. "When this one had that brilliant idea," he said through gritted teeth, nodding toward Chase, "the only way it could bite him back was if Hannah found out, which she did. But this is different. It's public. A potential business partner is involved. What do you figure will happen if he finds out about the ruse? He'd scream at the top of his lungs that Griffin Sterling isn't an honest man."

His words hit me right in the gut. Deep down, I didn't think

Jude would be the type to actually scream anything at the top of his lungs. But you could never be sure.

"All right, I'd like everyone to get off my case right now."

Chase looked at me. "I'm assuming the charade is over now, right?"

"That's what Phoebe and I agreed on." My tone was clipped. Yes, I'd agreed to it, but I didn't like it. Not one bit. What she'd said was true. She was still recovering from the fiasco with that jerk. She wasn't in a good place for anything. And yet I couldn't stop thinking about her.

"Okay, so since we couldn't go back to our brainstorming this morning," Chase said in a clear attempt to move on, "should we do it now?"

"That's not a bad idea," Duncan said, "Especially since the girls aren't here, so we can't bore them to death."

"Actually, I did want to talk about something else with you," Chase said. It seemed serious, judging by his expression. "I'd like to invite Hannah to join our weekly meetings. She's very smart."

There was a murmur of agreement.

"I think that's a good idea. She'll have a fresh perspective on things. Maybe she'll even keep us in check," Knox said.

"We actually need that," Finn added.

Wyatt cocked a brow at them. "What's gotten into you two?" Then he glanced at Chase. "I'm all for her joining us because I think she's smart as a whip, but not her trying to hold us in check or whatever this nonsense is that everyone has in mind."

Chase starting laughing as he took the last mouthful of his bowl, then said, "I'll ask her to join us. She'll be happy. And I don't think Hannah's going to keep anyone in check."

"Not that she could," I countered. We were definitely a handful, but Hannah fit right in with us. And despite what Duncan was saying, I could actually see a future where Riley might join our ranks too. I understood that for someone starting out, working as a corporate lawyer might seem like settling for something less. She still wanted to acquire knowledge, and that was best done in a big law firm.

After we finished eating, my brothers and I picked up where we'd left off this morning. Somehow, we seemed even more productive than usual. And I wasn't the only one who noticed.

"We should do this in the evening more often. Our brains work better," Knox said.

"Or you have more time to come up with ideas during the day," I teased. It was common knowledge that he always flew by the seat of his pants.

Besides, I felt the need to annoy him as payback for ratting me out to Mom and Dad.

"Ha ha, very funny," Knox said.

"We'll see," Duncan hedged. "I prefer to keep things like this in the office."

My brothers and I needed to discuss one more thing tonight: which wine to fast-track at our winery in Napa. I was heading down there tomorrow to talk some rebranding details with the team.

We had to decide between a chardonnay, pinot grigio, and Riesling. We ended up with a tie, each type getting two votes.

"Riley and Hannah can be the tiebreakers," Duncan said. We all agreed.

I wanted to hear Phoebe's opinion on this too. She liked her whites, and I was curious which one would be her favorite.

My brothers stayed for another hour or so. As they left, Chase and Duncan each took three bottles with them, one of each type.

Once I was alone, the impulse to call Phoebe grew stronger. I couldn't deny myself any longer. Why should I? We'd never specifically agreed on not calling each other. I pressed her number, putting the phone to my ear. It rang three times, and then she answered. My shoulders relaxed instantly.

"Hey, Griffin. Good evening," she said.

"Hi, Phoebe. How are you?"

"I'm good. I just got home, actually. It was a crazy day at the office."

"I figured. That's why I didn't call you at all today."

"You wanted to call me?" Her voice turned soft.

"So many times."

"Did anything happen? Does Jude want to meet again?"

"No, this isn't about Jude at all. Listen, I need your opinion on something."

"Okay."

"It's an in-person kind of thing." She laughed. I was a fucking genius. "I need to choose between three different wines. We want to focus on one and fast-track it. I'd love your opinion."

"Ah," she replied playfully, "because I'm such a wine drinker."

"You're very discernible with your whites."

"That's because white wine is all I drink. I get a hell of a headache from the red one. What did your brothers say?"

"We're on the fence. It's a tie."

"I'm happy to help you. Do you want to stop by the house? I'll order something to eat."

"I have one of your favorite bowls ready to bring with me. If you're in the mood for that, of course."

There was an awkward silence, and I realized this must sound insane. "My brothers were here. Jeremy too. I bought a pizza for him in addition to the bowl. He didn't even glance at the bowl, obviously."

"All right. Sure. I can't wait." Her voice was breathy.

"I'll see you in a bit," I replied before hanging up.

I was a straightforward kind of guy. Never used ruses to get what I want. It wasn't who I was. But ever since I'd met Phoebe, I'd gone against the grain. First with the pretend relationship and now this. But I needed to spend more time with her, and I didn't much care how it happened. I grabbed the bowl and the bottles of wine and headed to the car.

Thirty minutes later, I was already pulling in front of her

house. She opened the door before I even got out of the car. She had on a pink dress, but somehow it looked as if she was wearing nothing at all.

I groaned inwardly. *Get yourself under control, Griffin.*

But I was learning that when it came to Phoebe, that wasn't easy.

CHAPTER 18
GRIFFIN

"I COME WITH SUPPLIES," I said, heading toward the front door with the bottles of wine and the bowl.

"You want to get me good and drunk, huh?" she asked, looking at the bottles.

I laughed. "We're just tasting them. We don't have to drink everything."

"Oh, good. You're tasting them with me. I was feeling a bit weird about drinking on my own."

"I won't leave you in the lurch."

"Come on in." She smiled but averted her gaze. Before she turned around, I realized she was blushing a little bit. My imagination spiraled out of control again.

I should have turned on the lights during our night together so I could see her. Was she blushing like this when I was inside her? When she came? I needed to find out.

"This place is a bit of a mess." She looked over her shoulder, smiling sheepishly. "I didn't have time to put things back in order after I unpacked everything, and today was crazy."

It looked like someone had dropped a container of clothes in the middle of the room. "I was about to reassure you that it's fine, but I'm taking that all back."

She laughed. "Sorry you get to see me in all my messy glory."

"But I like that," I said before I could stop myself. "You don't have to pretend for me. Never, Phoebe."

Her smile deepened, as did her blush. I fucking loved it. I put the wine bottles and the bag with the bowl on the table.

Phoebe immediately took the bowl out and dug into the food with the wooden fork strapped to the container.

"This is delicious. I was starving."

"Where's your bottle opener?" I asked. One of the things we liked about the existing design of the bottle was that it wasn't a screw cap. You actually needed to uncork it. Some people hated the idea of it, but I liked it. It was classy.

She headed to the counter, opening a drawer. "Here it is."

I remembered the cabinet where she took the glasses from last time and opened it. The door promptly fell to the floor.

Phoebe shrieked, putting the bottle opener on the counter. "Are you okay?"

"Yeah, I'm fine," I assured her. "I have good instincts and jumped back quickly. It seems to have fallen off the hinges."

She grimaced. "Sorry about that. I realized last week that it was a bit loose, so I was being careful about opening it. I didn't have time to fix it."

"Never mind," I said, picking it up. I was determined not to make another comment, though I was tempted to buy her a brand-new kitchen. Wait a second, there *was* something I could do. "I can fix it for you later if you have the right tools."

"I do," she explained. "I bought everything last week. I just didn't get to do it, as I said. You know how to use tools?"

I nodded. "Yes, I do. After my parents divorced, my brothers and I fought for the title of 'man of the house.' There's not much I can't do."

"Oh! Okay. I'll file that here," she said, tapping her temple. "But let's leave that for later. Wine first."

I left the cabinet door on the kitchen counter and took out the glasses as she finished eating her bowl. I uncorked all of the bottles before bringing more glasses. "We're going to taste each one in a different glass."

"That's smart."

I poured two fingers of each one. It was enough to taste but not so much that we'd get drunk. "We also need water."

"I'll go get it." She dashed to the counter, filled two glasses from her filter, and put them on the table. "All right, which one are we tasting first?"

"The chardonnay because it's the easiest one."

"Mm-hmm." She nodded. "And a crowd pleaser."

"You do know your wines."

"We did so many tastings for Marshall's birthday party last year—" She froze with a look on her face I couldn't describe. "Never mind."

"You can talk about him if you want to. You guys were together for six years, so I'm sure it's hard not to."

"Actually, it's the last thing I want to even think about."

I wiggled my eyebrows. "I'm here to provide distraction on demand, as always."

"You're very generous, aren't you?" She wiggled her eyebrows right back, taking me by surprise. I never knew when she'd have a funny reply or when she'd get shy on me. I hadn't yet learned where that fine line was. But I was happy to do whatever it took to discover it.

"This is a good chardonnay," she said.

"I agree. Sometimes they can be too watery."

"Exactly! But this one's good." She took a sip of water, and we moved on to the next one.

"Is this a sauvignon blanc?" She pointed at the second set of glasses. Then she glanced at the bottle. "Oh, it's a pinot grigio. Nice."

We both took a sip. "All right, this wins hands down over the chardonnay."

"I thought you might say that." I didn't tell her what my favorite was because I wanted her to be as unbiased as possible.

She took another sip. "Hmm, I might ask for a refill of this one later, but not before I try the last one."

We both took a swig of water, and then we moved on to the Riesling. Her eyes widened from the second she smelled it. Then she took a sip and immediately closed her eyes, humming. "Tell me the truth. This is your favorite, isn't it?"

"Yes," I said.

She opened her eyes and sighed. "You should have led with that. I think this is one of the best Rieslings I've ever had. I mean, the pinot grigio is very good as well, but if you want to fast-track one, I'd suggest this."

"Yes, exactly. That's my opinion too."

"May I have some more?"

I stood up, pouring it in her glass.

"Won't you have more?" she asked.

"I'm going to fix your door first. I can hold my liquor, but I prefer to be in charge of all my faculties when I handle tools."

"So very responsible," she murmured.

"You sound like you're having a hard time believing it."

"I'll bring the toolbox right away." She blushed, then scurried off.

I went to the counter, looking at the cupboard's hinges. It wasn't a difficult fix. She came back with the toolbox a few minutes later, setting it on the counter.

"I bought this too."

"You know your stuff."

"Yes. That's why I wanted to flip this place myself. I'm very good at it."

"How come?" I said, then got to work.

"My parents flipped houses on the side, and I helped all the time. They insisted on paying me, but I mostly did it because I liked hanging around with them. Wait, I can help you."

"No, you go enjoy your wine. Since I'm here, I can make myself useful. You helped pick a wine, so I'll help fix your door. What was our catchphrase? 'You scratch my back, I scratch yours'?"

"We're good at that, aren't we? Looking out for each other."

I swallowed hard, then looked at the door. If only she knew how much I'd like to take care of her.

I got to work, hurrying to finish the cupboard so I could focus on the person who'd captured my attention.

Phoebe

I stood right next to him as he fixed the door. When he finished and turned to face me, I realized I was closer than I'd thought. Feeling the heat of his body against mine reminded me of our night together. We'd agreed that it was a onetime thing, so I wasn't really sure what this was. Were we friends? He'd refused to even entertain the idea when I'd brought it up, and I totally understood why.

Being friends with this hot-as-hell hunk was asking for trouble.

"What are you thinking about?" he asked. "You tensed up."

I took another sip of my wine, laughing nervously. The alcohol wasn't helping. "Griffin, I, *erm*… I'm not sure what this is or why…"

"Why I'm here," he finished for me.

I nodded feverishly, thankful that he'd been the one to phrase it that way.

"I don't know either," he replied.

I looked up at him in surprise. His eyes were a bit darker. He leaned forward, touching my jawline with the backs of his fingers. I didn't pull away. In fact, I did quite the opposite. I leaned into his touch, closing my eyes briefly.

I'd missed him. How was this even happening?

"I know what we agreed on," I said, "but we didn't say anything about staying away from each other."

"Which is good because I can't seem to be able to do that. All day I've been thinking about you. About if they treat you right at your job, or if something else broke in this place."

"You missed me that much?" I sucked in a breath.

Griffin shook his head. His eyes were darker still. "Forget I said that. I remember our conversation. It's just that fighting my instincts is harder than I anticipated."

"For me too," I confessed.

He closed his eyes. I shouldn't have said that; it just made things more difficult.

"I don't know what to do," I confessed, but I didn't move away because I needed the heat of him, the strength of him, to continue. "All my life, I felt like I knew exactly where I was headed and what was next. Now everything's wide open. I'm battling multiple fronts, and I'm barely able to keep afloat. The one thing I know for sure is that I'm not ready for another relationship."

"I know, Phoebe. And even if you were, I'm the last guy you should start one with."

I frowned. "Why?"

"This whole thing started because I'm not a relationship type of guy."

I licked my lips. "That's right."

An idea was forming in my mind. I smiled.

"Why are you so happy about that?"

"Because if neither of us wants a relationship," I said, choosing my words carefully, "then that would mean that we're just… er, what's the word? Casual. Yeah, I could do casual."

His mouth was on mine the next second. The kiss was unexpected, but I opened up to it immediately because I needed it more than anything else—even air. Griffin kissed and kissed, and I didn't want him to stop. I felt the edge of the table poke into my ass, but I couldn't care less.

His hands went from my face down to my shoulders and then my elbows before resting on my waist, his thumbs pressing into my rib cage. I wrapped my arms around his neck and stood on my toes. I was at the same level with him, yet it still wasn't enough. Even though I was kissing him with all I had, I wanted to have his hands all over me.

I only pulled back when I was gasping for breath. *Hmm, turns out that I do need air after all.*

"Phoebe," Griffin said. He groaned, then cleared his throat. He was keeping me pressed against him, but that was quite fine by me. I *needed* to be close to him. "Are you sure?"

I nodded. "Mm-hmm. Yes, I am."

He narrowed his eyes. "What if the wine clouded your judgment?"

"No, I just took a few sips. But you just being here, close to me, might cloud my judgment."

His eyes flashed. He was on the edge, and so was I.

"Fuck, Phoebe. You don't know how much I want to kiss you again right now."

"So why don't you?" To my dismay, he stepped back. "No, that's the opposite of kissing."

I took a step forward and then realized my balance was just a tiny bit off. I glanced at the bottles.

"Mm-hmm," Griffin said as if I'd just confirmed his worst fears. "I know we didn't have a lot of wine, but I think it was too much for you."

"It gave me liquid courage. Otherwise, I wouldn't have had the guts to say all that."

He stepped closer, kissing my cheek. Taking a deep breath, he kissed my forehead, wrapping his hand in my hair. And then he took another step back.

What was this sexy man doing? Confusing me, that was for sure.

"Listen, I'm going to Napa Valley for a few days."

"Okay," I said, unsure why he was sharing this with me.

"Think about everything while I'm gone. If you still feel the same once I'm back..."

"You'll believe me?" I asked him. "What can I do so you believe me now?"

"Phoebe, don't tempt me, okay? You have no idea how much I want to kiss you again. Make you mine again." He all but growled those last few words.

Honestly, I appreciated that he was holding back. I certainly had a bit more liquid courage than I needed. I didn't think I'd regret this tomorrow, but better safe than sorry.

"Okay, I guess."

"Just for now, okay? I'll be going, then."

"Oh," I said. "You don't have to."

"Phoebe, if I stay, I'll forget everything—my honor and my best intentions to do what's right."

"Oh."

He leaned over to grab a glass of water and brushed the side of my boob in the process. I let out a low, guttural sound, and Griffin took in a deep breath, rolling his hand into a fist.

Holy shit, he'd really meant every word. He was hanging on by a thread. The devil on my shoulder wanted me to bring out my inner vixen and push him over the edge. But I hadn't had *that* much wine.

Maybe some distance *would* do us good—although, if today was any indication, it would do just the opposite. I'd been brimming with tension and need for him.

"Good night, Phoebe."

"Good night, Griffin."

After he left, I felt a deep pang in my chest. Damn it, I'd been looking forward to spending the evening with him. I hadn't even asked him if he'd already met with Jude. Or how long he was going to be in Napa.

Since I was already on a slippery slope, I poured myself one more glass of his delightful Riesling.

To distract myself, I texted my parents. I really missed them. I'd planned to have my life a bit more on track before inviting them to visit, but who knew when that would happen?

Phoebe: Hey, I really miss you guys. I'd love to have you over.

Mom: YES! Sure. When? Just say the date and we'll be there.

I smiled big-time. I loved my parents to the moon and back. I scrolled through my calendar app, looking at all the weekends two months from now, and shared one with my mom.

Phoebe: How about this one?

Mom: We're on it.

Ah, tonight was truly amazing.

I sat down on my couch and thought about starting a new series on Netflix, but that was always a dangerous idea. For some reason, I couldn't watch a series like a normal person—just a few episodes at a time. Rather, I had to binge-watch every episode that was available. I rarely started a show when they were only one or two seasons deep because I got frustrated if Netflix ended up canceling them. But if I found one with multiple seasons, let's just say I'd end up having very little sleep over the next few days. Instead, I followed another dangerous impulse—I texted Griffin.

Phoebe: I forgot to ask how it went with Jude. Did you already meet with him?

Then I decided to go all out.

Phoebe: I wish you'd stayed.

Griffin: You have no idea how much it took for me to pry myself away from you. All I wanted was to kiss and touch you.

My entire body lit up like a live wire at his response. The pent-up desire I had for this man was unlike any other.

Griffin: I set up a meeting with Jude. Things are moving forward.

Phoebe: How long are you staying in Napa?

Griffin: Three days. Will you miss me?

I grinned, deciding to tease him.

Phoebe: Hmm… not sure I'll have time. I have two full days of training for work—we got new software.

Phoebe: But don't worry, I'll think about you know what.

Griffin: Phoebe, fuck.

Two words was all it took to ignite a fire inside me. I wasn't even sure why I was so on edge. I wasn't such a sexual person. Then again, no one I'd been with before made me feel like Griffin did. He seemed to know exactly what would drive me crazy. My heart was beating fast just thinking about our time together.

Was he correct? Was I setting myself up for heartbreak? I'd never had a casual relationship, but my life had just unfolded that way.

I wasn't even completely certain that I understood what it implied. Would we see other people?

Hell no. I swallowed hard. Shit. I wasn't going to share him.

I couldn't believe I was already stressing out. I was pretty certain that was the opposite of casual.

Biting my lower lip, I glanced at the phone. I wanted to tell him so many things, but I couldn't type them out. So I wrote the most important thing of all.

Phoebe: I can't wait for you to be back.

Griffin: Me too.

I sighed, then decided to chat with Veronica. She was going to lose her shit when I told her I was considering starting something casual with Griffin.

She answered after a few rings. "Hey, what's up?"

"I've got some news."

"Uhhh, of the sexy variety?"

I laughed. "You could say that."

"Yesssss!" she squealed. "I'm all ears."

CHAPTER 19
PHOEBE

MY TRAINING WAS in a small building not far away from the San Diego Superior Court. It was very intense, and the group was small. There were five of us, and our teacher asked us not to check our phones except during breaks. I felt like I was back in school. Then again, the accounting program was so complex that if you didn't pay attention for a few seconds, you could easily get lost. Since my work was paying for this, I was keeping my fingers crossed for them to hire me full-time.

I realized how addicted I was to my phone when I practically ran toward the back of the room during the first break. Taking it out of my bag, I unlocked the screen as quickly as possible. I had no message notifications, and my stomach sagged with disappointment.

Correction—I wasn't addicted to my phone but rather to Griffin.

Then I decided to check the messages anyway, and lo and behold, I did have one from him. It was from this morning. I'd missed the notification somehow. He'd sent a picture of a bottle of wine.

Griffin: This is the winner, and a certain gorgeous woman helped me pick it out.

A bout of jealousy, coursed through me. *A woman?*

Oh, he meant me.

Wow, that was interesting. I was jealous of myself.

Phoebe: Glad I could help.

Griffin: How's your training?

Phoebe: It's very intense, and we have a very strict teacher. We're only allowed to check messages during breaks. I'm going to be super burned out by the end of this.

Griffin: Lucky I'll be back to take care of you.

I bit the inside of my cheek. I was desperate to know exactly how he planned to do that, but he needed an answer from me first. And I didn't have it yet.

Before I could think of anything to say in response, the instructor announced that our break time was over. I put my phone back in my purse with a sigh.

The rest of the day was grueling. By the end of it, I was so exhausted that I even forgot to check my phone. I only took it out when I got home, seeing that I had two messages from Griffin.

Griffin: When are you done?

Griffin: Just send me a text when you can talk.

I immediately typed a reply.

Phoebe: I'm home.

He called me the next second.

"Hey. Sorry, I didn't see your messages. I just got home."

"Long day, huh?" he asked.

"Very. But you sound tired too."

"It was busy."

"What did you do today?"

"We toured the winery, and they explained the production process. Even though I'm not going to be involved on a day-to-day basis, I like to know the ins and outs of any company I invest in."

"That's a very solid approach in business," I said. "So, it was productive."

I was trying to gauge if he was done and there was a chance that he'd come back earlier. But I didn't want to be too obvious.

"We were busy all day. Tomorrow will be as well."

I pouted. *Damn it.* I wasn't going to see him tomorrow after all.

"What are you having for dinner?" he asked me.

"I'm in the mood for sunny-side ups. Although, I could make myself some fried rice. You?"

"I'll go to dinner with my brothers and our new business associates here. I actually have to go in a few minutes. Just wanted to hear your voice."

"Oh! I was hoping we could talk more."

"I'd promise to call you after dinner, but I don't know how long it'll last."

"No, no, that's fine. We can talk plenty once you're back."

I stopped in the act of pulling the fridge door, instead putting a hand on my chest. I had to say this to him. I'd been thinking about it all day, and I didn't want to postpone it any longer.

"Griffin, I'm ready."

"Fuck yes," he exclaimed, and my face morphed into a grin. I didn't even have to explain what I was talking about. He simply knew.

I jumped up and down for no reason at all, joy coursing through my body. I'd never experienced anything like this before. To be wanted by someone so completely made me feel special. *Griffin* made me feel special.

"Mr. Sterling, we're ready for you," a voice said in the background.

"Go have fun at dinner," I told him.

"I won't be able to focus. I'll only be thinking about you and all the things I'm going to do to you once I'm back."

"I could say I'm sorry for distracting you," I said with a shaky voice, "but I'm not. Not really."

"I'll see you soon, Phoebe."

"Oh yeah."

His words rang in my ears long after I disconnected the call. Even after I finished my dinner, all I could think about was the next time I was going to see him. Griffin was going to turn my world upside down. I had no doubt.

And I couldn't wait for that to happen.

The next morning, I woke up with a huge smile on my face. Instinctively, I reached for my phone, wondering if Griffin had texted.

Instead, an email from Marshall caught my attention.

I opened the message with shaky fingers.

Subject: Splitting profits.

Hey, Phoebe. So, I've been thinking about this for a while. The realtor says he has a good feeling about the price and that we'll be able to sell fast. Since I paid most of the down payment, I figured it's only fair for me to get most of the profits.

I blinked. *Is he shitting me right now?* We'd already planned to split the money from the sale in a way that made sure he hadn't lost any money with the down payment, but now he wanted to… what? Take more of the profits?

I don't think so. Over my dead body.

Did he know what a financial hit I took because of his cheating ass? I should have billed him for everything I had to buy for this place.

I'd even chipped in for our trip to Maui. Not with a lot, but I didn't want to feel like I wasn't contributing at all. And he took *her* on that trip.

I wiped my eyes. Damn it. I couldn't believe I was tearing up.

I texted him immediately.

Phoebe: Let's talk about this in person.

I didn't want to go back and forth over email. Marshall needed to know that I wasn't a pushover.

To my dismay, he answered right away.

Marshall: Okay.

I looked on Google Maps at potential meeting places around the courthouse and found a bar two blocks away. I sent the link over to Marshall before I could chicken out.

Phoebe: Let's meet there at 6.

Marshall: Great! I'll be there.

I took in a deep breath, steeling myself. I could do this.

My phone beeped again. I almost didn't look because I really didn't want to know what other crazy ideas Marshall had. But the message was from Griffin.

Griffin: Gorgeous, I changed my flight, and I'm coming back this evening.

Huh. Guess whose day just turned much better?

Yep, that's right. Mine.

I opened the fridge to get milk for my coffee and forgot that I was supposed to be extra tender with the door. I broke the handle *again*. But even that wasn't enough to ruin my mood.

Phoebe: That makes me so happy.

Griffin: Want me to pick you up from the office? Or is your training somewhere else?

I frowned. I could postpone Marshall, but I wanted to get it over with.

Phoebe: The training is near the Superior Court, but I'm meeting Marshall after that. He wants to discuss some details about the sale of the house. I figured it'll be faster in person.

The screen showed "Griffin typing" for a long time.

Griffin: Want me to pick you up from where you're meeting him?

Phoebe: Sure.

Griffin: I'll take care of you for the rest of the evening.

Oh wow. This was exactly what I was hoping for. Spending time with Griffin was the perfect way to end the evening.

I sent him the address and then went about my day.

On the way to training, I emailed my boss, stating my hope

and intention to get promoted as a full-time employee. The pay right now was crap, but I'd done some digging. They had much better programs for full-time employees.

To my astonishment, he responded right away.

Thanks for sending this. We'll let you know if something comes up.

I didn't know what to make of his answer. Since this was my first real job, I didn't know how to navigate office politics. I decided to push the issue to the back of my mind.

I could scarcely focus on my training today, though I did my best because this was quite literally my lifeline.

But once the teacher dismissed us and I headed to the bar where I was meeting Marshall, I grew uneasy. At least I could look forward to seeing Griffin later. He'd texted me the location where he planned to wait for me. It was a block away from the bar.

I was determined to stand my ground and was hoping Marshall wouldn't make a scene. I hurried there with quick steps, fiddling with my laptop bag on my shoulder. The strap was cutting into my skin, so I moved it to the other shoulder.

Marshall was already inside the bar when I got there. He noticed me right away and waved at me.

I walked over, ready to get this over with as soon as possible. Then I could focus on a glorious evening with Griffin.

CHAPTER 20
PHOEBE

"PHOEBE, I'm so happy you wanted to meet so quickly." He was smiling.

Hang on. Is he under the impression that I asked him here to accept his lousy terms?

Well, he had another think coming.

I sat down. "I figured we should crush that delusion you're under as soon as possible."

His smile fell. "What?"

"I'm not going to give you more of the profit than what we discussed beforehand."

He frowned. "Phoebe, you can't be serious."

"Yes, I am."

"But you know that I put up most of the down payment."

I swallow hard. "And you're getting all that back."

"Yes, but here's the thing. If I'd invested that money elsewhere, I would have made a profit, so that needs to be reflected in my share."

Marshall had always been dismissive of my needs. But this was different—downright callous.

I stared at him, focusing on breathing in and out. "And if I had invested the last few years in someone else, I might have had more to show for it than a huge amount of debt on my shoulders and a flailing career. So I guess we both made bad choices."

"It's not even remotely the same thing, and you know that. This was calculated on a spreadsheet. It's demonstrable."

I swallowed hard, feeling bile rise up my throat. He was sipping a yellowish drink that looked like vomit, which didn't help my nausea.

"Who calculated that for you?" I asked.

"That's none of your concern."

"I'm just curious."

"Adriana has a financial adviser."

Adriana. Her name felt like a punch to the gut.

I laughed. "Right! So you're asking your current girlfriend how to scam your ex-girlfriend."

"This is not scamming. That was my money."

"Which you're getting back," I said. "In fact, you know what I'll do? I'll send you a bill for everything I had to pay to move."

"What are you talking about?"

"The hotel on that first night." I swallowed hard. I'd been too heartbroken to even go to my best friend's house. "All the things I had to buy for the house." I could feel tears pooling at the corners of my eyes. I really, really didn't want to shed any more tears over this asshole.

He shook his head. "I'm not accountable for that. Look, Phoebe, let's be honest. The reason things didn't work out was because you pushed for a wedding."

"I..." My voice died in my throat. "You were going to propose on the trip," I stated. "I didn't imagine that."

"Yes, after you've been dropping hints for years at weddings. You kept pointing out that all your friends were getting married and how their boyfriends proposed."

I was determined not to let him see me cry. I crossed my legs, pressing them together tightly, and put my hands on the table.

"No, Marshall. The reason it didn't work for us is because

you stuck your penis in someone else. I'm not budging on this. You have no legal right to more of the profits."

"Don't be difficult."

I laughed without humor. "That's exactly what I'm going to be from now on. For years I kept agreeing with everything you wanted. And perhaps that was my mistake. I never challenged you enough. I never asked you to treat me the way I deserved. But I sure as hell won't allow you to walk all over me anymore. Now, if you'll excuse me, I need to go. I've said everything I wanted to."

I got up from the table and left the bar without another word. I headed straight to the corner where Griffin told me he'd wait for me.

"Phoebe, come on. We haven't finished the conversation."

What the hell? He followed me?

I stopped in my tracks. I was almost at the corner. I wondered if Griffin was already here.

"*I'm* finished."

"I'm counting on that money. I want to make some investments in the future."

I sucked in a deep breath. *His future with her?* But it didn't matter. "You are not getting more than we agreed on."

"What's going on?" Griffin asked as we rounded the corner.

"Oh, for Christ's sake, what the fuck? Do you follow her everywhere?" Marshall sneered.

"He's picking me up," I said.

"Right. *That's* why you've been belligerent. Because of him. Why would you even need the money from the sale with a sugar daddy around?"

"Shut the fuck up," I snapped at the same time Griffin said, "Watch your mouth." He was much better at this than me. He was calm and composed. His voice held power despite the fact that he wasn't yelling. In comparison, I sounded like a wreck.

"What's going on?" Griffin asked again, eyes focused on my face.

"He wants a bigger share of the profits on the house because he put more on the down payment. Claims that if he'd invested that somewhere else, he would have gotten more return."

Marshall looked at Griffin. "You're a businessman. You know I'm right. That's how capital works."

In an instant, Griffin transformed. His face was red, his eyes dark and intense. "Let's get one thing straight. You are the lowest of the lowest scum."

"What the fuck?"

"No, I wasn't asking. And you don't have to agree with me. It's a universal truth, no matter if you see it or not. If you had any sort of self-respect, you wouldn't even ask for any of the profit. No real man would do that. Then again, no real man would ever treat Phoebe the way you did."

"She doesn't deserve that fucking profit. The bitch didn't even—"

The next thing I knew, Griffin grunted, there was a loud whomp, and Marshall stumbled backward into the wall behind him.

"What the actual fuck, dude?" he exclaimed.

"Phoebe is not alone, you understand?"

Marshall stared at me. "You're actually going to let this moron treat me like this? He punched me."

"You deserved it."

He snorted. "Whatever. Forget I ever said anything."

"That's right," I said. It was a stupid idea to meet him. I should have just told him to go fuck himself over the email.

Marshall shook his head, looking between Griffin and me. "You know what? This type of guy is exactly what you deserve."

Griffin stared him down until he turned around, walking back in the direction of the bar.

Only when Marshall was out of our eyesight did Griffin turn to me. "Sorry about that. I shouldn't have lost my temper."

"Are you okay?" I asked, inspecting his hand.

"Yes. It doesn't even hurt."

"Are you sure? We can put some ice on it."

He cupped my face with his other hand. "Really, I'm fine. I just… hmm…" He looked down and then back up. "I've never lost control of myself like that."

I bit the inside of my cheek. "Don't blame yourself. Marshall just knows how to piss people off."

"He actually had the guts to ask you to meet him?"

"Well, uh, no," I said, stammering for some reason. "He emailed me. I told him I wanted to meet so I could tell him to his face what an asshole he was. I'm really sorry that I asked you to pick me up here. I figured it could give me something nice to look forward to after meeting him, but I didn't want to put you in this position."

"I don't mind. Whenever you need me by your side, just tell me. Okay?"

My mouth parted slightly. "Really?"

"Fuck yes."

"But…"

"You're hesitating. Tell me why."

"This doesn't exactly sound… casual."

"One thing doesn't have anything to do with the other. Whenever you need me, just say the word."

I nodded. "Well, I do need you tonight."

His expression slowly morphed into a smile. God, I'd missed him.

"All right, then let's hop in the car."

Once we were both inside, he leaned in slightly, like he was sharing a secret. "I'm planning to cook for you tonight at my place."

"You mean serious business," I teased.

He growled. "You can say that twice."

"How was Napa Valley?"

"Productive. I was actually talking to my brothers about renting a house in the area year-round. Then we could take turns going there. But maybe it's best to rent something on an as-needed basis. I'll calculate it. There's no point being wasteful."

I liked that Griffin was conscious with his money even though I was sure he had plenty.

"How was your course?" he asked.

"Very insightful. I'm grateful that the company is paying for me to do it even though I'm just a part-time employee. It's going to help me do my job better."

"I like your enthusiasm."

"I like what I'm doing. Though between the two of us, even if I didn't like it, I'd probably still do it. But I'm glad that I'm enjoying it." I smiled. "Aaaand I've told my boss that I'd love to be full-time with them. He said he'll consider it, whatever that means."

"I'm proud of you for taking the initiative." He leaned over, kissing my shoulder.

"Hey, eyes on the road."

He smiled as he focused his gaze forward. "You're a fighter. I like that about you. I think it's one of the things that attracted me from the beginning."

I turned to look at him. "What do you mean? I thought you were just playing the knight in shining armor because Veronica asked you."

"I heard you talking before that. I liked the fire you had."

"Well, I was talking Veronica's ear off about what an asshole Marshall was—actually, let's not talk about him anymore."

Griffin cleared his throat. "It's fine if you need to."

"And ruin this perfect evening? Nah. I just want to put everything behind me. I'm not naive enough to think that I'm rid of him, but I refuse to let him overshadow everything. I, for one, am looking forward to this. Can you believe I've never been to Point Loma?"

Griffin stared at me. "That's impossible."

I started to laugh. "I'm not even sure how that happened. I guess I just never ventured here. It's possible that my parents might have brought me here when I was a kid, but I just can't remember."

"I like it. It's very laid-back."

It looked upscale to me. We passed a few houses that were downright mansions.

"One of your brothers also lives here, right?"

"Yes, Chase and Hannah. She inherited the inn from her grandmother, and they live right next to it."

"That's so sweet."

As we turned sideways onto a smaller street, I was oohing and aahing at the homes. Some were bungalow style and clearly a bit older, while others were large and modern.

Griffin stopped in front of a huge gate. He pressed the button, and it opened up, revealing, without a doubt, the most stunning home I'd ever seen. It put everything we'd just passed to shame. I didn't even think that was possible.

"Griffin," I said. "This is breathtaking."

"You haven't even been inside." He smiled as he turned off the engine.

"You've got all these old trees."

"It's why I bought it. A developer built it, and then the couple who commissioned it decided to move elsewhere. They have a lot of kids, apparently. It's far too big for what I need, but these trees sold me. It feels like I'm alone in a forest."

All that glass was amazing. And when we stepped inside, I was even more impressed. I couldn't keep myself from gasping as Griffin showed me around the first floor. The view from inside was the most beautiful thing I'd ever seen. "Most love the ocean, but I'm a forest girl. I like being surrounded by trees."

"So do I. You're the first person to ever say that. Half my friends asked why I didn't buy something that has an ocean view."

"Pfffft. Someone criticized this beauty? How could they be so heartless?"

Being here, it became clear as day how different Griffin and I were.

No wonder he thought my house was a dump. Until today, I'd never been truly aware of how wealthy he was. He didn't flaunt it, but it was clear that he'd spared no expense on his home.

Oh, don't ruin the mood, Phoebe. Who cares that you and Griffin are from totally different circles? You two agreed to have fun together.

And we were going to do just that.

CHAPTER 21
PHOEBE

GRIFFIN WENT INTO THE KITCHEN, and I followed him. The stress of the day was simply melting away.

Standing in front of the island, Griffin pressed a button on the stone surface, then put a pot on the stone itself. Seconds later, he poured in oil.

"Wait, where is the actual cooking surface?" I asked, realizing there was no ceramic glass anywhere.

He smiled. "This is it. It uses an induction, so it's under the stone."

My jaw hung open. "Wow. I never knew something like this existed."

"It's fairly new," he said, "and expensive."

That's why it never popped up in my research for flipping the house.

"I can't accidentally burn myself, can I?"

"No. The induction doesn't heat up the stone, just the pot itself."

"Clever," I murmured.

Griffin put rice in a special pot and then started taking out ingredients from the fridge. "Is there anything you don't eat?"

"No. What do you want to cook?"

"Rice with egg and veggies."

"Sounds right up my alley." Honestly, I would have eaten anything. Being here was all that mattered. "Need me to chop anything?"

"No, I'm used to doing it by myself."

"Most people who live by themselves don't like to cook."

"I know, but Mom instilled that habit when we were kids. She always said there was no point spending money on takeout and insisted that cooking is an important life skill."

"She's right."

"Besides, it relaxes me. Can I interest you in wine?"

I clasped my hands together. "You brought back goodies from Napa?"

"You know it." Grinning, he showed me a small fridge of wine under the counter. "Which one do you want?"

"Surprise me."

"Your wish is my command," Griffin said.

The words completely lit me up, and he didn't even say it in a sexual way.

He took out a bottle of red, then put it back and said, "White! You get headaches from red."

I smiled wholeheartedly. His comment made me feel seen and heard.

I noticed the wineglasses in the cabinet behind a tinted glass door and took out two. He poured generously in both glasses, and then we clinked them together.

I swirled the liquid lightly, smelling it first. "Oh. My. God!" I closed my eyes, immersing myself in the scent.

"Phoebe," he growled.

I opened my eyes. He was staring at me with hunger.

"You drive me crazy when you do that."

"What?" I asked, thoroughly confused.

"That sound you make after you smell wine. I want to kiss you senseless every time."

I brought a hand to my mouth and giggled. I took a sip of the wine, then let out a "Hmm."

Griffin put his glass down. A second later, I set mine down, too, and then everything faded around us. It was just me and him. He gently took me by my shoulders and kissed me deeper than I'd expected. This kiss was hotter than any other we'd shared so far.

His lips wiped every thought from my mind. When I felt his hands under my ass, I didn't even question it. I was so lost in him that he could do anything he wanted with me.

After lifting me to the counter, he moved his mouth down my neck and farther to my chest until he reached my dress. Then he straightened, breathing hard. He brought his hands from around my ass to my outer thighs.

"The things you do to me, Phoebe."

"You've been holding back," I whispered.

"You have no idea. Every single time I'm with you, I want to devour you. And after our night together at the vacation house, I wanted to pounce on you the next day. And on Monday."

Clearing his throat, he stepped back. "Right. Dinner."

He gave me back my glass of wine while he focused on the pan.

I leaned in, whispering, "Cooking somehow makes you even sexier."

He chuckled and undid the cuff links on his shirt. Then he pushed the sleeves up to his elbows.

Oh, this man, really. Did he want to kill me? Did he even realize how hot that was?

I watched his every move intently. He cracked four eggs, then quickly chopped veggies before putting them in the pan. At the same time, he added the precooked rice.

Sitting here and looking at those hands was giving me sexy ideas. I hopped down and went behind him, massaging his shoulders before moving to his neck and down his back.

He groaned. "Phoebe, what are you doing?"

"You're cooking. The least I can do is make sure you're relaxed." I moved my hands farther down to his ass. "These muscles seem like they need some pampering too." My voice was a bit breathy.

Griffin groaned again, and I took my hands away. I didn't want him to burn dinner, after all. I could fondle him to my heart's desire after we ate.

He finished cooking just a few minutes later.

"This was quick," I said.

"Most of the things I cook take no time at all."

We ate at the huge table next to the window. He had a small sitting area beside the kitchen island, but his dining room was too beautiful not to use it. I carried the place mats and glasses, and Griffin brought the plates and cutlery. I realized I was super hungry after taking the first mouthful.

"This is delicious."

"I'm glad you like it."

I ate very fast, as did Griffin. I only slowed down after I'd almost cleared my plate. I still had a few forkfuls left, though, and I didn't plan on ignoring them.

After I swallowed the very last one, Griffin put a hand on my knee under the table, skimming his thumb up and down. I had no idea that was a sweet spot for me, but it was. I pressed my thighs together, sucking in a deep breath. I didn't think he'd noticed, though.

"So damn responsive," Griffin said.

Damn. He most definitely noticed.

His smile was smug as he focused on his food. I took another swig of wine, thinking how much different it tasted after eating. It was like all the flavors were enhanced.

"Want to move over to the sitting area?" he asked after swallowing his last mouthful.

I nodded enthusiastically.

We cleaned up the table in no time, starting the dishwasher too. Then he put an arm around my waist, leading me to the couch. He brushed his fingers up and down my rib cage, and I could swear that I felt that stroke between my thighs too. It was as if my entire body was a sweet spot.

As we sat down on the couch, I noticed the armrests had a wood surface on top for drinks.

"I love this house. It's so smart," I said as we set our glasses down. Then I straddled him.

Griffin cupped my ankles with his fingers before drawing his hands up my calves to my thighs. He looked at me intently.

"You're serious all of a sudden," I murmured.

He moved one hand up, caressing my jawline. "Phoebe, you're sure about all of this?"

I nodded. "Yes. I've honestly never been more certain about anything."

He smiled. "That's exactly what I wanted to hear."

He moved both his hands on my shoulder blades, pressing his fingers into them. I groaned, dipping my head back.

"Oh, wow," I exclaimed.

"You gave me that idea," he said. "You need to relax."

Then I felt his lips on my neck. "I've missed you. I've wanted to explore you for days."

I loved the sensations I felt when he spoke against my skin. Hot air blasted against my neck with every word.

Then he straightened up, coming level with my mouth, pressing his lips to mine.

And I was lost to him.

CHAPTER 22
GRIFFIN

I'D NEEDED this woman all week. I lifted her into my arms, holding her knees over my elbows. She kept kissing me as she placed her hands on my shoulder blades. I didn't have enough patience to take her up the stairs to the master bedroom, so I carried her to the guest bedroom instead. We didn't even make it to the bed. I plastered her against the wall, deepening the kiss, taking everything I needed while giving her everything she craved too.

At the back of my mind, I realized this evening was probably a bit emotional for her. I took my mouth off hers. Her eyes were closed, and she was humming.

"Phoebe. Tonight you can just sleep here. I don't want to take advantage of you."

Even as I said the words, I knew it would be fucking hard for me to stay away knowing she was under the same roof. But I'd get myself under control if that was what she needed.

She opened her eyes with a start. "No, no, no. I want you so damn much." She licked her lips and then brought her mouth to my ear. "I want you inside me."

I pulled back, staring at her. She was blushing. Fuck yes, she was trying to talk dirty to me, and I fucking loved it. I looked her up and down, calculating the fastest way to get her naked.

I loved that she was wearing a dress. I bunched it at her waist and then yanked it over her head, or at least attempted to.

It got stuck just as she said, "The zipper!"

"Fuck," I exclaimed.

I found the zipper at her back and quickly lowered it. Then I finally got rid of the dress. She was wearing a matching bra and panties.

"You look so fucking sexy in this."

She smiled shyly. "I know. It's new. I bought it especially for tonight."

I licked my lips. "For me?"

She nodded. "Yeah."

I liked her mix of sassy and shy—I never knew what to expect.

I traced the edge of her white lace bra, her nipples peaking beneath the cups as I kept brushing the upper part of her breasts. Continuing my ministrations with one hand, I lowered the other one to her panties, slowly teasing her. I wanted her soaking wet.

While kissing her, I moved my hand to her backside, cupping each buttock in turn. There was a strip of lace covering her crack. I ran my fingers up and down the right cheek until I felt her skin turn to goose bumps. She moaned against my mouth, and I slowly brought my hand to her navel, feathering my fingers in slow circles down to the edge of her panties. Then I pushed them inside the fabric and lost my mind when they slipped on her skin.

"Fuck. Why are you so damn wet already?"

She whimpered in response. This woman was making me lose control even faster than I'd thought possible.

I circled her clit before sliding a finger inside her. She was wet enough that I could add a second one without an issue. I pressed the heel of my hand on her pelvis and clit, feeling every muscle in her body change from being tense to completely relaxed. Her fingers dug into my shoulders.

"Phoebe," I groaned.

Then I yanked her panties down. Or at least that's what I attempted to do. I felt them rip apart, so I dropped them to the floor. Phoebe didn't even realize it.

I got rid of her bra next, and then I stepped back, admiring her.

"You're so beautiful."

The room had been completely dark when we'd been together last time, but now I wanted to keep all the lights on.

"I want to watch that beautiful body while you give in to pleasure."

I needed to see her face, her reactions. I wanted everything when it came to Phoebe.

And I knew just where to start. There was a huge mirror next to the dresser. Taking her hand, I led her in front of it, then stood right behind her.

"I like seeing your naked body like this."

"I want to see you too," she said.

"As I said before, your wish is my command."

I took a step back and undid the top button of my shirt. She watched me in the mirror. I liked that she was following the rules of my game without my having to explicitly say them. She wasn't turning around to look at me; she was glancing in the mirror, watching my reflection.

I took off my shirt slowly, enjoying the way she fixed her gaze on every button. I removed my pants much quicker, mostly because I needed to free my cock. The confinement was downright painful. Even the touch of the boxers' fabric was too much. She gasped slightly when I removed them, straightening up. Her eyes were glued to my erection. I was sporting a full hard-on already.

Then I stepped closer so half my body was behind hers. I put my hands on her shoulders, then lowered them down her torso, stopping at her breasts. I looked straight at her in the mirror while I twirled her nipples between my fingers. She pressed her knees together.

Was she even wetter than before? I had the overwhelming need to check. I kissed her shoulder while I moved one hand farther down. With the other, I was teasing her breasts. Watching her in the mirror was exquisite. I saw every arch of her back and sharp inhale. I was able to see her in a way I never could if I weren't focusing on her pleasure only.

My cock pressed against her right buttock. I could barely hold back from bending her over and driving inside her. But it wouldn't be long.

When I brushed her clit with the tips of my fingers, she dropped her head back against my shoulder and cried out my name. And I changed my plan. Yes, I still wanted her to orgasm before I made her mine, but I'd thought of a much more delicious way to make that happen than with my fingers. But first I needed to know something.

"Phoebe, are you okay with foreplay without a condom? I'm clean."

"Yes. Me too. And I'm on birth control," she said, licking her lips. "We don't need a condom at all."

That chipped away just a bit more at my self-control. "Phoebe, are you sure?"

She nodded. "Yes. So, so sure, I promise."

I moved us backward another step, then said, "Grab the edges of the mirror and watch."

I bent her forward just a bit so she was at an angle where I could rub the length of my cock against her opening. It was pure torture for me, but it was more pleasure than torture for her, which was exactly what I wanted. I watched her knuckles turn white as she clenched the edges of the mirror tight.

She closed her eyes too. I started circling her clit with the tip of my cock.

"Watch," I commanded.

She opened her eyes. They were slightly watery. "Griffin, please," she begged.

Those words nearly melted my resolve. Nearly.

I moved my cock slowly, focusing only on her clit. She came almost instantly. I held her tight, but her legs became unsteady. I'd been determined to wait for her to ride out her orgasm, but I pushed inside her. She cried out louder. The feeling of her pussy clenching around my cock was out of this world. I hadn't been prepared for the overload of sensations so fast. She was so damn tight that I had trouble controlling my breathing.

As I pulled out, she started to beg. "Please, please."

No way could I continue the foreplay. I needed her too much. But I couldn't have her like this, still hanging on to the mirror.

"Let's move to the bed, Phoebe."

She whimpered. Damn, she was killing me with those reactions. I sat down on the part of the bed that was facing the mirror and said, "Sit on me backward." She licked her lips and then turned around, moaning when she noticed our reflection in the mirror.

"I want to watch you until the end."

She lowered herself slowly and gripped my cock at the base, positioning it so that I could slide inside her all at once. She was truly exquisite, and she was all mine tonight to explore and please. I was going to do both those things in spades.

I thrust inside her from below. She took my cues, moving up and down at the same rhythm. I never stopped watching her in the mirror, loving the way her face changed when she started pulsing around me again. It was a damn sight.

I didn't have the freedom of movement I needed like this. "Stand up, and I'll fuck you from below."

She positioned herself just as I'd told her. Fuck yes, now I had more space to move.

"Touch your clit," I said. "Watch yourself in the mirror while you do it. Keep your eyes on your hands."

She blushed. I was inside her, and yet my words made her blush.

She nudged my cock with the sides of her fingers as she touched herself. I dropped my head back, letting out a guttural groan as her muscles tightened around me. We were both already too far gone.

Opening my eyes, I glanced in the mirror while I thrust inside her from below. I could still see glimpses of her reflection. She was following my instructions. Watching herself would make this even more intense for her.

I knew she was going to come before she cried out—not just because she was so tight that I almost gave in to my climax, but also because she took her fingers off her clit. She touched her breasts instead, closing her eyes. Then her shoulders jerked uncontrollably. I heard her cry out my name while I spasmed and my vision blurred. I came so damn hard that for a few seconds, I forgot where we were and what day it was. Then I slowly pulled out and lowered her onto the bed. She stayed on her back, hands at her sides, eyes closed. Her hair was ravaged.

I leaned on one side, bending an elbow, as I brushed the hair out of her face with the back of my hand. She opened her eyes slowly. They were unfocused at first, but then she looked straight at me, and a glint appeared in them. She smiled. Then she darted her tongue out, wetting her lower lip. She opened her mouth, inhaling deeply, laughing on the exhale. I leaned forward, kissing her sternum. Laughter reverberated through it. She traced my curved back with her fingers, her palm on my rib cage.

"This is a fantastic room," she murmured.

"What?" I asked.

"This bed is so amazing. No wonder you could—" She licked her lips. "—fuck so well." She blushed even though she was grinning. "Then again, you were excellent back at the house, too, so maybe it's not the bed. Maybe it's just you."

"I'd say so," I said, leaning over and kissing the top of her nose.

"I need to clean up."

"We have to go upstairs for that. I don't have anything in the bathroom here."

I grabbed my discarded shirt, using it to clean up before taking her hand and leading her to the upper level.

"You've never had guests?" she asked.

"No. But I'll have my nephew over soon enough. I want to decorate his room before he visits, though. His Spider-Man obsession is still going strong."

She kissed my bicep. "I like when you talk about him. Your voice softens."

I shrugged. "I care about him."

"Whoa," she exclaimed when we reached the top of the staircase.

The hallway upstairs was bigger than necessary. I'd turned it into a home gym of sorts, putting a treadmill and weights by the window.

"This house is stunning."

Once we stepped inside the bathroom, she looked around once, her mouth open. "You've got a huge walk-in shower *and* a freestanding bathtub."

I grinned, pointing to the corner. "And don't forget the Jacuzzi."

She blinked, following the direction of my finger. "Holy shit. I could just live in this bathroom. I'd sleep in the tub, cook at the sink. How can this even be real?"

"Which do you want, the tub, the Jacuzzi, or the walk-in shower?"

Turning around, she put her hands on my shoulders. "How about we give all three of them a try?"

I laughed, kissing her forehead. "I'm all for that."

CHAPTER 23
GRIFFIN

I LIKED my house best in the morning. The position of the sun warmed up the patio, but it wasn't so hot that you couldn't enjoy the outdoors. I made a point of going outside every morning to drink my coffee. Today was no different, except I didn't have a coffee. Phoebe was still sleeping, so I didn't even start the coffee machine because it was too loud. One big minus of the house was the open floor plan. I liked it, but you could hear everything from afar.

My phone rang at exactly eight o'clock. I wondered who it could be at this hour. Then I noticed that Mom had sent a message twenty minutes ago.

Mom: Do you need us to bring anything?

I frowned, not really understanding what she meant.

Mom: Before you say no, I've made muffins this morning. Everyone loves them.

Fuck. Fuck! I'd completely forgotten that I'd asked my family for breakfast this morning. How the hell did that happen? I'd planned to tell Phoebe yesterday, ask her if she was okay with that. And then I got completely lost in her.

I headed back inside and hurried upstairs, happy when I heard the shower. My family was going to be here in less than an hour. I knocked at the door of the bathroom before stepping in so I wouldn't startle her. She turned around, grinning.

"Turn off the water," I said. "I need to tell you something."

"Huh?"

I leaned in to turn off the water, getting my arm wet. "Listen, I need to tell you something."

"What is it?" Her smile faded.

"I forgot that I asked my family to drop by for breakfast today."."

"Oh my God. Um, okay. I wouldn't have washed my hair if I knew that because drying it will take forever." Her eyes widened. "Shit, we came in your car. Can you drop me off somewhere?"

"Phoebe," I said sternly.

"Huh? Yeah?"

"Has it occurred to you that I might want you to stay?"

She straightened up, lowering her hands by her sides. She must be cold without the water running, because her nipples were perked up.

Or maybe it was her reaction to me.

Her smile was back. "Wait, your family knows who I am?"

I cleared my throat. "Get dressed and we'll talk later," I said, looking anywhere but at her nipples.

"Why? Am I too distracting?"

"Fuck yes, you are. I'm close to mauling you right here in the shower, and we don't have time for that."

"Whoops, okay. Then shoo, shoo," she said.

"You're dismissing me?"

"This goes both ways, you know? You look very delectable standing there in your white T-shirt. I'm having all sorts of ideas, like turning on the water and pulling you under it. It's best if you wait for me downstairs."

I chuckled. "Sure."

I headed out of the bathroom, leaving her to get dressed. Descending the steps, I tried to anticipate how the day would go.

It wasn't really possible, though. I could predict my family's individual reactions, but when we were all together, things could escalate quickly and in ways I couldn't foresee. The dynamics changed according to what mood everyone woke up in. Since the entire family would be here today, this could go all sorts of ways.

I should have probably warned everyone, but it was too late now. If I wrote to my parents to give them a heads-up, they'd immediately call and question me about what was going on. And my brothers were better off without a heads-up anyway.

I checked the contents of my fridge. It was fully stocked. I had everything I needed for breakfast, but I knew it made Mom happy to contribute.

Griffin: Sure, bring whatever you want.

While I took food out of the fridge, I heard steps coming down the staircase, and then Phoebe walked in shyly with a towel wrapped around her.

"Um, my clothes are here," she said, pointing to the guest bedroom.

"Sure. I forgot, or I would have brought them upstairs."

She went into the bedroom. I was fighting all my instincts not to go after her. She was irresistible to me, even wrapped in a towel.

She came out a few seconds later, sighing.

"What's wrong?" I asked.

"I was going to just turn my panties inside out, but they're ripped."

I grinned, remembering last night. "That's all my fault, sorry. But I can't wait to be alone with you for the rest of the day. Unless you have plans?"

"Not at all." She fidgeted, pulling at the bottom hem of her dress. "Thank God it's long enough. I'll make sure to sit cross-legged."

The thought of her going commando was not helping my self-control.

She looked at everything I'd laid out on the dining table. "How many people are coming?"

"My parents, that's two. Then all of my brothers, which is another five. And then Hannah and Riley, too, plus Jeremy. So ten."

She jerked her head back, laughing nervously. "I'm meeting your entire family, and I've got no panties on!" She covered her face with her hands. "All right. I need coffee before they arrive."

"If you're hungry, help yourself to whatever you want."

"I'm not much of a breakfast person," she admitted. "I just run on coffee in the morning, and then sometime around eleven, I usually have a hunger attack."

I made coffee for both of us, and we drank it at the breakfast table.

Phoebe was completely silent at first, but after a few sips, she asked, "How is your family going to react when they see me?"

"Not sure. Last they knew, we were faking being a couple."

Her eyebrows shot up her forehead. "Holy shit! They knew about that?"

"Yes, and Mom handed me my ass."

"Wait, what are we now? We're not in a relationship because neither of us is real—"

"Phoebe, do we have to discuss this now? We're together, got it? Who cares what we call it?"

She laughed. "You're right. Just enjoy each other. We're having fun, only your family doesn't need to know that."

That's the truth.

"Exactly. Otherwise, my mom might beat me up all over again."

"I can't imagine anyone doing that."

"No one usually does except Mom. I let her get away with a lot." I grinned and noticed Phoebe looking at me with warmth in her eyes.

"So, when exactly are they coming?"

I checked the clock on the oven. "Half an hour, give or take."

I was wrong. Mom arrived ten minutes later, with Dad, Knox, and Finn—who'd apparently picked everyone up—in tow.

"Darling, I also baked some cookies and—" She stopped midsentence, noticing Phoebe.

Her eyes darted to me. Dad cleared his throat. Knox had a shit-eating grin, but Finn looked absolutely perplexed.

"Griffin, darling, you didn't tell us you had company," Mom said.

"Mom, Dad, everyone, this is Phoebe."

Mom jerked her head back but was polite enough to extend her hand. "Nice to meet you. I'm Susan, and that's Bruce," she said, pointing at Dad.

"And you," Phoebe said, shaking hands with everyone as they introduced themselves.

Knox was still grinning. "You've been holding out on us."

"Clearly," Finn said. He even *sounded* stunned. "Could we have an update? Phoebe, is he blackmailing you somehow to help his sorry ass?"

Phoebe's eyes bulged. I was used to my brother's antics and his direct ways, but she wasn't.

"Finn, behave," I warned.

"Hey, don't talk to me like I'm a dog."

Knox kept looking from me to Phoebe. My parents had the good grace to not say anything.

Then the rest of the family arrived. Chase and Hannah came first, followed by Wyatt. At least Jeremy wasn't here yet. I preferred to get this explanation out of the way before he arrived. I didn't want him to get wind of my charade with Phoebe, however brief it was. I wanted to be a good example for him.

"Everyone, I want to introduce you to Phoebe."

Hannah looked at Chase in confusion.

Wyatt cocked a brow. "Is this the next stage in whatever you two are planning? You need feedback from us?"

"Feedback?" I parroted.

"Yeah. Someone to tell you if you have any real chemistry or that you look like puppets in a show or something?" He locked straight at Phoebe. "And no offense to Griffin, but this is something we never thought him capable of. Sounds more like something I'd do, or these two." He pointed at Knox and Finn.

"Yeah," Finn said lazily. "We're the ones with crazy ideas."

"What has gotten into all of you?" I asked.

"Son." That came from Dad. He sounded very serious. "We're surprised, that's all. Phoebe, forgive my boys."

"They're a bit much," Mom supplied.

"And when we're surprised, we're a lot much," Finn finished for her. "Quite frankly, I feel like Knox and I are always on that level. Larger than life."

I realized that Phoebe had been completely silent since introducing herself. I wanted to explain this as succinctly as possible.

And then a light went on in my head. *Wait a fucking second. I don't have to explain myself. Not even to my family.* Things were different, and that's all they needed to know.

So, I put an arm around Phoebe's shoulders. "We're not pretending anymore."

Mom stared at us intently. Hannah frowned. Chase looked at Wyatt with a questioning glance, clearly feeling like he'd missed something.

"Hell yeah, I called it," Knox said, turning to Finn. "Told you."

"Yeah, man, I thought you were just bluffing."

What the hell are they talking about?

"Um, wonderful. So, that means you two are dating," Mom said. She looked like I'd just told her Christmas was happening twice this year.

Dad was smiling too.

Phoebe, however, was completely silent.

"Now, before you make Phoebe feel uncomfortable—" I began, but Wyatt interrupted me.

"Oh, that ship has sailed."

"We're very sorry, Phoebe. It's just the way we are," Knox explained.

"Why don't we have breakfast?" Mom asked. "Phoebe, you're the only person here who hasn't tasted my cookies and muffins. I'd like to know what you think."

"Sure," Phoebe said slowly.

Thank fuck for Mom. She seemed to be the only one with a good head on her shoulders.

"Someone text Duncan," I announced as we headed toward the dining table. "Tell him what's going on so he doesn't ambush me too."

"Duncan wouldn't do that," Wyatt replied, then turned around to Phoebe again. "He's basically the only one of us who's got some manners."

"Hey, I do too," Chase countered.

I realized it was the first thing he'd said since I announced that Phoebe and I were an item.

"That's debatable," Hannah said. "You were a royal ass the first time I met you."

Phoebe started to laugh as Chase groaned.

"Hannah," he warned.

"Sorry." Hannah grinned sheepishly. "A grump. Is that better?"

"We get the gist," I assured them.

"Anyway," Knox cut in, "Duncan does have manners. He wouldn't make a fool of you in front of Phoebe."

"Well," Finn said, "when taken by surprise, sometimes he forgets all about his manners and is just as much of a Neanderthal as the rest of us. I'll text him."

"Thank you," I answered sardonically.

"Who wants coffee?" Phoebe asked.

Everyone said they would like a cup, and Phoebe darted right to the coffee machine. It took a while to get breakfast ready. Then, after putting all the food on the table, my family sat down and immediately started eating. This reminded me so much of my childhood—we were especially loud and crazy during mealtimes.

I walked to Phoebe, kissing her shoulder. "Babe, are you okay?"

"Your family is not what I expected," she commented quietly.

"Sorry about them."

"What? No, don't be sorry at all. I just thought... Well, it's going to sound wrong, but I'll say it anyway. I figured they'd look down on me."

I tilted her chin up, looking at her. "Why the ever-loving fuck would they do that?"

"Because you're the Sterlings. I was clueless about the family when I met you, but not anymore. I like that they're all down-to-earth, even in the way they tease you. But still, we're different."

"'Tease' is a nice word."

"Told you he's not lying to us." Finn's voice filtered toward us.

Phoebe and I turned to look at the table at the same time. Every single person was staring at us.

"For fuck's sake!" I exclaimed.

"We're sorry. We're sorry," Mom apologized. "Boys, back to the food."

Hannah was trying to control a fit of laughter.

"Sorry, man," Chase said. "Knox was throwing around the idea that you might still be faking and that you're using us as an audience to practice on."

Phoebe started to laugh, as did I.

"But we get it now. We were barking up the wrong tree," Wyatt admitted. "Either that or you're very, very good at faking it."

"Yeah, I wouldn't put that past him," Finn announced.

"I wouldn't think he's capable of that," Knox added.

"I'll have you know that we *were* very convincing," Phoebe stated, and I was astounded at the sass in her voice. Were my family's antics rubbing off on her?

Knox was looking very smugly at me.

I brought my mouth to Phoebe's ear. "That's because I was so damn attracted to you that it's a miracle I didn't kiss the panties off you that first evening at the restaurant."

"That would explain a thing or two." She blushed as we brought a few cups of coffee to the table.

"You two aren't getting any coffee," I informed Knox and Finn.

"Why the hell not?" Finn blurted.

"Because you've pissed me off, and you're already fired up with your BS. You don't need more ammunition."

As Phoebe and I made coffee for everyone except those two, Duncan, Riley, and Jeremy arrived. Duncan behaved well, introducing the three of them to Phoebe. Amusement was obvious in his eyes, but he didn't say anything that would put Phoebe on the spot.

I owed him one. Even though she'd said she liked this group, it could quickly become too much for someone who wasn't used to us.

After we all sat down at the table, Phoebe headed to the kitchen. She returned with two coffees, putting them in front of Knox and Finn.

"I like you two," she said, smiling at me.

"Thank you, Phoebe. We like you too," Knox replied.

"We're very likable," Finn said. "Duncan's and Chase's girls have taken a liking to us. In some cases, even before they took a liking to our brother."

"Who?" Phoebe asked.

Hannah cleared her throat. "Yeah, that's me."

Chase raised a brow. "What do you mean?"

"As we established before, you were a grump of the highest order when we first met. And the second time too. And your brothers seemed to have all of that humor you lacked," Hannah explained.

"That's not true," Chase said as Wyatt, Knox, and Finn started to laugh.

I kissed Phoebe's cheek. Mom was quieter than usual, watching us intently. I was certain she'd give me a piece of her mind after.

Dad leaned forward, whispering something in her ear, and Mom softened. At least I could count on him to have my back.

"Jeremy, your uncle tells me you're going through a Spider-Man phase," Phoebe said.

He nodded enthusiastically. "Yes, and he said I can have a room here with Spider-Man."

"That you can, buddy," I assured him. "But I need you to go shopping with me. I don't even know where to begin."

Jeremy climbed on his chair, clapping his hands once. "Yes. Can we go today?"

Duncan turned to him. "We need to schedule that in advance, Jeremy," he said patiently. "You can't just expect people to do what you want whenever you want it."

"But he asked," Jeremy said.

"I have plans with Phoebe today." I put my hand on her upper thigh. I was trying very hard not to think about the fact that she was commando.

She smiled up at me and said, "The three of us can go shopping if you want."

I couldn't believe that she'd suggested it.

Jeremy's deafening yelp of joy filled the room. I chuckled as Duncan tried to quiet him a bit.

"Duncan, Riley, would that be okay with both of you?"

My brother didn't reply right away. I knew exactly what he was thinking. He didn't even know Phoebe. But after Riley whispered in his ear, he nodded.

"Sure," Duncan said. "We'll pick him up before dinner."

"That sounds like a plan," Phoebe said.

Jeremy got down from his chair, running right between us. He gave me a half hug, and I kissed the top of his head.

"You're awesome, Uncle Griffin. Awesome."

Knox and Finn were looking at me with suspicion. I knew they were onto me. They were Jeremy's favorite uncles, but they didn't have a Spider-Man room for him at their respective places because they each had a bachelor pad. Slowly but surely, I was buying my way onto my nephew's favorites list.

And Phoebe's too.

CHAPTER 24
PHOEBE

THE FAMILY STAYED for another two hours. When it was time to leave, I realized that Jeremy was negotiating with Duncan and Riley again. Everyone else had left, and the three of them were by the window in the living room.

"What do you think they're talking about?" I asked Griffin. We were quite a few feet away, near the coffee machine.

"I bet he's asking Duncan if he can spend the night here when we're done shopping."

"That would be so cool. We could make it a movie night, buy popcorn and stuff." I stopped talking and glanced at Griffin. "Shit, I just realized I invited myself for a second night. It wasn't my intention."

"Funny, I planned to convince you to stay."

"Really?"

He grinned wolfishly. "Fuck yes. I want you here with me another night." He brought his mouth to my ear. "And a third one."

I fidgeted against him, sucking in a breath when he pressed his chest against my boobs.

I put a finger over his lips and shook my head. "We're not alone, remember?"

He straightened up. "No, actually. It happens to me all the time when I'm with you. I forget there's anyone else around."

I completely swooned, but then Jeremy's voice broke the magic. "Dad!" he exclaimed.

"Let's go help him. Are you sure you want him to spend the night here?" Griffin asked.

I nodded. "Yes. I'd love that."

His eyes changed. They softened somehow, but I couldn't quite understand why. Taking my hand, he led me to the trio. "Hey, guys. Phoebe and I were talking, and we don't have any plans. We'd love for Jeremy to spend the night here, if you're good with it."

"Yes! I told you, Griffin loves me."

"Of course I do, buddy," he said, and Jeremy ran straight to him. He wrapped his arms around Griffin's torso as if he wanted to grab as much of him as possible. That was so cute.

Duncan looked straight at me. "And that's okay with you?"

I nodded. "Yes, of course. I was thinking we could have a movie night."

"Yes!" Jeremy pumped his fist in the air. "You're my favorite person. I love movie nights."

I looked at Duncan for a sign that I'd committed some sort of faux pas. For all I knew, maybe Jeremy had a TV curfew.

Duncan just laughed. "I see you're hitting it off, so we can't say no." He looked at Riley, who was smiling.

"Then it's settled," Griffin said.

Jeremy was still hugging him. "I'm going to make a list of what I want to buy. Where can I find a pen and paper?"

"On the kitchen counter."

"Okay. Bye, Dad." He didn't even wave at his father before darting toward the kitchen.

"Thank you for doing this," Duncan said.

"If anything happens or you need help, just call us," Riley added.

"We've got this," Griffin said. "You two have fun."

"Yes, we will," Duncan said before turning to his fiancée. "I'm taking you out on a date."

Riley smiled even wider. "Sounds like my kind of Saturday night."

As we walked them to the door, Duncan kept giving us tips about Jeremy's nighttime routine.

Griffin frowned. "Dude, come on. It'll work out. Don't stress too much. I'll call if we forget something."

"How will you know if you're forgetting anything?" Duncan asked.

"You have zero trust in me. He has sleepovers with Knox and Finn all the time."

"It'll be his first one with you."

Oh, that explains the very detailed instructions.

"Duncan," I said, "we probably won't remember all the steps. How about we call you later this evening? Or you can text the instructions if it makes you feel better."

Duncan seemed much more relaxed. "Yes, I'll do that. I'll text Griffin everything."

"Great!" I exclaimed.

We bid them both goodbye before they left.

"Are you done with that list, buddy?" Griffin asked loudly the second we closed the door.

"No, I keep getting ideas," he said, running toward us. He'd scribbled in bold letters on the white sheet of paper. I only had time to read the first one, which said **Batman bedsheets**, before Griffin took it away, looking at it.

"No more Spider-Man?" he asked.

"No, I already have two Spider-Man rooms. Now I want to have a Batman room too."

"Do you actually know where we'll find all this stuff?"

"Target," he and I said at the same time.

Griffin frowned. "Let's see where I can find the nearest one. I haven't been in years."

I jolted my head back. "What? How is that even possible? You don't shop at Target?"

"No. I usually just go to a grocery store when I need food, and I order everything else online."

Jeremy grinned. "Don't worry. Dad didn't know about it either, but Riley took me once. She says she *hooked* me on it."

I laughed. "Let's hook your Uncle Griffin on it too."

We learned that the nearest Target was twenty minutes away. During the drive, I asked Jeremy to recite his list a few times until I'd memorized the items. I also wanted to buy a change of clothes and some panties, since a certain handsome man ripped mine to shreds.

Once inside, I suggested we divide and conquer, but the boys wanted us to stick together.

"I can see the appeal. They have literally everything," Griffin said after we'd knocked off most of Jeremy's list in under two hours.

He looked at the list while pushing a full cart. I was pushing the second one that was only half full. Jeremy was helping me too. He stood right by my side the whole time, and I loved it.

"Buddy, if you've got everything you need, we can head over to the cash register," Griffin said.

"How about some Batman-themed shower gels and shampoo?" I asked. I didn't actually know if there were any, but I was keeping my fingers crossed.

"Yes, yes, yes," he exclaimed, and we headed to the aisle with personal hygiene.

"You're good at this," Griffin murmured as we arrived in the section with shower gels for kids. Of course there were Batman-themed ones too.

I smiled softly. "I just let him inspire me. There are so many cool options. Imagine being a kid today."

"You'd be a great mom, Phoebe."

That touched me in ways he couldn't possibly know.

"Thanks," I murmured as Jeremy grabbed a Mickey Mouse shampoo as well.

I wondered how come he liked Batman *and* Mickey Mouse, but maybe I'd find out when we picked our movie for tonight. We were now very well prepared for that. We didn't just buy popcorn but an air-popper to make it. What was this life?

Before going to the cash register, Jeremy decided he wanted to buy a Batman figurine too. They all looked identical to me, but the boys went back and forth about it for a solid twelve minutes before I gave up.

"You know what? I'm going to buy something for dinner. I'll meet you at the cash register, okay?" I said.

Griffin nodded. Jeremy wasn't even paying attention.

Smiling, I headed straight to the grocery aisles, wondering what they would like. *Ha! Pizza!* I was sure it would be a hit. I didn't buy a frozen one but rather picked up all the ingredients so we could make one together. Afterward, I ran over to the women's clothing section and quickly grabbed some panties that were on sale as well as a cute cotton dress.

I met the two of them at the cash register. It took a while for us to pay—Saturday was a very popular shopping day for Target. When we finally reached the car, Jeremy yawned.

"Buddy, if you want, you can wait inside the car while we load everything," Griffin suggested.

"Okay," he said and immediately got in the car.

We emptied the carts fairly quickly, and then I took them back to the store while Griffin arranged things in the trunk. By the time I returned, he was already in the car.

On the way home, Jeremy talked our ears off about all the things he bought.

The second we arrived at the house, Jeremy exclaimed, "Yes! I get to decorate the room."

Once he got out of the car, we unloaded the trunk. We needed two trips to carry everything inside the house. I put the groceries in the fridge. Everything else belonged in Jeremy's room.

"Do you have a quick-wash cycle so we can clean these before we put them on the bed?" I asked Griffin, pointing at the sheets.

"Yes. I'll take care of it," he replied, taking them from the bag.

After he left, Jeremy and I started opening the other packages.

"This will be even cooler than the room I have at Mom Shona's house," Jeremy said.

"Where is that?" I asked, a bit confused.

"In Dublin."

"Right," I said.

"Mom Shona is my real mom, but since she doesn't live here with us, now Riley is my actual mom. Actually, I never told Mom Shona that I think Riley is my actual mom. But I think she might know that anyway."

"You can never have enough moms. It's cool that you have two."

He nodded. "You're right. It is cool. I don't even know many people who have two moms. Some kids at my school say that their dad has another woman, but that one isn't their mom. They say bad words about her."

Oh my God. Kids at school discuss this stuff?

While Jeremy walked around with his huge Batman figurine to find the best place to put it, I was fearing that the room might look a bit like a bat cave—pun intended. The sheets were dark mauve and black. But Jeremy was happy, and that was all that mattered.

My phone vibrated while I helped him put a poster on the wall. My stomach somersaulted when I saw I had a message from our realtor.

A couple will make an offer for the house today. I'll keep you posted. Hopefully, I'll have more details next week.

Yes, yes, yes. I was keeping my fingers and toes crossed. This had to work out.

It had to.

When Griffin joined us a few minutes later, I debated telling him about the news but ultimately decided not to. I'd fill him in once I had more info.

"The sheets need one hour. What are we doing now?" he asked.

I looked at the clock. "We could make dinner before starting movie night."

Jeremy jumped up and down. "Let's start the movie night. We don't need dinner. We have popcorn."

Griffin looked at him with a stern expression. "Your dad sent me the list. He said that dinner is mandatory."

Jeremy's face fell. "But I never have dinner when I'm with Uncles Knox and Finn. I eat so many sweets that I'm not even hungry."

Griffin looked at me in confusion, then back at Jeremy. "And your dad is okay with that?"

"No!" It sounded as if he wanted to add the word *dummy*. "Dad doesn't know about it. I don't tell him, and my uncles don't either."

I smiled. Growing up, I'd played that exact same card with my grandparents. They spoiled me to the moon and back, and my parents never knew anything about it.

"I can make pizza. I bought all the necessary ingredients when we were out shopping."

Jeremy's eyes widened. "You know how to make pizza? It's my favorite."

I grinned at him. "Yep."

"I can help. I always help Dad cook."

"Sure," I said. "Between the three of us, we can prepare the pizza really quickly. I bet we can start watching movies within an hour."

"Yes, yes, yes. I love it here. Can I come more often?" Jeremy asked Griffin as we went to the kitchen.

He chuckled. "Sure, buddy. I love having you here."

Opening the fridge, I took out the tomato sauce, mozzarella, basil, and the dough.

"Which part is your favorite?" I asked Jeremy.

"I like to put the tomato sauce on the dough."

"Then you start with that. I'll shred the mozzarella. If you want, you can sprinkle that on too."

"Yes, I do," he said. His eyes were glinting with happiness.

As I rolled out the dough, Griffin opened the can of sauce. I wondered if life could actually be like this. I could see us doing this exact same routine on a Saturday in a few years, going shopping with our boy and then cooking together. My heart started to ache—that's how much I wanted it.

At first, I thought I didn't want a relationship, when really I just didn't want another bad one. But this? Yeah, I wanted this.

But was it truly possible?

Just be happy about today, Phoebe. Enjoy every second.

Grabbing the can with both hands, Jeremy started pouring the sauce very carefully. He was biting his tongue with the tip stuck out.

Griffin came to me on the other side and kissed my cheek. I shifted my focus from Jeremy to him. "You're good with him."

"I'm enjoying this."

"Thank you for this amazing day."

He looked at Jeremy and then at me for a second before helping Jeremy.

And I couldn't help but wonder if maybe I wasn't the only one imagining something more.

CHAPTER 25
PHOEBE

"DARLING, HE SOUNDS SO WONDERFUL," Mom said.

"I know, right?"

"I don't know many men who would decorate a room at their house for their nephew."

I was such a genius. I knew telling Mom about that particular detail would sell her on Griffin right away. Hell, *I* was still melting just thinking about it.

Ever since we'd been at his house two weekends ago, I kept looking at the pics I'd taken of the two of them. Unfortunately, Griffin had been crazy busy since then. I was discovering that the man was quite a bit of a workaholic. But even though he had a lot going on, he texted me a few times a day and even dropped by with dinner about three times a week. The fact that he was carving out time for me made me feel important.

But things were starting to get busier and busier on my end as well as the tax season began. I was keeping my fingers crossed that it would mean I'd get that full-time job offer soon, but I wasn't holding my breath. The way I saw it, I had to prove to my boss that I was an invaluable member of the team, and the rest would just work out.

"We can't wait to meet him when we come visit," Mom said.

"Yes, I'm so excited about that too."

"Listen, I've got to go. I love you darling. Take care, okay?"

"Sure. You, too, Mom."

After hanging up, I started wondering how I'd coordinate the visit if we did manage to sell the house before my parents arrived. Although, unfortunately, I hadn't heard from the realtor yet.

Biting my lip, I decided to push a bit and messaged her.

Phoebe: Hey! Any news about the house? It's been a while.

Beth: I have an email with the offer in drafts but was waiting for some details to finalize it. Never mind, I'll just send it like it is.

I read the message three times before it sank in.

Oh my God.

We have an offer on the house.

I immediately opened my inbox. The email from Beth was there. They were offering $15,000 over the asking price, which she said was to be expected.

I felt my body loosen up. My muscles almost turned liquid with relief. This was yet another thing I'd started to believe wasn't going to happen after all. I felt like I'd be stuck making payments for this house forever.

See, Phoebe? It pays off to keep moving forward and expect good things to happen.

The profit on the sale was slim, but at least I'd get rid of the mortgage payment. I wasn't going to look a gift horse in the mouth. So I instantly replied to Beth and CCed Marshall, so he'd be in the loop.

The only caveat was that they wanted the house empty in three weeks. That didn't give me much time to find something else, but beggars couldn't be choosers.

Whatever. I want to accept.

I inhaled deeply, then immediately forwarded the offer to Veronica.

I was relieved, but at the same time, I couldn't believe this stage of my life was ending. I was *so* ready to leave this house behind and the memories of how I got here. Only a few months ago, I wouldn't have thought that was possible. This house had embodied a lot of my dreams, but not anymore. I knew it had a lot to do with meeting Griffin. I'd started healing even before we were *really* dating.

I smiled at the thought. I was moving on, and it felt glorious.

My phone rang with a call from Veronica.

"Congratulations!" she said as soon as I answered.

"I'm so relieved."

"Girl, you're on fire."

"That's exactly how I feel."

"Have you started to look at places to live?" she asked.

"No, I haven't."

"Oops, sorry. I didn't want to rain on your parade But the email did say that they need you to vacate quickly."

I sighed. "I know."

It was already causing me anxiety. My budget was modest, and San Diego wasn't cheap.

"You can sleep on my pullout couch while you find something. You don't have to hurry the process."

I bit the inside of my cheek. "Do you mean that?"

"Sure. It'll be like back in college."

"I just don't want to inconvenience you."

"You wouldn't. Look, it's the least I can help you with. I wouldn't offer it if I didn't mean it."

That was true. She'd offered that after the breakup, but I'd figured since I was paying the mortgage on this place anyway, I'd better stay here.

"I'll keep that in mind. Thank you. I'll only stay until I find something suitable."

"Something nice."

I laughed. "I won't be moving into some luxurious condo."

"Not yet," she said.

I grinned. That was why Veronica and I were soulmates. We both liked to put a positive spin on things. I'd lost my way a bit after all the heartbreak, but I was getting back on track.

"I'm so happy for you. What did Griffin say?" Her tone changed a bit, though I couldn't understand why.

"I haven't told him yet. I just found out myself. And it's not final anyway. Marshall still has to agree to it, but I think he will. He's even more desperate than I am to sell the house."

"I can't believe he's ready to move on with someone else."

I shrugged even though she couldn't see me. For some reason, the thought of it didn't hurt anymore.

"I really don't care what he does. I just want to sever all ties between us."

"Good for you. I'm so happy you got over him. I can barely believe it, honestly."

"Why?"

"I don't know. It hasn't been that long."

"That's true," I said, "but I think some wounds run so deep that you can't help but stop caring for that person."

"And it does help when someone new comes along, huh?"

"You're fishing for information," I said, going into the backyard and sitting down on the swing. I wasn't going to miss the house, but I was definitely going to miss the small yard. I'd probably have to rent a studio or something. It would be a long while before I could afford a house.

"Well, you're a bit tight-lipped about Griffin, and I wonder why."

"I'm not doing it consciously," I assured her. "I'm starting to fear that if I talk about how good things are, they'll fall apart."

She gasped. "Holy shit, friend."

"Oh wow. I don't even know where that came from."

"Well, wherever it did, I hope things change soon. You deserve to be happy, Phoebe."

"Thanks, Veronica."

"Okay, I have to go. I'm being summoned by the boss from hell. What if I come to your place after work and help you pack?"

"That would be amazing, but I'd feel super guilty to hijack your free time."

"Ha! No need. You can take me out for a drink on Friday as repayment."

"Consider it done."

"Then I'll see you this evening."

"Yes, ma'am. I love you."

"You too."

For the rest of the week, Veronica came to my place after work, and we filled box after box. I'd decided to move in with her next week already.

"Sooo, finally telling Griffin tonight?" Veronica asked Friday evening as we were preparing to leave the house.

"Yes. I'm so excited to see him."

He'd called me this morning to make plans, and when I told him that Veronica and I were going out, he simply suggested catching up later. He was meeting with Jude's team today, and he wasn't sure how long it would take.

That was fine by me. I'd have fun with Veronica in the meantime. She couldn't stay late anyway because she was working tomorrow too.

"That makes two of us. I've been hoping to see him again for quite some time."

I frowned. "Why? You've already met him."

"Yeah, but this is different. He's actually dating my best friend now."

"Right… Please don't scare him away."

She grinned mischievously. "I'm not making any promises."

Griffin

I was passionate about my work—always had been. But meeting with a new team on Friday afternoon hadn't been my best idea. I kept glancing at the clock, wanting this to be over so I could start my evening with Phoebe.

At least this meeting was going exactly the way I wanted it to. I'd arrived at Jude's office thirty minutes ago, and we'd gone straight to the main meeting room, along with his CEO, CFO, and a marketing manager. I always made a point to meet the management team before I decided whether I really wanted to invest in a business or not. Clicking with the founder was important, but I needed to click with the management team as well. Although, in all fairness, the management team could always be changed. But so far, Carlos, Moira, and Eve had made a good impression on me.

"We'd funnel a new investment into acquiring more users," Carlos said.

"What age groups are you focusing on?" I asked.

Carlos and Moira exchanged a glance. "We're focusing on twenty-five and up. People who are on their first, possibly second job already."

Eve leaned forward. "We figured that's when people start having a stable enough income to pay our yearly fee."

Jude shook his head. "It's not all about the money, Eve."

"Well, I, for one, am happy the CFO is thinking about the money," I said, and Eve laughed.

Moira, who was in charge of marketing, added, "Our focus groups also tell us that starting at that age, people are more inclined to pursue long-term relationships or look for something serious."

I fundamentally disagreed with that. Twenty-five? The last thing I'd wanted back then was a long-term relationship. But not all people were the same.

"On which channels does the acquisition happen?" I inquired.

"We're casting a wide net. But most of our users come from the ads we run on Facebook and Instagram. We've got someone covering TikTok, but ads don't perform very well there. And we're not making headway with organic content on the platform yet."

"I say focus most efforts on the channels that are yielding a good return. Sometimes we have a tendency to run after the new shiny thing, even though we're better off doubling our efforts on the places that already work for us," I said.

Moira looked at Jude. "I like Griffin. Finally, an investor who isn't obsessed with us trying out every social media platform known to mankind."

"He's got a good eye for business," Jude agreed.

"Well, I think this has been productive." It was one of the longest meetings I'd had with a potential new investment. "I'll be in contact with Jude."

I rose to my feet. So did Jude. I shook hands with Moira, Eve, and Carlos.

"I'll walk you out," Jude said. "Actually, I'm leaving too. My wife's waiting for me with pot roast." He rubbed his palms together. "It's one of my favorites."

We headed out from the meeting room and walked straight toward the exit.

"Send my regards to Phoebe."

"I will."

"You know, that girl is the reason I gave you a second chance," he added as we stepped outside.

Guilt ate at me. I detested lying, even for a good cause. But I couldn't imagine a scenario where I told Jude the truth and he wouldn't be pissed off. Even though things were different now, they weren't exactly as we'd portrayed to them. Regardless, some things were better left unsaid.

As we parted ways, I pushed the matter to the back of my mind. I was meeting my woman, and I intended to focus on her completely.

CHAPTER 26
GRIFFIN

AS SOON AS I got in the car, I checked my messages. Jeremy had sent me a picture of him in his Spider-Man room with the caption **I like my room at your house more.**

Fuck yes. Mission accomplished. I liked having the little guy over and was hoping to convince him to spend the night at my place again soon. Duncan was probably the one who needed convincing, though. I didn't really blame my brother. When Jeremy was younger, Duncan couldn't trust me to be alone with him. Mostly because I didn't realize kids needed to be watched constantly.

Then I noticed another picture—Phoebe had sent me a selfie with Veronica. They were holding cocktail glasses.

Griffin: I'll be there in twenty minutes.

I couldn't believe how much I'd missed her. It felt bizarre. I was going to show that to her in every way possible.

During the drive, I called my CFO to discuss the details of the transaction. It was all standard, but I liked to follow those types of investments closely.

I arrived at the beach club soon enough. Music was blasting from outdoor speakers. I was about to call Phoebe when I entered to ask where exactly she was, but then I saw her and

Veronica in one corner in front. They weren't alone. There was a guy with them, and I instantly disliked him.

I walked straight to them, and when I got closer, I heard the douche ask my woman, "Tell me, Phoebe. You like to come to these places often?"

"No, it's the first time I've been out in ages."

"You should get out more often. This place could definitely use someone as hot as you."

What the actual fuck? I'd never heard anyone sound so fucking corny. "Who the hell are you?" I asked without further ado as I joined them.

Phoebe's mouth opened. Veronica actually started to laugh.

The guy looked at me and sneered. "I'm with the ladies tonight. Fuck off."

I leveled him with my stare. His bravado faltered, his shoulders drooping. "I don't know what game you're playing, but you're definitely not." I pointed at Phoebe. "She's with me."

The guy glanced from me to Phoebe, stunned.

What the hell? He thought she was available?

"I'm free for a dance if you want," Veronica told the guy.

He still looked confused as fuck, but then he glanced at Veronica and said, "Sure, sure."

After they left, I slowly turned to Phoebe.

"My, my," she said through fits of laughter. "You've got a jealous streak. I wouldn't have taken you for having one."

"Why was that guy under the impression that you were single?"

"Huh?" she asked, still laughing, but the corners of her mouth turned downward.

She looked around, and I realized some people were eyeing us cautiously.

"Griffin, come on. Don't make a scene."

I took her hand, walking with her out of the premises and farther away from the group. The beach was deserted.

"There, now no one can hear us."

"Okay," she said.

"So, answer me."

She ran a hand through her hair. I looked her up and down. She was stunning, wearing a dark green dress and high heels.

"Veronica picked him up. He was there flirting with her."

"That's not what it sounded like."

"I was her wingwoman."

"He was flirting with you." I emphasized every word.

"I wasn't encouraging it in any way."

"What if I hadn't joined you?"

She jerked her head back. "I don't like what you're implying."

"Which is what?" I asked.

"You tell me."

I stepped closer to her, putting both hands on her neck. "I don't like what I saw. A guy who didn't know you were taken was flirting with you."

"Taken?" she whispered.

"Fuck yes. I don't want anyone flirting with you. I want everyone knowing you're fucking mine." I tipped her head up. "I want to be the only one who gets to see you wearing that dress."

"Now, see, that's not going to work, Griffin. You can't tell me what to wear."

I kissed her before I said anything else that I'd end up regretting. Fucking hell, I knew she wasn't flirting with that dude. He was the one who'd complimented her. It was all on him, and I was acting out.

She pulled back a bit. "Don't think you can kiss your way out of this," she murmured. "You can't talk to me like that, Griffin. Or even think like that about me. I will not tolerate it."

"I know. I'm sorry."

"Just don't do it again."

"I can't make any promises," I said. "But I'll try my best."

I kissed her lower lip, pulling it between mine.

She cleared her throat. "Let's go find Veronica."

"Sure."

We walked back to the club, carefully navigating the mass of people. But not careful enough, apparently, because only a few steps in, someone bumped into me.

Phoebe shrieked, and I instantly tensed, zeroing in on her. The woman who'd bumped into me had spilled her bright blue cocktail right on Phoebe's dress.

"Shit! I'm so sorry." The woman was slurring her words a bit.

Phoebe pressed her lips together, waving her hand. "Whatever." Turning to me, she added, "I need to change out of this. But I want to tell Veronica goodbye first."

"We'll find her quickly."

We walked deeper inside the club. I noticed several guys checking Phoebe out. I took a deep breath, trying to rein myself in. My instincts were in overdrive when I was with her. Usually, it was so easy for me to assess a situation and react accordingly. But not tonight. Not with her. Telling Veronica we were leaving was the polite thing to do, but all I wanted was to throw Phoebe over my shoulder and take her to the car.

In the end, my rational side won.

But if that guy flirted with her again, I wasn't liable for my actions.

I put an arm around her shoulders and focused on her and her alone as we entered the room. We found Veronica and that guy dancing in a corner.

She stopped moving when she noticed us. "What happened to your dress?"

Phoebe sighed. "Someone spilled a drink on me. I need to go home and change."

"Sure, you two have fun. It was great seeing you again, Griffin."

I nodded at her. "Likewise."

"And you totally earn points for the caveman behavior."

Phoebe stared at her with an open mouth. I started to laugh.

The guy smiled sheepishly at Phoebe and then at me. "Sorry, dude. Didn't mean to make things awkward. Veronica filled me in on everything."

I nodded but wasn't able to do more than that. For fuck's sake, I had manners. Mom had taught me better.

"No problem" was all I said.

After waving at them both, we went outside to my car.

"I'm starting to feel cold," Phoebe said once we were both inside.

"We're gonna be at your place in half an hour tops, and you can change. Or… you can take it off on the ride. I definitely wouldn't mind."

She cocked a brow. "Really? How about all the people who would see me through the window."

I gritted my teeth. "No!"

Phoebe burst out laughing. "Thought so."

After a beat, I added, "I really am sorry about the way I acted back there."

"In all fairness, if I found you at the club and some woman was all over you, I might throw a jealous fit too."

"That does my ego good."

She giggled, crossing her legs. I had a fantastic view of her left thigh. Clearing my throat, I focused on the drive, keeping my eyes on the road.

We arrived at her house a short while later and headed straight inside. As soon as I stepped in, something felt off. I looked around. "You've tidied up." Everything was in boxes. I frowned. "Wait. You're packing?"

"Yes! I have a bit of news, and I wanted to share it with you tonight," she said, putting her hands together and smiling from ear to ear. "The house has an offer, and I accepted it. Marshall too. It's going to officially go over to the new owner in three weeks."

"That's fantastic. When did you find out?"

"At the beginning of the week. Although, the realtor did

mention that someone wanted to make an offer way back when we had our weekend with Jeremy."

"Why didn't you say anything?"

"Honestly, I didn't want to jinx it. I was afraid it would fall through at some point, but it didn't. The check cleared, and the bank approved the loan."

Something wasn't sitting right with me. "When did you even start packing?" Then I realized what it was. "When are you moving? And more importantly, where?"

Her smile widened even more. "I'm going to room with Veronica starting next week. Until I find a new apartment."

"Why didn't you tell me you have to move?"

She shrugged. "I didn't want to burden you with all that. You have enough on your plate already."

"You should have told me."

"Why?"

"Because you're part of my life." I frowned. "Am I not part of yours?"

Her smile fell. "Of course you are. Why would you think otherwise?"

I pointed at the boxes. "It doesn't feel that way. I get you not telling me about every step in the sale of the house, but you should have told me about moving. Unless I'm misreading everything that we have?"

"No, you're not." Her voice was a bit high-pitched, and she looked at the boxes and then at me. "I just... didn't think it mattered where I lived. Besides, you have enough going on, even more so now with your deal."

"I will always be busy, Phoebe. But I still want to know everything going on in your life."

"Why?" she murmured.

"Because I care about you so damn much."

Her eyes widened. Honestly, the confession caught me off guard too. I hadn't even been thinking the words. They just came out. "You look so fucking surprised. That means I haven't done my job well enough of showing you just how much you mean to me."

She licked her lips, running a hand through her hair and then putting both hands on my chest. "Griffin, I..." She swallowed hard. "I always figured you wouldn't want a relationship."

"I thought that, too, but what the fuck did I know?"

She gave me a soft smile. "I care about you too."

"Do you mean that?" I asked her. "Because if your feelings aren't there yet, you don't have to... I don't want to push you if you're not ready."

"Why would you think that?"

I pointed at the boxes.

She sighed loudly and rolled her shoulders. She was tense, and I didn't want to make her feel that way, but she needed to understand what she meant to me.

"I don't even know how to share things, Griffin. I was in a long-term relationship that... Well, Marshall didn't care much about me in any respect. Most of the time, I was doing my own thing. Even when I was doing stuff for us, I was planning everything, and he just went along with it. It didn't occur to me that you'd like to know what's going on in my life, let alone the details."

"I so fucking would. Play by play. Everything." I tilted her head up. "You're not alone in this. I might not know much—or anything—about relationships, but I want to do things together. Our lives are merged now, babe. We're together, yes?"

She closed her eyes and smiled. "Say that again."

"Together. We're together," I repeated. "Are you ready for that?"

"Yes. That sounds amazing. I really was going to tell you tonight that I was moving, though."

I started to laugh. "You didn't think the boxes would tip me off?"

"I didn't even think about that. Do you want something to drink?" She groaned. "Crap, I already packed the glasses. I'm sorry, I really didn't think this through. Should have left out more things. Want us to go to your place for the night? I'll just grab something to change into tomorrow."

"When exactly are you moving to Veronica's?"

"Next week." Turning around, she headed to her bright pink suitcase, opening the top.

I gritted my teeth. "We really have to work on your communication skills."

She looked at me over her shoulder, blushing, then closed the bag again, straightening up. "Know what? We can actually just take this huge-ass bag with us. I have most of my seasonal clothes in here."

I narrowed my eyes and said, "Take everything you need until then."

"Why?"

"To stay at my place." I realized I wanted her there. "There's no point in you staying here until next week. It's even more depressing than before with everything in boxes."

She smiled. "True. But are you sure? I don't want to get in your hair."

"I'm fucking sure. Why do you keep questioning me every time I say something?"

She shrugged. "I'm not used to this, Griffin. It's new territory."

I stepped closer, gently putting my hands on the sides of her neck. "For me, too, but I need you to take what I say at face value."

Her smile was impish now. She put a finger on my chest and pushed me away. "When we were concocting stories for Jude, I remember thinking you were a great actor."

"I've needed you from the very beginning, Phoebe. And I haven't stopped needing you since." This was another confession that came out of nowhere. I wasn't prepared to even think these things, let alone say them.

"I need you too," she whispered.

"And that scares you," I concluded.

She gasped. "How can you tell?"

"Because your entire body tightened up."

"I am afraid. I'm trying not to be, but I can't help it."

"Phoebe, you've been through a lot. That's understandable. And as I said before"—I lowered one arm to her waist, pressing her closer to me—"I don't want to rush you. We'll take things as they come. Now, go change into something dry and let's go home."

CHAPTER 27
GRIFFIN

ON THE WAY to the house, we spoke a bit more about her living arrangements with Veronica. This whole thing still wasn't sitting well with me. I didn't like that she felt she couldn't share everything with me and that she might be a burden. I was going to have to work on that.

On the other hand, who was sending mixed messages? Me. I knew it, but I'd never in my life thought I'd ever want to be with one person. That one person could be all I needed.

And the clincher? That I wanted to be the only one she needed too.

Once we arrived, I headed upstairs with her, carrying her luggage and depositing it in the master bedroom next to the dresser. I didn't even bother turning on the light.

"Do you want to take anything out now?" I asked.

"No, not really." She walked closer to the window. "I like how big the moon is tonight and that you can see it in all its gorgeousness through this huge window."

She was standing right in front of it, and I walked behind her. I liked having her here in my house and my bedroom. More than that, I liked that she was staying for a few days.

I pushed her hair up, wrapping it around my fist, and tilted her head forward so I had access to the back of her neck. Then I kissed her exposed skin slowly, trailing down between her shoulder blades.

"I love this dress." It left so much skin for me to explore and touch and lick. "Keep your hair here," I instructed. I wanted both hands free to explore her.

She immediately took over, holding her hair out of the way.

I feathered my hands slowly down the sides of her body as I moved my mouth farther down until I reached the edge of the fabric. I lowered the zipper with my right hand, kissing every inch of exposed skin as I went. She moaned, and that sound filled me with pride.

As I uncovered almost all of her back, my patience ran out. Yanking the zipper and then tugging her dress down, I lowered myself to my knees as I held her by the ass so she could step out of the outfit.

I couldn't get over how gorgeous she was. It was such a privilege to see her take off her clothes for me. She looked incredibly sexy in her high heels and lingerie. Phoebe was petite but not fragile. She was curvy and fit. I loved how thick her hair was and the way it fell over her breasts, highlighting how perfect they were. Her hips were full, her skin perfectly smooth. She was absolutely beautiful.

I turned her around, looking up at her. She bit her lower lip, averting her gaze, and I kissed the front of her thighs while tilting her pelvis with my hands. I wanted her at a certain angle. Dragging my thumb over her panties, I grew rock hard the second I realized that she was already wet. I slipped one finger inside, between her panties and her slick skin, wanting to double-check just how wet she was for me.

I immediately undid my belt and jeans with the other hand and then shoved it inside my boxers. Gripping my cock, I squeezed it tight while I moved my thumb over her bare skin. She moaned again, even louder. I made eye contact with her for a brief second. Her eyes widened, and she zeroed in on the hand

I had in my pants. Then she averted her gaze again, but I felt her become even wetter. I alternated between focusing on her clit and dipping my thumb inside her.

When she began to shudder, I realized that she needed to lean against something. I didn't trust myself to hold her up with my hands, so I moved us farther back until she reached the wall. It was much closer than the bed. I was going to make her come here first, before I even took her underwear off. Then I'd continue pleasuring her on the bed.

I squeezed my cock tighter. I didn't have much room to move with my jeans still on, but it was enough. Besides, she was all that mattered now. But I needed another angle for her.

I put one of her thighs over my shoulder and moved the fabric—just the part covering her pussy—to one side. She put one hand on my head, wrapping her fingers in my hair. *Fuck yes.* I turned her on so hard that she wanted to ride my face. I loved making her lose control. I took her panties off, then pressed my thumb on her clit. Then I pushed my tongue inside her while squeezing myself tightly.

I felt the throb of pleasure course through her body. She tightened her grip on my hair and pushed her pelvis forward just a fraction of an inch, as if she needed my tongue deeper. What she actually needed was my cock, but we both craved this fast release.

Her legs started shaking, and I realized this wasn't fair to her. She needed to sit on the bed so she could fully focus on her orgasm, not be afraid that she'd fall over. I pulled back and led her to the bed, but I didn't sit her down there. Instead, I turned her around and pushed her onto her knees on the bed. Then I pressed a palm on her back so she was on all fours.

Moving her farther away from the edge, I kissed her buttocks while I worked her clit with one hand. With the other, I lowered my pants, dropping them to my ankles along with my underwear and then stepping out of them without even pausing from touching her.

She was close, and I wanted to feel her let go. Her body began to shake lightly. I needed her to come because I wanted to sink inside her as soon as possible. She clenched her knees together, trapping my hand right before exploding. I positioned my cock at her entrance the very next second and slid in. She cried out even harder.

"Fuuuuuck yes." I felt as if I was finally able to breathe for the first time since we'd stepped inside the bedroom. Her orgasm intensified with every thrust. I dropped my head back, closing my eyes and losing myself in this woman. I enjoyed the way she tightened around me, the sounds she made.

Her moans quickly turned to pleas. "Griffin," she murmured. "Please."

I breathed in through my nose while slowing down. I wasn't thrusting like a madman anymore; now I was pushing in excruciatingly slowly, wanting her to feel every inch of me.

"Please!"

I knew what she wanted. She needed me to touch her clit, and I was going to do it, just not the way she imagined.

I pulled out of her and then drew my cock over her pussy, rubbing the length of it across her opening. Then I touched her clit, moving back and forth over it, coating her in her own wetness.

"Oh my—ohh!" Her voice shook as she grabbed the sheets, pressing her forehead against the bed. She rocked back and forth, mirroring my rhythm.

It was pure torture for me, so I slipped back inside her. A groan reverberated through my chest—hell, my entire body. I needed her on a visceral level, and not just right now or tonight. I needed her to be part of me forever.

Leaning over her back so I had access to her clit, I played it like a harp with my fingers while I thrust inside her. Pleasure took over my body. I needed to be even wilder. I needed to thrust with all I had.

"Touch yourself while I fuck you."

I heard her sharp intake of breath. Then her hand hovered next to mine.

Fuck yes. She didn't even hesitate in following my orders.

She came the next second, and I stilled. Feeling her tighten around me was impossibly good. I nearly gave in to my own climax, but I managed to stave it off. I didn't move one inch while she thrashed and clenched, just internalized her cries of pleasure and the way it coursed through her body.

My woman was going to come three times tonight. I was determined.

Once I felt her inner muscles relax and her breathing become more even, I pulled out of her. She didn't move an inch. I liked seeing her spent like this, and I wasn't even done with her. I climbed off the bed, looking around for her panties. I had an idea.

After retrieving them from the floor, I went back to bed and turned her over. She was putty in my hands, soft and trusting. Once she was on her back, I smiled at her. She blinked slowly, looking up at me.

"Put your hands over your head, beautiful."

"Why?"

"I want to tie them."

Even though she'd been spent just a few seconds ago, her eyes were suddenly alert. She licked her lips while I wrapped her panties around her wrists. Then I pushed my cock up and down her opening, massaging her clit, not sinking in yet. I couldn't stop watching her, soaking in every reaction. But I wouldn't last long.

When my cock started to pulse, I lifted her ankles, putting them on my shoulders. As I touched her clit with my thumb, I pushed in and out of her relentlessly. She came fast, and I followed seconds after, giving in to the pleasure. I let it wash over me, thrusting until I'd given her everything I had.

Spent, we lay down next to each other, the sound of our ragged breaths filling the room. I recovered first and turned on one side, propping my head on my hand. With my other one, I traced her abs and her breasts. She was lying on her back, eyes closed, but she wasn't asleep. A smile tugged at her lips.

"I like when you can't stop touching me," she said.

"You mean always, then?"

She tugged at her wrists. "How about untying this?"

"I could," I teased, "but I like seeing you all tied up for me."

I kissed her neck before straightening up again, but I did free her hands. I'd wanted to heighten her senses, not make her uncomfortable.

She blinked her eyes open, looking at me. "I'm so happy I'm staying until Tuesday. I can't wait to see how many more delicious things you'll do to me."

I leaned in again, kissing her neck once more before moving down between her breasts. "You have no idea how many things I want to do to you. There won't be enough time to cover everything. Don't move in with Veronica. Move in with me. Then I'd have all the time in the world to do everything I want with you."

The muscles in her stomach clenched beneath my lips. I only realized what I'd said when the words were out. When I looked up at her, her eyes were wide.

"You want me to move in here for sex on demand?" Her voice was teasing, but it also held an edge that it didn't have before.

"Interesting way to put it," I said in an even tone, carefully choosing my words. I was always excellent at building up arguments and laying out the pros and cons in any situation, but now my mind was blank. So I told her the one thing I was completely certain of. "It would make me happy to have you here."

She licked her lips, and I kissed farther up.

"Griffin," she murmured. "But when we met, you said—"

I shook my head and put a finger over her mouth. "There's no point in bringing up what I said when we first met. I'm different now. I think you know that. And it's because of you."

She smiled against my finger. "Why don't we revisit this

conversation in the morning, once the post-orgasm fog has lifted from your brain."

"Phoebe, I'm not going to change my mind. And it's not just for sex, though that is an added bonus. I just want you with me. Now, if you don't want to, I completely understand."

"Oh, I want to," she said, a huge grin on her face. "I do want that. It wouldn't be for long anyway. I plan to find an apartment soon."

That didn't sit well with me, for reasons I couldn't even explain. Things were happening quickly, I realized that. I was just pissed that I hadn't met her before she met her asshole of an ex. Then maybe she wouldn't hesitate at the thought of living together. *Damn it.*

"And even though you didn't outright ask me to do it, I'd happily be your sex slave. I just want you to… you know…" She shrugged. "Be completely certain about us."

"I am." I emphasized each word.

She pushed me onto my back, climbing over me and kissing my chest. Then she wiggled on top of me. "I was so good and spent before, but look at me now. I don't think I'm going to be able to sleep a wink."

"You're that excited?"

"What do you think? Look at this." She pointed at her mouth. Her grin was enormous. I'd never seen her so happy.

"Well, it's a good thing we aren't going to bed yet. First, I'm going to cook for you. Then I have a few more delicious ideas for the rest of the night."

"Sold. Hook, line, and sinker. I'm all yours."

CHAPTER 28
GRIFFIN

WHEN I WOKE up in the morning, Phoebe wasn't next to me. I didn't get up right away. Instead, I rolled over onto her side of the bed, replaying last night in my mind. Smelling her perfume on my sheets filled me with an inexplicable sense of joy.

I got out of bed a few minutes later, putting on boxers before going downstairs. I was about to call out for Phoebe when I noticed her sitting on the floor next to the window, looking outside. She was wearing a robe.

"Good morning, gorgeous," I said.

She glanced at me over her shoulder. Her eyes were hazy with sleep. "Oh, I'm sorry. Did I wake you up making coffee?"

"Yes, but I don't mind." I sat next to her, taking a sip from her cup.

"Hey, don't steal my coffee," she mumbled.

"You're adorable in the morning."

"Hmm… I need the sustenance today after the extensive *workout* from last night. I didn't get to sleep too much."

I laughed. "Same here. Do you want to go to your place later and bring the rest of your stuff?" I asked as I pulled her robe down her shoulder.

"Oh, already?"

"Yes. Why wait?"

"Okay. If you're still sure."

I looked up at her. "Phoebe, stop saying that. Of course I'm sure."

She closed her eyes. "I'm sorry. I didn't even realize how annoying it is to keep questioning your intent."

"It's not annoying, but I would like to understand why you're doing it."

She sighed. "I think it's because I'm just not used to this, what we have. I was always the one who pushed for things in my past relationship. And here you are *offering* to make more space for me in your life. It's almost bizarre. And I guess I'm just afraid it won't last, that you'll think better of it."

"Don't. I want you here."

"Okay." She put the cup of coffee down and climbed onto my lap.

Fuck me, she was commando under the robe. Why didn't I realize that?

I pushed it farther off her shoulder, then kissed from the top of the fabric up to her neck. She leaned a bit away and looking at me while chewing on the inside of her cheek.

"I'm not sure if we should bring the things today, though. I still have to pack some stuff, and I have a lot of boxes. They won't fit in your car. I was actually thinking about splurging on a moving company."

"I can call the one that helped me move here. I paid for a full package and still have some hours left."

"What? No, no, no. You don't have to pay for it," she said. "I can afford it."

But I knew for a fact that she couldn't. I wanted to give her the best life possible. But I knew she wouldn't agree, so I had another idea.

"Or we can use my brothers' muscles. They all have big cars. If they all join, we can bring everything in one trip."

She smiled. "They wouldn't mind?"

"No, they wouldn't. They'd give me shit, that's for sure, but they'd be happy to help."

"That would be terrific. I'll make a delicious meal for everyone to enjoy afterward."

Her reaction touched me unexpectedly. Phoebe couldn't receive anything without giving something back. It was endearing. Cooking after spending the whole day moving sounded exhausting, but I knew it was important to her.

"I'll text them right away."

"If they don't have time, there's no hurry, really. I just need to be out of the house by Thursday the week after next." Her shoulders sagged.

"When are you meeting the realtor?"

"On that Wednesday."

"And Marshall will be there."

She nodded, and all my muscles tensed up.

"I'll come with you."

She looked at me intently for a few seconds, then shook her head.

"No. I'm tempted to say yes because having all these muscles," she said, tracing my arms and my abs, "and this smile"—she touched my lips—"always fills me with good energy. But I want to do this on my own. Just firmly close the door on that chapter in my life."

"Phoebe, every time you face that guy, he hurts you."

"I know. But this will be the last time I ever have to see him. And it'll be good for closure, you know?"

I actually didn't. I had no experience with closure or anything even remotely similar.

"All right. I understand," I said. "Where are you meeting them?"

"Near the Central Library."

As she told me the exact address of the realtor's office, it got me thinking.

"Know what? I'm meeting Jude that day."

"Wow, you do like to schedule stuff in advance."

I nodded. "It's absolutely necessary in my line of work. I can have our meeting at a coffee shop nearby. And after you finish, you can come straight over. We'll wrap everything up quickly, and then I'll be all yours."

Her face lit up with a smile. "You'd rearrange your day for me?"

"Oh yes, babe. I'd do a lot more than that for you."

The real question was what I *wouldn't* do for this woman. I wanted her to be happy and content. I was feeling on top of the world because she was moving in with me.

"All right. Let me text my brothers."

I wrote to all five of them, expecting them to respond over the course of the day. To my astonishment, they all answered before I even had time to make coffee for myself.

"That's weird," I said as I poured beans into the grinder.

"What is weird?" Phoebe asked.

"They're all willing to help us today."

She frowned. "So? You said they'd be happy to help."

"Yeah… but they all answered quickly. Almost as if they spoke with one another."

I bit back a laugh, absolutely sure that I was right.

"When do we want to go?" I asked Phoebe.

"It's up to them, really."

"Knowing my brothers, they probably cleared their schedules and are ready to pounce. I'll tell them to meet us at your house in an hour."

"Perfect," Phoebe said and then widened her eyes. "Let me just check your fridge."

She dashed to open it, then perused the contents. She rose on her toes, inspecting the top shelf as well.

"Okay, this looks good. I have everything I need to throw lunch together. By the time we get back from the house, it's going to be lunchtime for sure. Then they'll have the rest of the afternoon off. I'm excited."

"Chase asked if you're taking any furniture."

She shook her head. "No. The new owner said he's got plans for it. I only packed the smaller stuff, like glasses and plates and…" She paused, looking around at the kitchen. "You don't actually need any of that."

"We'll figure out later what we'll do with them."

I was so damn ecstatic that this woman was going to live with me, I couldn't even explain it. Nothing had ever given me so much joy. Not even sealing a business deal.

While I drank my coffee, Phoebe went upstairs to get dressed. Mom called as I finished making myself a second cup, and I answered right away.

"Good morning, darling," she greeted.

"Hey, Mom. How are you doing?"

"Fantastic. How's your Saturday?"

"It's going great. Do you need help with anything?"

"Oh no. That's not why I called. I was wondering if you have plans for dinner."

"Why?"

"Oh, well… I spoke to Jeremy today, and I couldn't help but overhear…"

I started laughing before she even finished her sentence.

"Don't laugh at me, young man."

I cleared my throat. "Sorry. Please continue, Mom. What is it that you couldn't help but eavesdrop on?"

She gasped. "I didn't eavesdrop! Oh my. I can't believe my own son would accuse me of something like that."

"Mom!" I urged.

"Well, he was saying that Duncan is going to help move some boxes from Phoebe's house to yours."

"Exactly. All my brothers are coming."

Mom didn't say anything for a few seconds. "You're going to make me ask, aren't you?"

"Yep" was all I said, because I was too busy fighting a smile to form sentences.

"Do you have anything to share with the family, son?"

"What do you think, Mom?"

"I think Phoebe is moving in with you."

"You're correct." Now I did burst out laughing.

"Oh, stop that! I wouldn't have to go around eavesdropping—"

"Thanks for owning up to it."

"—if you'd share things with me, honey. Oh, I'm so proud of you. This is a very important milestone."

"We only just decided it, Mom, and it's temporary," I replied, keeping it vague. I couldn't possibly give her details about when and how I'd popped the question, so to speak.

"Well, no matter how it came to be, I'm very happy for you."

"So, why did you ask about this evening?"

"Oh, no reason."

Now I was suspicious and earnest. "Mom."

"Nothing is set in stone, but you'll receive news over the course of the day."

I'll receive news. That sounded ominous somehow.

When I heard Phoebe come down the stairs, I quickly added, "Mom, I've got to go. Have a great day."

"And you too."

"I'm ready!" Phoebe called. Then she stopped in her tracks, looking at me. "And you're still in your boxers."

"Yeah. Mom hijacked my time."

"Everything all right?"

"She's up to something, but I'm not sure what. She was ecstatic that you're moving in."

Phoebe jerked her head back. "You told her?"

"I didn't have time to. But news in my family travels in mysterious ways."

I walked up to her, kissing her forehead. "I'll be down in a minute."

"So, what exactly did your mother say?"

"That I'll receive news over the course of the day. Those were her exact words."

"Oh." She laughed. "Your family's something else."

"Yeah, you can say that again."

CHAPTER 29
GRIFFIN

WHILE GETTING DRESSED, I kept thinking about what Mom meant. She'd probably ask us to dinner at her place. I wouldn't mind—not at all.

Ten minutes later, we were on the way to Phoebe's house.

During the drive, I shared our location with my brothers. To our astonishment, Chase arrived before us. He was leaning against his car, flashing me a shit-eating grin.

"Good morning, you two. Phoebe, nice to see you again."

"Hey, Chase. Thanks so much for volunteering to come over," she said.

"Always happy to help out."

She smiled at me. "Generosity really does run in the family. Your brother didn't even hesitate asking me to stay with him until I find something else."

"It was indeed a surprise to everyone," Chase said.

I decided to lay out all my cards. "Did you talk to Mom?" I asked him as we went to the front door.

"No. Why?"

"No reason." Mom would let me know what she was up to soon enough.

Phoebe cleared her throat as soon as we stepped inside. "So,

I've actually packed a lot already, but I still need to gather some things together. All these boxes are ready, obviously." She pointed to the corner stacked with boxes and two huge suitcases. "These are bursting at the seams, so I won't open them again. I'll pack the rest of the things in a small carry-on."

"That's okay," Chase said. "Take your time. Meanwhile, the two of us will load as much as possible in our cars. When the rest join us, we'll split the boxes among ourselves."

"Thanks so much. I'll hurry, I promise."

Once Phoebe went into the bedroom, I expected Chase to start asking questions, but he just got to work. Finn and Knox arrived almost immediately after.

"The other two are on their way," Finn said the second he stepped inside the house.

"Where's Phoebe?" Knox asked.

"I'm here," she announced, coming out of the bedroom at the same time that Duncan and Wyatt came into the house.

"Oh, you're all here," she exclaimed. "Do you want anything to drink? Jeez, I didn't even think about offering before."

Wyatt chuckled. "Relax. We're your packmules today. Just put us to work, and we can celebrate afterward."

"Celebrate?" Phoebe asked.

Wyatt flinched, and Chase grunted.

I stared at Chase. "Man, I thought you were hiding something, but I figured I was just being paranoid."

"All I'm saying is, keep an open mind," he said, looking at Phoebe apologetically.

"Don't overwhelm her, Chase," I warned.

Phoebe frowned. "You lost me."

"Great job, dude," Knox said.

"I told her I was suspicious that you all replied at the same time. It almost seemed like you've been talking to each other."

No one said anything for a few seconds, and then Duncan sighed. "Oh, what the hell. Yeah, we might have spoken on the phone before agreeing to reply."

Chase cleared his throat. "So, Mom and Hannah were talking. We want to throw a barbecue at the inn for dinner."

"That's so sweet," Phoebe said.

"Aha," Finn said with laughter. "I feel like we owe it to you to warn you. Mom will prod you and Griffin with questions about the decision to move in together."

Phoebe's eyes bulged, but then she shook her head. "I wanted to cook lunch for you, though."

Finn shrugged. "We can eat a lot. We'll be happy if you feed us for lunch and we get barbecue for dinner. It takes forever for us to barbecue anyway."

"That's true," Chase said. "Whenever we all gather for that specific purpose, we somehow end up taking a million years to do it."

"Yeah, that's because everyone is too busy gossiping. Like now," I said. "Come on, let's load up our cars. Phoebe, you need help packing what's left?"

She shook her head. "I'm already done with that, so I'll help you. I'll carry the boxes that aren't too heavy."

"Let's all get to work," I said.

I appreciated that they were all going above and beyond to put Phoebe at ease. And I had to give Finn more credit. He'd picked up immediately how important it was for her to cook a thank-you meal.

I'd always enjoyed doing things with my brothers. We were extremely good at pulling ourselves together when we had a goal. The result was that we finished loading up the boxes only two hours later.

It was a good thing that all of them came over. We could barely fit everything in six cars. I'd initially wanted to load up my Toyota, too, but the engine wasn't starting. That was a problem for another day.

"Do you need to do one more check of the house before we leave?" Finn asked.

Phoebe shook her head. "I'm good. I already checked it a few times."

"Let's hurry," I said. "We've got another two solid hours of work ahead of us."

Phoebe winced, though it was almost imperceptible. I only caught it because I knew her so well.

I took her hand as we walked to the car, and she whispered in my ear, "I feel guilty."

"Trust me, they're enjoying it."

"Hmmm… that can't possibly be true. But I like spending time with your brothers."

I kissed her hand. "I'm glad."

She sighed, looking over her shoulder at the house before we got in the car.

"I can't believe I'm finally leaving this place. I'm so excited for the next phase of my life," she exclaimed as I gunned the engine.

"So am I. And if my brothers weren't tailing us the whole way, I'd show you exactly how excited I am."

"Don't worry, I've got lots of ideas. I can't wait to finally be alone. I keep making mental notes right here." Phoebe tapped her temple.

My cock twitched. Damn, I was very close to finding an excuse to pull over somewhere. But they were all following me, so that was out of the question.

We arrived at the house a short while later. As soon as we got out of the car, Phoebe said loudly, "Guys, we actually do have drinks and stuff here. What do you want?"

"No! Work first," Knox said, making the rest of us pause.

Chase was staring at him with bulged eyes. "You actually said that?"

"Yeah, there's merit to that theory. And then Phoebe can feed us. I've already worked up a huge appetite."

Phoebe put her hands on her face, fingers splayed wide, eyes narrowed as she looked at the floor, clearly thinking hard.

I stepped closer to her, putting an arm around her shoulders. "Babe, don't stress out."

"I'm not. I'm just trying to remember everything you had in the fridge and figure out what I should cook."

"Relax," I told her. "We'll eat anything."

"Yeah, literally anything," Wyatt said. "You can even order pizza."

Phoebe lowered her hands, straightening up. "No way."

"Babe, you've got plenty of time, okay?" I said. "It's going to take us about two hours to unload these boxes and carry them to the bedroom."

"Oh, that's right," she said, as if she'd completely forgotten that two hours was indeed a lot of time. "Unless you guys are hungry right now."

Knox shook his head. "Don't worry about us, Phoebe, okay? We're not hungry. We all had breakfast, so take your time."

"All right. Do you mind if I leave you alone to carry everything in so I can cook?"

"Not at all," I assured her.

She rose on her tiptoes, giving me a quick kiss. I fought my instincts with all I had so I wouldn't kiss her back hard and make a spectacle out of us. I still kept her close to me for longer than intended, only letting her go when I felt her smile against my lips. She hurried up the stairs to the house.

Only when we heard the front door close did Knox say, "Anyone else feel like we're missing a piece of the story?"

"What do you mean?" I asked.

"Let me see if I got this straight," he said. "You two started by faking this so you could get in Jude's good graces. Then you started having a fling, and now you're moving in together."

I grinned. "You've got it."

"Come on. Throw us a bone," Finn said. "How exactly did this happen?"

"I don't even know," I said. "It just did. And now I'd appreciate it if you wouldn't make Phoebe uncomfortable with your questions."

Wyatt dropped his head back theatrically. "Dude, give us some credit. We've been on our best behavior."

"Yeah. Why do you think we waited until she was gone to corner you?" Knox asked.

Chase shook his head.

Duncan pointed at them. "Be careful, because questioning your brother can quickly turn into you not being able to keep your mouth shut around Phoebe either."

Knox and Finn exchanged a glance, and then they both looked at Wyatt.

"You're right," Wyatt said. "Our older brothers are judgmental assholes sometimes."

"No, we're not," Chase said coolly. "We just know you three very well."

"So, let's just nip this in the bud," I concluded.

They grudgingly agreed, and then we started unloading the boxes.

I'd have to warn the rest of the family, too, when we went over to Chase and Hannah's later. I knew everyone had the best intentions, but Phoebe was gun-shy as it was. I didn't blame her. She'd been through a lot. But if everyone started questioning my decisions, she might get the wrong idea.

I wanted her to have no doubt that I really wanted her here. She thought this was all temporary. But I wasn't so sure about that.

CHAPTER 30
PHOEBE

WHILE COOKING, I texted Veronica, informing her about this unexpected twist. My friend was over the moon.

Veronica: That guy is a KEEPER. Yes, yes, yes! I'm so happy for you.

Phoebe: Thanks, V.

I smiled, dancing around the kitchen the entire time. Despite insisting that they wanted to load up all the boxes first, the guys took a break after about an hour. It turned out that carrying them from the car up to the house took much longer than bringing them from the bungalow to the car back at the old house. Plus, the guys genuinely liked one another, so there was a lot of banter among themselves that slowed down progress.

"All right, I'm going to spoil you for a bit," I said as I brought lunch to the table.

The casserole didn't take long. I didn't want to sing my own praises, but this recipe was delicious.

"Why are you in such a good mood?" Griffin said as we sat down.

"I just like cooking in this kitchen. I feel like it's made my food even better."

"No, babe, that's all you," he said. "You're a fantastic cook."

My heart gave a mighty sigh. I hadn't even cooked that often, but I loved that he was praising me.

"Holy shit, this is good. I wonder if it seems even better because we've been doing manual labor," Knox said. Laughing, he added, "It's objectively fantastic."

Duncan and Wyatt were both scarfing down food so fast that they weren't even talking. Only after Duncan cleaned half of his plate did he say, "Damn, this is good. I was starving."

"Oh my God. Why didn't you say anything before?"

He shrugged. "I didn't even realize until I started eating."

Knox looked at Griffin and me a few times with disbelief. I'd give a penny for his thoughts.

"So… you've got a plan for living with this bozo?" Knox asked.

"I didn't know I need one," I said between bites.

"Ha!" Finn exclaimed. "Well, it's his first time living with a woman, so I'm betting you're going to need a book of plans to deal with him."

He's never lived with a woman before? Was that my face turning into a smile? No, it was a downright grin.

"Dude," Duncan said, "you don't have to put her on the spot."

"To be fair, he's putting *Griffin* on the spot," Chase added.

My God, I loved these guys.

Griffin held his hands out, shrugging. "Well, I haven't, and I'm not ashamed of it. I know Phoebe and I will sail through this without any issues."

"I'm counting on you to tell me the truth," Knox said, pointing at me.

"Yeah," Finn added. "Take notes, you know, for any proof to the contrary that we can hold over his head."

I laughed after taking another forkful. The two of them looked at me, stunned. I took my time swallowing and then said, "Yeah, that's not going to happen. I have my man's back through and through."

Griffin pulled me closer to him, kissing the side of my head, and Duncan whistled. Chase actually burst out laughing.

"One of these days, you two will learn what it's like to feel this sort of loyalty to someone," Chase said to Finn and Knox.

"Interesting that you've left me out," Wyatt said.

Chase waved his hand. "I meant the three of you, obviously. But I actually pointed those two out because I think the probability of you getting hitched before them is higher."

Now it was Wyatt's turn to look stunned. Knox and Finn had almost identical grins.

"Take that back," Wyatt said.

Chase frowned. "Why?"

"I don't want that sort of thing out in the open."

"In case of what, karma?" I asked.

He didn't even answer. Clearly, the idea scared him witless. But I suspected that Chase and Duncan had started out that way. He might come around still.

"All right, if it makes you feel better, I'm taking it back," Chase said. He was obviously fighting laughter.

"Thank you," Wyatt replied.

"I'm putting it out in the open again," Knox added cheerfully.

Wyatt turned his head to look at him. "Why would you do that? I thought we were a team."

"I don't know. Habit, I guess," Knox replied. "You being part of the older group, we being the younger ones, it's just what we do."

"No, we don't," Wyatt said. "We're not five anymore."

"Sometimes we are," Finn cut in. "Like right now." He looked at me apologetically.

"Hey, don't stop on my behalf. This is fascinating. I've had friends who had siblings growing up, but at most one or two, and it wasn't so..."

"Insane?" Duncan suggested.

"Lively," I replied. "Is it always like this?"

"Usually, it's worse," Griffin said. Then his face turned into a devilish grin that I'd never seen him use around me. "And I'm one of those causing most of the trouble."

"He is," Wyatt agreed. "Don't let him fool you with this facade he's putting on now."

"This group is getting more interesting by the minute," I murmured.

"You wait until we're all together this evening with our women," Chase warned. "For some reason, we're even worse around them."

"You'd think that you'd try to impress them or something. But no, that only happens in the beginning," Knox said, focusing on me again. "Now that I think of it, these two bozos also pretended to be above bickering when they first met their girls. Actually, no, wait, Duncan really is like that."

I didn't know what to reply, so I just laughed.

"All right," Griffin exclaimed, "how about we finish our lunch and get to work? You can give me all the shit you want later."

"I was going to give you more shit later anyway," Knox said, "but you do have a point."

While we finished the rest of our lunch, my phone vibrated in my pocket. Taking it out, I noticed a message from Mom.

Mom: We finally got tickets. We can't wait to see you.

Oh, I was ecstatic. It was a bit early for her to send me the ticket details, but who cared. Usually, I told her to send them two or three weeks before so I had all the info.

I froze when I looked at the ticket dates. Oh my God, they were coming the weekend after I was handing the house over. But I knew for a fact that I'd told them to buy the tickets for the end of next month.

Taking a deep breath, I scrolled farther up until I found the message.

Nope, I'd told them to come this month. *Ah, damn it.* I bit the inside of my cheek, deciding not to tell them about my mistake. The tickets were nonrefundable.

Crap, this was not a good time at all. I'd have to think about how to best bring it up later with Griffin. Right now, I wanted to focus on taking care of the guys.

"Anything wrong?" Griffin asked.

I shook my head, putting the phone in my pocket. "It's all good."

He didn't say anything, so I chanced a glance at him. He was frowning slightly. I figured he didn't buy my quick excuse, but he didn't insist.

Once everyone finished, we carried the plates to the kitchen.

"I need a coffee now," Chase said. "I'm starting the coffee maker."

"See, that's why I didn't want us to pause for lunch," Knox said. "I knew we'd be tired afterward."

"Guys, you know you can just take the boxes out of your cars and put them by the wall," I told them. "I'll carry them to the bedroom later."

Chase looked at me like I'd lost my mind. "No. That's not how Sterlings do things. We'll carry everything upstairs. We just needed a boost."

"Well, then, I'll take a coffee too," I said.

I usually didn't drink any caffeinated drinks in the afternoon, but I wanted all my energy today.

The second we emptied our cups, Knox said, "Let's stop procrastinating or we'll never get this done."

Finn nodded. "Yeah. We don't want to be late to Hannah's either."

It turned out that he was right. It took almost two hours to carry up the rest. The guys were completely spent by the time they'd finished.

"I really need to think about doing something more to thank them," I murmured as Knox, Chase, Finn, Wyatt, and Duncan went up with their last stack of boxes.

"No, you don't, babe," Griffin said, coming up from behind me. "Trust me, it's good to put them to work. Otherwise, they'd spend *all* of their time giving me shit. This keeps them occupied and focused on something else."

He pulled me out of view of the staircase and into the living area. Then he pushed me against the wall and kissed me so deliciously that my fingers curled. I rose to my toes, deepening the kiss.

"You know, I think we should go before we become cock-blockers," Knox said.

I gasped, literally jumping to the side. My face felt completely red. My insides were on fire. I slowly walked in front of the staircase so they could see that nothing untoward was happening. Griffin joined me after a few seconds, glaring at his brothers.

"Oh, we already are." Knox nodded. "Got it. We'll be out of your way."

"Actually," Chase said, looking at his phone, "our parents are already there. Hannah said that you're welcome to join us, and then we can make it a whole afternoon event. If you don't have plans."

I glanced over my shoulder at Griffin, who zeroed in on me. By the feral intensity in his eyes, I was 100 percent sure that he *did* have some very sexy plans for me this afternoon.

"That's fine by me," I said.

That intensity flared up a bit. Oh, I was enjoying this. I would love to seduce this amazing man right here, right now, but we couldn't turn Hannah down.

"Sure, we can go," Griffin said.

"I'm not going to start unpacking until tomorrow anyway," I added.

"Good idea," Griffin replied. "I wouldn't let you today anyway. You need to relax."

He pressed his fingers into my shoulder blades as he led us out of the house. His brothers were right behind us. I didn't actually do anything—they'd been the ones carrying stuff around—but when he pressed his thumbs into my skin, the tension released instantly.

Huh, look at that. My man knew me even better than I knew myself.

As we descended to the car, I said, "I'm actually glad for the excuse not to be home; otherwise, maybe I would feel so guilty that I would start to unpack and organize things."

He growled in my ear. "No chance of that, babe. I had far better ideas for the afternoon."

Oh yeah, I'd been spot-on.

CHAPTER 31
PHOEBE

AFTER WE GOT into the car, I asked, "Want me to put the address in the GPS?"

"No, it's a few minutes away, and I know the route."

"Right."

I was giddy to explore more of the neighborhood. I'd only seen areas surrounding Griffin's house until now, and I was curious about the rest. Especially about the inn.

When Griffin told me the name, I'd immediately googled it. It was a gorgeous Queen Anne-style home, and I couldn't wait to see it.

As Griffin said, we only needed a few minutes to reach the gate. As we drove in, I kept looking around. The property was huge, lined with old trees, and the inn itself looked like something out of a fairy tale.

I sighed. "Oh, this is wonderful."

"You like historic houses?"

"I like to look at them, but…"

"Not live in one, right?"

"Exactly. Oh, I should have brought a host gift," I said as we got out of the car.

"What? No, you don't have to."

"Well, it's the first time I'm visiting their home."

"It's the inn, not where they live. And anyway, it's the thought that counts."

Hmm, I didn't agree with that, but there wasn't anything I could do. I made a mental note to buy everyone a gift when we went to their place the first time. I just needed a bit more of a heads-up.

I wondered where everyone else was. The front porch was empty.

"Mom would love this place. Whenever she and Dad travel, she chooses historic B&Bs," I said.

Instantly, I remembered that I had to plan my parents' visit. My palms got sweaty at the thought.

The rest of the guys arrived as Griffin led me through the front door. I looked around in awe when we stepped inside. This place had a lot of character, so thoughtfully decorated and exquisitely maintained. You could feel the love in each piece of furnishing. There was a narrow corridor and a staircase leading to the upper floor. We heard sounds coming from a side room.

Chase came up behind us. "Let's go to the kitchen."

He led the way through the inn. The rest of the brothers were behind us.

Stepping inside the kitchen, I couldn't help but beam. Riley, Hannah, and Susan were sipping from orange cups. Jeremy and Bruce were sitting next to the counter, playing chess. Jeremy looked up at me with a huge smile.

Hmm, Griffin was right. Once he likes you, he really likes you.

"Hey, Phoebe." He ran toward me, wrapping his arms around my waist. "I'm so happy to see you again."

"And you too." An unexpected bout of love hit me as I hugged him right back.

"Did everything go smoothly?" Susan asked.

"Yes," Griffin replied. "We got all of the boxes moved and upstairs."

"If you need help unpacking, let us know," she continued.

I was shocked by her offer. I was practically a stranger. She'd only met me once, and based on how all of this started, I wasn't so sure how accepting of me Griffin's parents were.

Maybe I was overthinking this.

"Thank you, but I have to do it myself. I have to look at everything and figure out where it fits."

She nodded. "That's true. It's hard to delegate that."

I glanced at the table. They'd already prepped stuff for the grill: a plate with meat and a separate one with veggies.

"This was a group effort," Hannah said, following my gaze.

"I figured. By the way, Hannah, you have a beautiful inn."

"Thanks! I love it. Especially now that I've finally repaired every single thing." She pressed her lips together before adding, "I hope I'm not jinxing myself. Every time I think I've fixed everything, something new breaks."

Chase stepped next to her, kissing the back of her head. "It's an old house, love. Things are bound to break down. But we'll take care of it, don't worry."

They were too cute for words.

"Enough small talk. How can we help?" Wyatt asked.

"Each of you grab something and bring it outside," Chase said.

I liked how the guys took over. I was wondering if Knox or Finn would give him shit because he was so openly into Hannah, but they didn't.

As we all carried things outside, Hannah and Chase were discussing what to grill first. I whistled when I saw the long-ass table they'd put there.

Hannah laughed, looking at me. "I know, right? It seems like it's never-ending. The guests like to gather here and chat among themselves."

As we set everything on the table, Chase said, "I'm going to start putting the veggies on the grill because they typically take a little while." He had corn and peppers and some zucchini.

"Did you two go to some sort of school without telling us?" Knox asked Chase as the latter grabbed a bowl with veggies.

"What are you talking about?" Chase asked.

"Just that you and Hannah and Griffin and Phoebe are starting to worry me."

I grinned to myself.

"What's that about, babe?" Griffin asked, eyes on my mouth.

I tilted my head toward Knox, but he and Chase weren't within earshot anymore. "I was wondering if they'd give him shit too."

"No good deed goes unpunished in this family," he replied.

Hannah snickered next to us. "That's right."

My phone beeped, and I took it out of my back pocket.

Mom: All good, hon?

Shit, I forgot to answer her. I typed back quickly.

Phoebe: Yep. Sorry, I'm busy right now but will call later to discuss in detail.

Then I slipped my phone back into my pocket.

"Babe, you're worried about something." Griffin tilted my chin up. "Is something wrong?"

I bit the inside of my cheek. Hannah was right next to us, putting salt and pepper on the meat. But I could still share this—I mean, it wasn't a secret or something I was ashamed of. "I messed up. I told my parents a while ago to visit me. I actually thought I told them to come at the end of next month, but it's this one. Mom just sent me the tickets with their flight schedule."

"When are they coming?"

"Two Saturdays from now."

I was expecting him to berate me for being so careless. Instead, he said, "No problem. They can sleep in Jeremy's bedroom. That's one of the reasons why I wanted a double bed there in the first place."

I hesitated, choosing my words carefully. "I was going to suggest they sleep at a B&B."

"Nah. It's high time they met me."

I smiled sheepishly. "That's true. But I just moved in..."

"I have an idea, if you don't mind me eavesdropping," Hannah said. "The inn actually isn't booked that weekend. We only have one other couple coming. I'd love to have your parents here."

My eyes bulged. Okay, so generosity wasn't just a Sterling gene. Apparently, the women who entered the family shared it too. "Hannah, that would be amazing. Mom would love this place."

I looked apologetically at Griffin. "I do think Mom would be a bit afraid that she might be in our way. I haven't even gotten to tell her I moved in with you yet."

"Do you think they'd feel better here?" he asked.

"Absolutely. I'll pay for the room, of course."

Hannah looked at Griffin. "She's not serious, is she?"

He chuckled. "Unfortunately, she is. But don't worry, I'll talk some sense into her."

"You're one of us," Hannah went on, turning to me. "I'd be happy to have them here."

"Thanks, Hannah. I really wasn't expecting this."

She smiled wholeheartedly. "Anytime. Just ask. If I don't have any guests, I'm happy to host anyone. And if I know far enough in advance, I just won't book anyone."

I made a mental note *never* to tell her in advance. The last thing I wanted was to cost her a guest.

She glanced at the grill. "I think it's going to take a while before he can put the meat on the fire. I'm going to bring some snacks and prepare some finger foods," she said before disappearing into the house.

Griffin turned to look at me intently.

"What?" I asked a bit defensively. I felt as if I were under a magnifying glass.

"I asked you at the house what was wrong. You said everything was fine, even though you were clearly stressing out."

"I just wanted to think about how to explain everything to

you first. I didn't want you to think I'm rushing you into meeting my parents. Or hosting them."

"Babe, listen to me." He cupped my face. "We're a team. You don't need to think about a strategy to talk to me. You just tell me what's going on, and we'll figure it out, okay?"

Was he for real? Because it sounded like a dream.

I nodded. "Okay."

"Promise?"

"I promise."

"Great," he said, leaning in and kissing my forehead.

Someone cleared their throat. I looked sideways and noticed Knox was only a few feet away, his gaze fixed on something. But wait, it wasn't on us.

I followed it and realized he was looking at his parents. They were behind Chase, leaning into each other, talking. Their bodies were angled toward each other in an intimate way.

"Dude, why are you staring?" Griffin asked him.

"I think our parents want to share something with us," Knox said. His voice was different than before. It wasn't teasing—quite the contrary. It was almost hesitant.

"Right…," Griffin murmured.

"What's going on?" I asked.

"Our parents have been growing closer," Knox explained.

"So… are they officially an item now?"

"Not sure what that is."

"You know what? That is none of our business," Griffin told his brother. "So don't even think about asking them."

Knox cocked a brow. "Why not?" Then he held up his hands. "Never mind. I won't say anything. But I bet someone will ask them what's going on sooner or later."

I chuckled, but I did agree with him.

Knox headed to the fire, and I focused on Griffin.

"How do you feel about this?" I asked him.

"Not sure. They divorced when we were kids. We're used to navigating a war between them."

"I'm sorry. Looking at them now, I wouldn't guess they were once at each other's throats."

"They avoided each other for some time after the divorce, so seeing them on good terms now is bizarre."

"I don't blame you."

"Can someone bring the meat?" Chase asked loudly.

"We're on it."

I grabbed one plate. Griffin took another one. Slowly, everyone gathered around the fire.

As we all stood around chatting, Finn pointed at their parents. "All right, anyone want to update us on this?"

I exchanged a glance with Knox, and both of us started to laugh.

Finn looked at us. "What?"

"Called it," Knox said. "I knew someone would ask."

"What are you talking about?" Bruce asked.

Finn narrowed his eyes at his dad, then pointed at Chase, Duncan, and Griffin. "You three are in relationships. You need to take this over."

"I'm quite content watching you do it," Griffin said.

I elbowed him playfully, and he just shrugged.

Chase cleared his throat. "Mom, Dad, is there anything you want to share with us?"

"Now that you boys mention it —" Bruce began, but Susan interrupted.

"In retrospect, darling, it was a bit naive of us to think they wouldn't figure us out at some point," she said.

"Nevertheless," Bruce continued, "as you know, your mom and I have been dating for a while. Now we've decided to take it to the next level and rekindle our relationship."

"What's the difference?" Knox asked. "Actually, no, I don't want details."

"I do," Finn said.

"No, trust me. You don't want to open that can of worms,"

Wyatt said, coming closer. Looking at his parents, he added, "We're happy for you."

"Yeah, we are," Duncan added.

"So, what does that mean? Are you moving in together or something?" Chase continued.

"Not yet. We just spend a lot of time together at the store. We'll see how it goes," Susan said. "But so far, we're very happy." She sighed, looking around. "I'm terribly sorry if this is confusing. And for putting you through the divorce and all that fighting. I know we can't make up for it in any way, but this chapter in our lives will be so much better."

"Let's toast to that," Duncan exclaimed.

"We have champagne inside," Chase said. "I'll go get it. I want to check on Hannah anyway."

"We'll come inside with you and bring glasses out," Griffin said.

Everyone dispersed in a flurry of activity as we went inside to get the champagne and glasses.

"There's always something happening in your family, isn't there?" I asked Griffin.

He grinned. "You can bet on that."

CHAPTER 32
PHOEBE

LIVING with Griffin was even dreamier than I could have imagined. Over the next two weeks, I got so used to pampering my man in that huge house that I wasn't even sure how I'd deal with moving out. Since public transportation wasn't great around here, I went to work on my bike every day. It was quite the workout, but I loved it.

I tried not to dwell on my life before Griffin because what good would that do? Though it was hard not to, as I realized this was all happening so quickly. But when you knew things were right, they just were. Just because our relationship was moving at lightning speed, that didn't mean it was wrong or that it wouldn't work. In fact, having dated Marshall for six years showed me what I *didn't* want in a relationship, so I was even more certain that what Griffin and I had was right.

When D-Day came around, I walked toward the realtor's office with my head held high. I'd splurged on an Uber to get here, and I was meeting Griffin after, and he was dropping me off at the office. I was happy to put all this behind me.

Just before I entered the building, my phone beeped with a message. I took it out, certain it was from Mom. I'd called her on the way, but she didn't pick up. She knew my meeting was starting now.

Mom: Good luck today. We're so happy you're finally selling the house and beginning a new, better chapter in your life.

Phoebe: Thanks, Mom. So am I.

Mom: Can't wait to see you. And meet Griffin. And Hannah.

When I'd told my parents that I was temporarily staying with Griffin, they were a bit surprised. But they got used to the idea faster than I thought. Then they insisted that they couldn't possibly stay with us, so I told them about Hannah's offer. Mom was ecstatic.

Mom: Want to call us?

Phoebe: I can't, I'm about to go into the realtor's. Love you, Mom.

Mom: Love you too.

Taking a deep breath, I stepped inside. Beth was waiting for me at the reception desk. "Phoebe, welcome. Let's head straight inside the meeting room. Everyone's here already."

"Oh," I said, surprised by that. "I'm not late, am I?"

"No, but I think everyone was very eager."

"Right."

I followed her down the narrow corridor. I'd never been here before. The agency's office seemed a bit claustrophobic. The reception area was small, and there were four or five other doors in the adjacent corridor.

I sucked in a breath when we stepped into the meeting room. There was a young couple on one side of the table, and Marshall was on the other one. He didn't even acknowledge me, and I did the same, moving forward and focusing on the couple.

"Hi," I said. "Congratulations are in order."

She beamed at me. "You're so kind. Thank you. I'm Sylvie."

He nodded. "And I'm Felton. We're so excited to buy the house."

"We have so many plans to restore it," she said.

"It's got a lot of potential," I said, because it was true.

"Right. Well, everything is settled. This meeting is mostly ceremonial," Beth chimed in, pulling out the documents. She showed each of us where to sign.

Marshall was still not acknowledging me, but I realized one thing: I was completely at peace. I was relieved to get this chapter over with. In the past, I was a mess around him. But sitting here, I simply felt nothing. He didn't have the power to hurt me anymore, and it was amazing. I was free.

"All right. Now, here are the last sets of keys," I said after signing, taking them out of my bag.

"Do you need to take anything else from the house?" Sylvie asked.

I shook my head. "No. I'm good."

Then she turned to Marshall. "And you?" Perhaps she didn't know our bitter history, but that was for the better. I appreciated that Beth had been discreet.

"No, I don't have anything there," Marshall said.

Beth rose to her feet. "All right, then. We're done. Congratulations on your new house, Felton and Sylvie."

She shook their hands. Marshall and I did the same.

Even though I was indifferent to him, I was eager to get out of here. Without rose-colored glasses on any longer, I realized that Marshall wasn't someone I wanted to be around. In the past, I'd made excuses for him. But I knew better now—he wasn't a good person.

As we exited the meeting room, Felton and Sylvie walked in front of me down the narrow corridor. She was giddy with laughter. I had a flashback of when Marshall and I first got the house and how I'd felt the exact same way. I'd been in love with all the possibilities it held. Was it their starter home, or did they just want to flip it? It didn't matter. It wasn't my business. I was just ecstatic that this had gone off without a hitch.

And as a plus, I was going to see Griffin in about ten minutes. The coffee shop where he met Jude was less than a block away.

The second we stepped out of the realtor's building, Marshall said, "I hope you're happy!" His tone was laced with accusation and hate.

I cocked a brow at him. "Meaning?"

"You've got your unfair share of the profit."

Oh, for fuck's sake, he's still going on with this.

"We sold at the agreed-upon price, and I am more than entitled to half of the profit."

"Keep telling yourself that. I never took you for a vindictive person."

I blinked. "So, giving me what's mine by right means I'm trying to take something away from you?"

"You're not like this. You never asked for one thing in all those years."

That hurt. He'd relied on me being passive when we'd dated. Why was I so insecure with him and yet the total opposite with Griffin? Whatever, it didn't matter anymore.

"That was my mistake. I put up with whatever crumbs you wanted to throw my way, and you got used to that. But I'm not the same person anymore, Marshall. You did me a favor by not proposing."

"Yeah, right." He burst out laughing. "Like you would have said no."

"That's the problem. I would have said yes. And then I would have been unhappy with you for the rest of my life. I probably wouldn't even know what real happiness is. But now I know what it means to be loved and respected. To be someone's priority. And all that was possible because we broke up, so thank you for being a huge ass."

Marshall shook his head. "I don't know what you're on about, but that guy isn't going to stick around. He's a fucking gazillionaire. He can have any woman he wants. And he usually chooses models, judging by the pictures I found online. Don't fool yourself. He's way out of your league."

I rolled my shoulders back, stepping closer to him. "Griffin is a real man, but that's not something I can explain to you. You just wouldn't understand because you're not even close to being one."

"That's it, start insulting me."

"Not my intention." I shrugged. "So, from the bottom of my heart, I wish for you to find as much happiness as I did."

Marshall didn't reply—he just snorted.

I am so done with this asshole.

Without another word, I turned around and headed in the direction of the coffee shop. The more distance I put between me and Marshall, the more my mood improved. I was free. I was meeting my amazing man and seeing Jude again. I'd put this chapter behind me, and it felt even more glorious than I thought it could.

I texted Mom quickly because she'd asked me to give her an update as soon as I could.

Phoebe: All done. Everything went well.

She'd been so great throughout all of this. Then again, my mom had always been amazing. I always felt like she was in my corner even when she feared that I wasn't making the right decision—such as working in Marshall's office for a pittance and not pursuing my own career. She was gentle about it, though, never outright criticizing me or making me feel bad about myself.

I still remember that day I told her. She'd asked, "Darling, are you certain about this? You might not be able to use everything you've learned in your degree, and I know you like to be intellectually stimulated."

"It's what I want to do," I'd told her, and she didn't push further.

I guess some things you don't learn unless you experience them yourself.

She responded right away.

Mom: I'm so happy for you, honey. Dad and I send you lots of love, and Nana and Granddad as well.

She then sent me a picture of the four of them, and I put a hand on my chest. Oh, that was cute. Nana looked exactly the same as she had when they moved away from here ten years ago. The only thing that betrayed my grandparents' age was the fact that they moved much slower these days.

I had to pay them a visit soon. I'd been so busy trying to keep afloat over these past few months that I couldn't even contemplate leaving. But now things were starting to look up.

I toyed with the idea of asking Mom and Dad to bring my grandparents as well on their visit, but that wasn't fair. Traveling was exhausting for them.

I couldn't wait for my parents to meet Griffin. I was sure they'd love him.

It was official—time to move on. At one time, I didn't want to rush things and jump into another relationship, fearing it wouldn't work or that it would be a rebound relationship and fall apart. But what Griffin and I had didn't feel that way at all.

I arrived at the coffee shop only a few minutes later. It was truly just one block away from the realtor's office. I still couldn't believe that Griffin had chosen his meeting's location specifically to be close by to me. He was amazing.

It was a lovely place. They had a garden outside with huge white umbrellas. A fence made out of greenery separated the perimeter of the coffee shop from its surroundings.

I spotted Griffin and Jude at a table for four, right in the center of the garden. The place was relatively empty.

I walked over to them with quick steps. Griffin glanced at me when I was only a few feet away. His face lit up, but his eyes scrutinized me. He cocked a brow in a silent question, and I nodded to let him know that everything had gone smoothly.

"Phoebe, darling, I was so happy when Griffin told me you'd join us," Jude said as he rose to his feet, shaking my hand and then leaning in to kiss my cheek.

"I'm happy to see you again," I told him earnestly.

I sat down next to Griffin, who put a hand on my lower back, rubbing it up and down. I leaned into his touch, immensely grateful that he was here. Even though the morning had gone well, I realized that I was still a bit unsettled. My entire body only calmed down at Griffin's touch.

The man has magic powers, I swear.

"What looks good?" I asked Griffin. He had a menu open in front of him.

"They have five types of waffles," he said with a smile. "And pancakes."

"This day calls for a waffle," I said.

He laughed, kissing the side of my head. "I thought you might say that, but I didn't want to order for you."

"How's Emma?" I asked Jude.

"She's great. She went to visit our grandkids and is spending the week there. We miss them a lot. We're both trying to convince our kids to move closer, but we'll see how that goes."

My God, these two were so sweet. I opened my mouth to ask if he planned to visit them soon as well, but my stomach lurched when I saw Marshall step into the garden.

Shit, did he follow me? No, that was ridiculous. He wasn't even looking around.

I nudged Griffin, and he frowned at me, raising a brow in question. I couldn't tell him that Marshall was here, but I turned to look in his direction. I was simply keeping my fingers and toes crossed that he wouldn't notice us.

Of course, I didn't have any such luck.

Marshall jerked his head back when he spotted us. To my dismay, he walked right toward us. That was when Griffin noticed him too. He went completely rigid.

Shit, shit, shit. This couldn't be happening. My mind was racing. Should I excuse myself and ask Marshall to talk to me outside? But that would just draw attention to the fact that something was off.

I wasn't sure what to do. It was like watching a train wreck in slow motion without being able to do anything about it. Hopefully, we could shut down the conversation before Jude suspected anything.

"So, you're both here," Marshall said, looking from me to Griffin. "Should have known you were close by. That's why she talked about you like you're the Eighth Wonder of the World or something."

"Excuse me," Jude said. "What is going on?"

"Leave these premises or else," Griffin said nicely, but the threat was clear.

"Or else what?" Marshall said, looking straight at Griffin. "You'll have me removed? You don't own this place."

"Get out. You're interrupting a business meeting."

"You bring your girlfriend to your meetings? Whatever, man. You'll come around to see things from my perspective when you've been with her for longer than a roll in the—"

Griffin rose from the table and grabbed Marshall by the collar. "Stop while you're ahead. Remember last time?"

I jumped to my feet too. Jude was simply looking at us with a stunned expression.

"Griffin, he's not worth it," I murmured.

Jude cleared his throat. "I don't know who you are, but I'm guessing you're an ex-boyfriend of Phoebe's. I suggest you move on. Phoebe and Griffin have been going together for eight or nine months now. And we have a meeting to conduct, so please leave us."

I sucked in a breath.

Marshall scoffed. "What are you on, man? Phoebe and I broke up three months ago."

Jude opened his mouth but didn't say anything else. He looked straight at me. I didn't have it in me to lie to his face again.

"Marshall, go! Just leave," I demanded.

"Whatever!" he huffed.

I was fighting tears, trying to keep my composure, but I held my chin high, not breaking eye contact. He was the one who looked away first, turning around and heading out of the establishment.

"Are you okay?" I asked Griffin.

"Yeah, don't worry about me. You?"

I nodded, nervously looking at Jude.

Griffin straightened up, turning to him, too, as if he'd just remembered that Jude had witnessed everything.

He was staring at both of us with a serious expression.

"Jude, I'm sorry you witnessed that," Griffin said. "The guy is a complete asshole."

"Normally, I'd say that this is none of my business," Jude said in a measured tone. "But something he said bothered me. When we went to dinner, you two told me and Emma that you'd been going out for about six months. Or did I have that wrong?"

I bit the inside of my cheek, glancing at Griffin. My mind was racing at a million miles an hour.

Should we make up something quick? He was kind of giving us the option, but honestly, I didn't have the energy.

As if reading my mind, Griffin took in a deep breath, then grabbed my hand under the table, squeezing it lightly.

"There's something Phoebe and I wanted to share with you."

I knew from the tone of his voice that he wanted to fess up, so I squeezed his hand right back under the table. I was shaking slightly from the encounter with Marshall.

I should have known this morning went too well.

"We didn't exactly tell you the truth from the beginning," Griffin continued.

"I just put that together," Jude said smoothly. His voice wasn't overly harsh, but it missed the usual warmth. "Why?"

Griffin looked at me briefly before going on. "When you and I met, you implied that you didn't like my reputation. And then, as luck would have it, I ran into Phoebe."

"And we started to pretend that we were dating," I finished for Griffin.

"So, you've been lying to me and to Emma all this time," Jude said. Now his voice *was* harsh, and I didn't blame him.

"I can explain," Griffin said, but Jude got up from his chair.

"There's no need. I don't want to know any details, but I don't do business with liars."

"We really—" I began, but he waved his hand, and I stayed silent.

"No, no. I've heard more than I need to know." He shook his head before getting up from the table. "I'm shocked that you tricked me and Emma. This is unbelievable."

I couldn't find my words—or any words at all—as Jude walked away. I felt horrible that we'd disappointed him. And I hated that Emma would no doubt feel the same as her husband.

I nudged Griffin. "Go after him. I'm sure you can calm him down, explain it all."

Griffin turned to me, cupping my face with one hand. "I'm not going anywhere. You're shaking, and I'd rather be here with you."

"Well, then, I can talk to Jude."

"Forget about Jude. I just want to make sure that you're okay."

"I think I'm fine, Griffin. I just need to process this for a bit. But I don't want you to lose this deal."

He frowned. "Don't worry about that. I'll let things cool down for a bit." Pressing his thumb on my lower lip, he asked, "Do you want to take the day off?"

"I can't do that. I told my boss I'd be in the office at nine thirty. He expects me there."

Griffin's gaze zeroed in on mine. "I want to take you home and spoil you all day long."

My heart exploded with joy. I wanted to climb him right here, right now. "It's not possible, though."

He groaned. "I know. I've got a full day, too, and I have to drop by Sterling Investments. But for now... do you want to order waffles?" he asked.

I sighed. "Honestly, I've kind of lost my appetite. Maybe I should just go to the office."

"I'll drop you off there."

"Do you think Jude will pull out of the deal?"

Griffin's smile faltered. He rolled his shoulders back. "It's possible. But I'll talk to him before he has time to do anything too rash."

"I'm sorry." I felt horrible about all this.

"Don't. You're more important than any deal, okay?"

I nodded, but I was still upset. I knew how important this deal was for him, and I felt incredibly guilty that Marshall had completely shit on it. Griffin would have to start doing damage control immediately, and I didn't want him to waste any more time on me.

"I think we should go," I said. "My boss will be happy if I show up earlier."

"Okay."

It took a while to flag a waiter and ask for the bill. After paying for the coffees, Griffin took my hand and led me to the car.

As we climbed inside, his phone rang. He immediately answered.

"Hey." He frowned, then closed his eyes. "For fuck's sake! Yeah, I literally just had a meeting with him. Hold off for now. I'm going to fix this."

"What happened?" I asked when he hung up. My heart was in my throat. I was afraid of the answer.

"Jude already informed my team that they are no longer considering us as a potential investor."

"Oh God!" It was all my fault. If it weren't for me and my ass of an ex, Griffin wouldn't be in this situation.

"I didn't think he'd act so fast."

Griffin said nothing else after that. His mind was probably

working at full capacity, thinking about how to fix things with Jude. I wished I could help, but I didn't have a single good idea.

The man was right. We'd lied to him, and I couldn't really imagine a more terrible way for him to find out.

"Hey, want to bounce ideas off me? We're good at coming up with stuff together," I said, trying to lighten the mood.

"No, I need to discuss the options with my team."

I didn't know how to reply to that, or how to make this better. But the silence felt heavy, and I had a sudden urge to fill it with chatter.

"Are you going straight to your office?"

"No, I'm dropping by Sterling Investments first. We need to vote on a strategic decision."

"Right."

We sat in utter silence for the remainder of the drive because I had no idea what else to talk about. My heart felt heavy.

When we arrived in front of my building, he got out of the car, opening my door. Deep lines marred his forehead.

After getting out of the car, I traced those lines with my thumb. "You're stressed out."

He took my hand, kissing my palm. "This is an unexpected development. But it's nothing I can't deal with."

Hmmm… that didn't seem entirely true, though. His shoulders were hunched. His jaw was set. He was worried, and I wanted him to know that he could be vulnerable around me.

I rose on my toes, pressing my lips to his. The kiss started out chaste, but then he deepened it. The next thing I knew, he'd pressed me against the car.

I pulled back slightly. "Griffin," I murmured, "we're at my office."

"Fuck. I completely forgot that." His frown had dissipated. *Ha!* This was progress. "No one makes me lose my head the way you do."

I grinned. "I feel very full of myself right now."

"You should." He splayed his fingers on the side of my neck, zeroing in on my lips. "I'm going to go before I make a spectacle of us."

"Okay," I whispered. "Have a great day."

"You too."

Even after he drove off, I stood rooted to my spot.

Tonight, I was going to take care of him just the way he deserved.

CHAPTER 33
GRIFFIN

"DUDE, YOU LOOK LIKE SHIT," Finn said the second I stepped into the meeting room at Sterling Investments.

"Thanks for the observation," I replied.

My brothers were all gathered here. Even though I had a lot on my mind with Jude, I was determined to focus on the here and now.

"Want to share what happened?" Wyatt asked.

I shook my head. "No, let's hit the ground running. I have a lot to do today."

"You know, we have been known to have good ideas," Knox said.

"Not to sing their praises too much, because it might go to their heads, but they're right," Duncan said.

Chase frowned, looking at me without saying anything for a few beats. But then he said, "Want me to have your back or work with them to convince you to fess up?"

Knox whistled. "Dude, that's not how taking sides works. You don't actually ask one of the parties involved."

Chase narrowed his eyes at him, shrugging. "You do things your way. I do them the way I want."

I tapped my fingers on the table, making a split-second decision. I actually did want to talk to my brothers. They were smart, and their input was valuable. But I also knew that if I opened up, I'd derail the whole meeting.

"This is what we'll do," I said. "First we'll vote on the creation of those new funds, and then we'll chat about my issue."

"Ha! So there *is* an issue," Wyatt said.

"Voting first," I insisted.

The team at Sterling had worked tirelessly since we'd spoken about adding funds into our portfolios that invested in green energy. They'd put together some options for us to consider. We had a golden rule: all of us had to approve any change in strategy for it to happen.

Chase cleared his throat. "The team has done a great job vetting funds. I, for one, fully believe that adding this area of focus will be beneficial for us as a company."

Duncan sat up straighter. "I agree."

"That means you both vote yes?" I asked.

"Yes," Chase replied.

I nodded. "Good. So do I."

Knox and Finn exchanged a glance, looking to me before speaking.

"I agree too," Knox said.

Finn added, "Count me in."

Wyatt began to laugh. "You do realize that we could have just done a group call if all we wanted to do was say yes. Which, by the way, I'm saying yes too. I thought we might have to discuss pros and cons."

"That's always a possibility," Chase said, unfazed. "Hence why we always do this as a meeting, so no one feels pressured into agreeing with the rest."

Wyatt waved him off. "We can't be pressured into anything."

Knox slapped one hand against the table. "Okay, the topic is adjourned. Now we can all hear what Griffin has to say."

This had been the shortest voting protocol we'd had in years.

I was certain they'd sped it up for my sake. Although, granted, we had all been in favor of the ideas since the beginning.

Now that quite literally all eyes were on me, I was second-guessing my decision to share this with them. I'd never hear the end of it. Not that I didn't deserve it, but still.

"The unthinkable happened," I said.

"Phoebe is pregnant?" Finn asked.

I jerked my head back. "Why would you jump to that conclusion?"

"And why would it be unthinkable?" Knox asked.

"Stop derailing the conversation. This is about something else," I assured them.

"Something serious," Wyatt said.

I wasn't smiling at all. "Jude found out I was lying to him."

"Fuck," Chase exclaimed.

Duncan just fixed me with his eyes. A few beats later, he asked, "How?"

"It doesn't even matter. The details aren't important."

"Just spin things around," Wyatt suggested.

"Impossible."

"See, that's why it's helpful for us to know details," Finn said.

"How did he find out?" Duncan asked again.

I cleared my throat. "You all know that Phoebe sold that old house. The closing was today."

"Fuck yes," Knox said. "I can't believe she actually lived there."

"Anyway, I figured it might be a difficult day for her, but she didn't want me to go along. I still wanted to be nearby, so I held my morning meeting with Jude at a coffee shop in the area. She joined us after signing the papers."

Chase actually smiled. "Good for you. You've got soft skills I wasn't even aware of. It was important to be there for your woman."

"I figured that, too, except that her ex also dropped by that very same coffee shop." There was a collective groan around the room. "He caused a scene and made it very clear that he and Phoebe were together until three months ago."

"Fuck my life," Knox said.

Finn's eyes were wide, and then he leaned back in his chair, putting his hands on top of his head.

"Now I'm getting the full picture," Wyatt said.

"There's no way to turn this around," I admitted. "And I don't want to lie to Jude anymore."

"Figured out that's a bad idea, huh?" Duncan said.

I looked straight at my older brother. "I know I fucked up. You were right. This whole thing backfired."

"What's your plan?" Chase asked.

"I don't have one."

"How did Jude react, exactly?" Duncan asked.

That felt like twisting the knife in a wound. But again, details were important.

"He stormed off, assuring me that he doesn't deal with liars. A few minutes later, I got a call from my team that we were no longer in the running as an investor."

"He moves fast, then," Duncan said.

Everyone was quiet for a few seconds.

"No words of advice?" I laughed but without humor.

"Honestly, I don't even know what to say," Wyatt said.

Well, that was a first. I'd managed to stump all of my brothers. This was not good. Not at all.

Chase cleared his throat. "I hate to point this out, but it's more than just your reputation at stake."

"I know." The reputation of my company and even of Sterling Investments was on the line. Besides, I genuinely hated that I'd disappointed Jude. "I'll fix this."

"You'd better," Chase replied.

"All right, well, if any of you actually comes up with an idea that could help me...," I said, rising to my feet.

"How about threatening him?" Knox asked.

I nearly stumbled backward. "I'm sorry, did I hear you wrong?"

Tilting his head, Finn said, "I don't see how that would work."

Wyatt turned to them. "Are you two serious right now?"

"We're just considering the options," Knox said. "We could find some dirt on him. Everyone has skeletons. Nothing too bad, just embarrassing enough for him to keep quiet that our brother faked a whole-ass relationship to get a business deal."

"Who are you, and what have you done with my younger brothers?" Duncan asked.

I was too stunned to answer for a few moments, then recovered.

"All right, I'm going to forget that you said that," I declared.

"Yeah, I'm not," Duncan said, "because what the fuck? Do I have to keep an eye on you?"

Knox rolled his eyes. "You're so dramatic, Duncan."

I threw up my hands. "Right, I don't have time to listen to bickering. If any of you comes up with usable solutions, you can call me anytime."

"How is Phoebe taking this?" Chase asked.

"I haven't had time to discuss it with her in depth. She was visibly shaken up by that asshole causing a scene."

"It's a good thing her family is coming to visit, then," Chase said.

"That's right." I knew how important family was to Phoebe. They'd make her happy. "Okay, I'm leaving. Let me know if you come up with ideas—*legal* ones."

Knox and Finn chuckled, and then Finn said something I hadn't thought of. "You know, if you had done this to me, I would have taken it personally—that I was stupid enough to fall for your charade, faking the relationship. I'd be pissed off for that reason rather than that you lied to get my business."

The others kind of collectively agreed. I did too. Being lied to didn't leave anyone with a good feeling, no matter how you looked at it.

We said our goodbyes, and I left the meeting room.

After I left headquarters, I went straight to my office. On the drive, I tried Jude a few times, but he rejected my calls.

"Fucking hell." I knew he needed to cool down, but time was of the essence. I needed to get to him. I couldn't allow too much time to pass.

My team pounced on me the second I arrived. "Griffin, what happened? Weren't you meeting Jude this morning?" Stella, my assistant, asked.

"I did," I said.

"Everyone was surprised when he called."

I hurried into my office, and she followed me, standing in the doorway.

I took a deep breath. "There's been an unfortunate development—of a personal nature."

"What can we do to fix it?" she asked.

I didn't answer right away. I'd come here determined to brainstorm with my entire team and fix this together. But the truth was, that wasn't possible. This was all on me. It was my responsibility alone to fix it.

"Only I can do that." Then a thought hit me. "Actually, you can help me with one thing."

"What's that?"

"I need to know Jude's schedule today and tomorrow."

She smiled. "I can find that out."

I frowned at her. "That easy?"

"His assistant is very friendly. She was shocked when she heard about Jude's decision. I called her immediately to double-check that it wasn't a mistake or something."

"All right, thanks."

After she left, I paced my office up and down. Jude was my utmost priority, but I couldn't just sit around twiddling my thumbs while she inquired about his whereabouts. I had plenty of other things to do.

Stella emailed me his schedule for today an hour later. Fuck, he was trapped in back-to-back meetings.

I immediately got up, heading to her office. She winced when she saw me.

"How about tomorrow's schedule?"

"I'll do my best, but his assistant is a bit more tight-lipped now that we aren't buddies anymore. But I'll get it to you tomorrow, I promise."

"Thanks."

I headed back into my office, sitting at my desk. Miraculously, I managed to get in a few hours of solid work. I threw in the towel at five o'clock and headed straight home.

Usually, I was easily able to push work issues to the back of my mind in the evening, but this was different. I kept thinking about the best way to apologize and get back in Jude's good graces the whole drive.

Phoebe was already there when I arrived. I smiled for the first time in hours. Fuck yeah. My woman was at home, and I was determined to give her the very best of me.

I jogged up the porch stairs and pushed the front door open. She simply fit my life in a way I didn't know was possible. I didn't announce my presence right away, just stood watching her for a few seconds before walking toward her with quick steps. She must have heard me, because she looked over her shoulder and smiled.

Yeah, watching her light up because I was there would always be one of my favorite things.

"Well, hello," she said.

"Hey, babe."

"I'm making meatballs and pasta. I figured we might both need some comfort food."

"Fuck yes!" I kissed her without further ado.

She gave in to my kiss immediately, just as she had this

morning. But now I could make it last as long as I wanted. I could devour her to my heart's content. Kissing this woman was exactly what I needed right now.

Then something warm touched my shoulder.

She jumped back and covered her mouth.

"Oh, whoops." She'd dropped the spatula on my shirt. "Sorry. You sort of made me lose my balance and my head." She wiggled her eyebrows. "You know, the usual."

She sniffed the air before abruptly turning to the stove. "Crap. I don't want to burn dinner. Don't distract me."

"Yes, ma'am," I said.

She looked over her shoulder and asked, "Want to tell me how today went? Did you talk with Jude?"

I shook my head. "He wouldn't take my calls, but I'm going to get to him eventually."

I'd managed to take my mind off him for a few seconds, but now the issue was front and center in my mind again.

Phoebe smiled at me. "Why don't you go change your shirt before dinner's ready?"

"Sure. I have to take a shower too."

Before going up, I wanted to do one more thing. Standing behind her, I put an arm around her waist, bringing my mouth to her ear. "I like coming home to you."

She melted against me and wiggled her ass against my crotch. "Good, because I love it too."

CHAPTER 34
PHOEBE

PREPPING dinner in Griffin's kitchen was hands down one of my favorite things to do. Singing to myself, I put the food on plates before setting the table. I didn't like putting the pan on the table. It was just asking for an accident to happen.

Everything was so good. Marshall was out of my life, I was spoiling Griffin, and my family was coming in two days. I was making mental lists of all the things I wanted to do before they arrived. Hannah had insisted that she was going to take care of everything, but that wouldn't do. I wasn't going to let her clean their room by herself or buy snacks, since she'd insisted on hosting my parents for free.

I finished setting the table just as Griffin came down. He glanced at the plate and smiled, but I could see that he was still a bit lost in his thoughts.

"Babe, this looks delicious."

"Thanks. I tasted it, and it is, in fact, delicious, if I do say so myself."

He smiled, pulling me close to him with one hand and kissing my cheek before lowering his mouth to mine.

"*You* are very delicious, and I can't wait to taste you after dinner."

I laughed, pushing my hips into him. He cast his gaze down once and then back up at me. His eyes darkened a bit, and he swallowed hard. I was absolutely sure that he was going to start seducing me right away. But to my astonishment, he moved to the side, pulling out two chairs. We both sat down at the same time. I was still simmering as I took the first mouthful of spaghetti.

Griffin groaned. "This is good. Thank you for cooking."

"My pleasure. I could cook all day long in this kitchen. By the way, I'm going to head to Hannah's inn tomorrow after work and try and help her in every way I can."

He stopped eating, frowning at me. "Wait, what for?"

"You know, my parents arriving the next day. I just don't want her to deal with everything."

He nodded without any enthusiasm. "Right. Sure. I'll join you too."

"You don't have to," I said.

"No, I want to be there. You're right, it's not fair to leave everything to Hannah. And I don't want you doing everything on your own either."

"Thanks. And during the weekend, I'll take them around town."

Griffin nodded absentmindedly. I pressed my lips together, deciding not to spam him anymore with my plans. He had other things on his mind. Besides, my parents were used to being with me whenever they came to the city. Marshall never made the effort to spend any time with them. He'd acted like they were a nuisance whenever they visited—which was once every two years.

Ugh, I had to stop thinking about Marshall. He was in my past.

Except, Griffin wouldn't have run into trouble with Jude if it weren't for that moron.

Midway through dinner, Griffin's phone pinged. He looked at it and frowned.

"What's wrong?" I asked.

"Stella sent me Jude's schedule for tomorrow. It's packed, but I have an idea about how I'm going to approach him."

"Do you want to talk it out with me? Ooor I can completely take your mind off it."

I wanted to lighten the mood, but Griffin just shook his head. "No. I need to make a game plan. I have to fix this."

His tone wasn't cutting or anything, but my heart leaped to my throat regardless.

He was a bit lost in his thoughts for the rest of the dinner, but once we'd loaded up the dishwasher, I set in motion my plan to seduce him. I ran my hands over his chest. Rising onto my tiptoes, I pressed my lips to his.

I felt the corners of his mouth lift up, and then I attacked him, plain and simple. I wanted to climb this man, wanted him to have his way with me. I hummed when he kissed me back deliciously hard. He groaned against my mouth, twirling our tongues. Then he cupped the back of my head, deepening the kiss even more, until we were both out of breath.

"Oh, fuck. I can't stop kissing you."

I smiled. "Well, the good thing is, you don't have to."

"You're cute."

I grinned.

"But don't distract me tonight, babe. I want to catch up on some things for work and make a plan for tomorrow."

"Oh," I said, biting the inside of my cheek. "So much for my seduction plan. I'll go in the bedroom and read, then, so you can have the living room all to yourself."

"Thanks. I really appreciate it."

"One more kiss before I leave you alone?"

"No, because you make me lose my head every time."

I smiled at him, but my stomach turned unpleasantly. Yeah, I was the only one who made him lose his head. But I couldn't help thinking that I was the one who'd caused him to lose the deal too.

I walked toward the staircase, then stopped midway.

"Griffin?" I asked.

He was already sitting on the couch, eyes trained on the screen of his phone.

"Yeah?"

"You're not mad at me for the deal falling through, are you?"

"What? No, of course not. Don't worry about it."

I did, though, because he didn't meet my eyes as he said it.

That night, I stayed awake later than usual, hoping to hug Griffin when he came to bed. But I was still alone when I fell asleep.

When I woke up the next morning, Griffin's side was untouched.

He didn't sleep at all?

I jumped out of bed, heading to the living room. He wasn't there, and his car wasn't either. Frowning, I went to check Jeremy's room and froze. The bed was made, but the sheets and the pillow had wrinkles that indicated Griffin had slept here.

Oh God. Why didn't he come to bed?

A million thoughts raced through my mind, but I didn't have time to procrastinate.

I hurried through my morning routine, not wanting to be late for work. We had a very strict in-office policy.

When I arrived at the office, I finally checked my messages. Mom usually texted me the day before she came, asking about the weather and whether I wanted her to bring me anything. But I didn't have any messages from her. Instead, I had one from Griffin.

Griffin: Hey, babe. You were sound asleep when I left. Hope I didn't wake you up.

I hesitated, wondering if I should ask him why he slept in a different bedroom, then decided not to.

Phoebe: I didn't hear you at all. Hope you have a great day.

I liked my job, but I wasn't able to focus today. I kept waiting to hear from Griffin. When was he meeting Jude? What was his game plan?

I checked my phone during every break, but I didn't have any other messages from Griffin. I didn't want to pry, but I really wanted to know how things were going.

When five o'clock rolled around, I couldn't help myself anymore and texted him.

Phoebe: How did it go with Jude?

Griffin: I'm only heading now to meet him.

Phoebe: Good luck.

Taking a deep breath, I added something else.

Phoebe: I'm really sorry that he found out like that. I feel very guilty about it.

I didn't want to trouble him with my worries, but it was weighing on me.

I waited for a few seconds, but he didn't reply. I wasn't going to overthink this, though. He had a lot on his mind.

Instead of fretting, I decided to call Hannah. She answered right away. "Hey. You got off from work?"

"Yes, I'm leaving now. I'll stop by Walmart and buy some food and snacks and so on."

"Really, that's not necessary. Honestly, I can—"

"Hannah, I truly appreciate that you're hosting them, but I want to help. I can't allow you to feed them as well."

"Right. I'll see you soon. I'm excited to meet your family. Hurry up."

"I will."

I really liked her. If I had a sister, I would have wanted her to be like Hannah.

I checked my phone again as I walked from the bus station to Walmart. Griffin hadn't replied, but I was still determined not to overthink it.

Come on, Phoebe. Get yourself together. The man has more important things on his mind than reassuring you. Focus on getting things together for your parents!

I usually avoided shopping on an empty stomach because I tended to buy everything in sight—which was exactly what was happening right now. I'd initially planned to buy food for breakfast and snacks for in between, but I ended up leaving Walmart with five bags chock-full of food. Oh well. It wasn't going to waste. Whatever my family didn't consume, Hannah could use for other guests.

I texted her before I got into an Uber. Griffin still hadn't replied. I was on pins and needles, but I didn't want to pester him any more.

I smiled as I entered the gates to Hannah's inn. I could completely understand why she loved running it. She was on the front porch, waving at me. Chase had an arm around her waist. They were adorable.

As I got out of the car, she and Chase walked toward me.

"I might have gone a bit overboard with the shopping," I admitted innocently.

Hannah started to laugh.

Chase chuckled. "You don't say. I'll carry these inside."

"I'll take one as well," I said. "It's not heavy, just full of chips and stuff that my family isn't even allowed to eat. But I know they'd love it."

"It's good to spoil them," Hannah agreed.

Yep, she was definitely my soul sister.

We carried everything inside quickly.

"I thought Griffin was coming with you," Chase said as we started to take the groceries out in the kitchen.

"Yeah, he said he'll drop by, but he's having a stressful day."

"Did he manage to get hold of Jude?"

"Oh, you know!"

He nodded. "He shared it with us. He was a bit on edge."

I bit my lip. "I know. Last night, he went to bed late. He stayed up making a game plan."

Hannah zeroed in on me. "You're worried."

"I… well…" I sighed. "I feel guilty about everything that went down."

Chase stopped in the act of opening the fridge, turning around to look at me. "What exactly do you think you have to feel guilty for?"

"If it weren't for Marshall and me, the deal wouldn't have fallen through." I didn't know if I should be sharing this with them, but it felt good to get it off my chest. "Yesterday, he seemed a bit off when he came home. He usually talks to me about everything, but he was a bit distant."

"That's just the way my brother is when he's got a problem. He fixates on it until he solves it," Chase said as he resumed putting groceries in the fridge.

"Right." That explanation did make sense, but I still couldn't help wondering if Griffin was mad at me or something. I couldn't bring myself to share that he'd slept in a different bedroom, though. That was too personal.

"You'll see. He'll show up here later as if nothing happened, back to his old self," Chase assured me.

"All right!" Hannah exclaimed, looking at the table. "I think we should focus on our to-dos, of which there are many. I still haven't made the bed."

"I'll do that," I replied, grateful for the chance to be useful.

"Let's finish putting the food away first."

"Yes, ma'am."

"Whatever doesn't go in the fridge belongs there." She pointed at the cabinets above the sink.

"I'll grill something for us," Chase said.

"Oh, but I wanted to treat you guys to something," I said. "Maybe order in."

"Grilling is my pleasure," he replied. "And I'm fast when I only have to do it for a few people."

Hannah clapped her hands. "Okay, we have a plan. We'll put the food away, Phoebe will make the bed, and I'll help you with the grill. And I'm just putting it out there that after dinner, we can also have s'mores. And pop open the bottle of wine."

"Now that's my kind of evening," I said with a grin.

CHAPTER 35
GRIFFIN

I COULDN'T REMEMBER the last time I'd been so sleep-deprived. Last night, I stayed up until very late, brainstorming for my pitch to Jude. As I headed to bed, I was so restless that I knew I would toss and turn the entire night, so I ended up crashing in Jeremy's bedroom.

This morning, I woke up at six o'clock sharp. I'd gone through the motions at the office the whole day. Not even my team approached me. They could clearly see from a mile away that I was in a shitty mood.

Stella found out that was Jude was playing golf tonight, which was why I showed up at one of the most prestigious country clubs in San Diego at six o'clock sharp.

Frankly, I was surprised that he liked to play the game. I'd tried it once because it was a good way to do business—people liked to talk shop while swinging clubs—but I found it boring as shit.

The parking lot was full, but that wasn't a problem because they had a valet service. I dropped off my keys, and they took care of everything.

A club employee approached me the second I stepped inside. "Good evening, Mr. Sterling. We're ready for you."

The guy was too hyper, but I didn't have the energy to shut down his enthusiasm. No one could come here without an appointment. Stella had taken care of that, and now they thought I wanted to be a member.

"I'm simply here to meet an acquaintance," I informed him.

His face fell. He was holding a notepad. I was betting my ass that there was some sort of form on it that he'd expect me to fill out.

"Right. Who is that person?"

"Jude Carson."

"He's still playing, but he should be done in about ten to fifteen minutes. Are you joining him on the golf course?"

"No." I wanted to catch up with him after he'd finished.

"All right. He always uses a cart, so you're welcome to wait for him either in the bar or outdoors by the golf cart parking lot. We have a refreshment area set up there as well."

"I'll wait outside."

"Please follow me. I'll show you where it is."

I was going to tip him well because he was being very professional. I'd expected him to be pushier about getting me to join.

I took a good look around while we walked straight across from the reception area to a huge double door. Even from here, I could see the expanse of the golf course. Once outside, he pointed at the sitting area.

All right, that isn't half bad.

The golf carts were parked quite a distance away, but from what I could tell, there was no way to get from the parking lot to inside the club without passing the sitting area.

"Perfect. I'll wait here."

"Do you need anything else?"

"No," I assured him. Then I took out a fifty from my wallet and handed it to him.

His eyes wide, he said, "Thank you," before turning on his heels and heading back inside.

I had too much energy to sit, so I paced around, replaying my pitch. Objectively, I had excellent arguments. His team had already accepted me. I'd contributed with ideas they could work on, and we had a good thing going.

Yet something about the pitch felt wrong. I just couldn't put my finger on it. What was I missing?

I looked up every time I heard a golf cart approach until Jude came twenty minutes later. Only after parking the golf cart and walking up to the sitting area did he spot me.

Jude paused, leveling me with a cold stare. "Griffin, I assume you aren't here by accident."

"Guilty as charged, Jude. I need to talk to you, to apologize."

He paused before replying. "Fine. There's a bar inside the building. Let's go there."

"Perfect. Thank you for the opportunity."

We left the parking area and headed inside. We sat down in the bar area, next to a loud group of six.

"How did you know I was here?" he asked.

"I can't reveal my sources."

He began to laugh. That was a good start.

"Griffin, I already informed your team of my decision."

"I know."

"And it's not reversible."

"I understand that too. In your place, I'd do the same."

His brows rose up his forehead. "You would?"

"Yes. Going into a partnership with someone who lied to my face is unthinkable."

"At least we agree on that. What the hell possessed you to do it in the first place?"

"Honestly, it was an unexpected turn of events."

"When did you even meet Phoebe?"

"That very night that you and I went to the restaurant. After you left, I stayed at the bar. She was there with her best friend, waiting to meet with that imbecile." I frowned, remembering that evening. It had been bizarre. "I started talking with her friend. One thing led to another, and I went to Phoebe's table pretending I was her boyfriend so she could get rid of the ex."

Jude jerked his head back. "You're joking."

"No, I'm not. You should have seen Phoebe's face. She was just as stunned as you were. I guess she trusted her friend because she went along with it. After that, I figured I wouldn't see her again. But as luck would have it, I did. We started talking, and she suggested helping me with you, just as I'd helped with her ex. Thinking back, I can't even tell you why I agreed to it. I knew it was a bad idea to negotiate under false pretenses. But I wanted to spend time with her, and that won out."

"Wait… are you currently dating her or not?"

"Yes. Things changed during that weekend at your house." What was I doing? My goal was to change his mind, not tell him about my personal life.

"Is that so?"

"Yes. We started seeing each other in earnest after that."

"Another success of my dating app, if I can say so myself." Jude looked smug, but his eyes were still cold.

"I'm sorry for lying to you, but I can't say that I'm sorry about everything that happened. Otherwise, Phoebe and I wouldn't be together right now."

Jude didn't reply, and I couldn't read his expression. I'd gotten used to him being open and fun around me. I hated that I'd disappointed him.

And right here, right now, I realized one more thing. I didn't actually care about sealing the deal anymore. In the past, I would have gone to great lengths to secure an investment, but Jude's friendship was more important to me than that. And it was all because of Phoebe. She'd changed me fundamentally

"My brothers often tease me that I'm too focused. That I go to great lengths to make sure things go my way."

"I agree with them."

"I will say that I've never lost a deal in my whole life."

Jude cocked a brow. "I find that hard to believe."

"It's true. But now I'm going for something else. I'm hoping to save our friendship."

He sat up straighter in his seat, pointing at me. "When I told Emma about the ruse, her exact words were 'Oh, but those two belong together.' And then she said, 'I actually liked them. I'd hoped to see them again.'"

"Forget about the deal," I said. "Honestly."

"You know what? I do appreciate your friendship as well. Let's order some champagne and celebrate that."

"That's good enough for me," I exclaimed, feeling as if a weight had been lifted from my shoulders.

Jude flagged a waiter, who instantly appeared at our table. "Bring us a bottle of your best champagne," he requested.

"Right away, sir."

The waiter quickly returned with a chilled bottle of Dom Perignon. He popped the cork and poured in two glasses. Jude and I clinked them as the server left.

"To interesting developments," he said.

I started to laugh. "I agree."

Jude started to tell me about the boat he planned to rent for the Mediterranean to take his wife on a cruise. He showed me several options, and I gave him my honest opinion. I disliked all of them. "They're far too small."

"You're right. If I want to stay with my wife for three weeks, we need something a bit bigger. Thanks for the honesty."

"Irony intended?" I asked.

Jude shrugged. "Maybe. You know, I really appreciate that you're not pushing the work issue."

It was another thing I'd learned from Phoebe—not to see everything in black-and-white.

I opened my mouth to reply, but then I heard my phone was buzzing.

I took it out and tried to silence it, then noticed it was Chase. He usually didn't call without a reason. "I have to take this."

"By all means," Jude said.

I answered right away.

"Where the fuck are you?" Chase demanded.

"In a meeting."

"And you couldn't let us know?"

Then it hit me. "Shit, I completely forgot I was supposed to come by the inn today."

"You don't say. I understand you had important business to settle, but you could have at least kept Phoebe in the loop. She's worried."

"About what?" I asked, then grimaced. I never replied to her message. My focus had been completely shot today. "Fuck. I remember. Is she still there?"

"Yeah."

"Then tell her I'm leaving for the inn right away."

"You'd better!"

After hanging up, I focused on Jude.

"You need to go," he stated.

"Yes."

"The missus is mad at you."

Before meeting Phoebe, the use of the word *missus* would have creeped me out, but now I didn't mind.

"Yeah. I made a blunder. I need to fix it."

"Good luck."

"Thanks. It was great catching up with you tonight, Jude."

"With you, too, my boy. Have fun. Send my best to Phoebe."

"I will. And please greet Emma for me."

He nodded. "She'll be happy to hear about us making amends."

"I think so too," I replied.

I'd had a glass of champagne, but my mind was surprisingly clear. Despite having been exhausted all day, adrenaline was running through my veins right now. Jude and I were on good terms again. Fuck yes! But I couldn't really enjoy the victory. I was apprehensive about Phoebe. I'd let her down.

I looked at her message before starting the car. Fucking hell, I should have reassured her somehow. I vaguely remembered that she'd mentioned it last night too. What had I told her? For the life of me, I couldn't remember.

This wouldn't do. My woman had to know that she was my top priority.

I drove at top speed, debating if I should call her on the way. But no, I wanted to talk to her face-to-face, look her in the eyes, watch every expression.

When I arrived at the inn, I parked right next to my brother's car. There was no one in the front, but that was no surprise. I assumed they were either inside or at the back of the house, around the fire pit.

I listened intently for a few seconds. Laughter resounded in the open air, and fire crackled. They were clearly in the back.

I hurried, walking around the house. When they came into view, I didn't announce my presence right away. Instead, I simply witnessed the scene in front of me.

Phoebe and Hannah were both laughing hard. Chase stood next to Hannah, shaking his head, but he was laughing too. Something in the way both women moved told me they'd had a bit to drink. Sure enough, there was an empty bottle of wine next to them.

"Hello, fam," I greeted.

Chase looked up. "Finally, you're here."

Phoebe turned around, her smile falling as her eyes went wide. She licked her lips before asking, "How did it go with Jude?" Then she tried to stand on her feet rather abruptly and swayed. In an instant, I was right next to her, steadying her with both hands.

"Babe, how much wine have you had?" I asked.

"Oh, a bit."

"You know what?" Hannah said, turning to Chase. "You and I should go inside and leave these two alone to talk things out."

"That's a good idea," Chase said.

Hannah stumbled a bit as she started to walk away. "Oops. I had a bit too much wine too."

Chase put an arm around her waist, leading her toward the house.

I was grateful to both of them for looking after my woman.

"I'm sorry for bailing tonight," I said in Hannah's direction.

"There wasn't too much to do," she replied. "Still, a phone call would have been nice."

"True," I admitted.

Hannah waved her hand as she added, "Doesn't matter. You're here now. All right, in we go."

Chase pushed the door open, and they both went inside.

The second the door closed, Phoebe asked, "How did things go? Is the investment moving forward?"

"Fuck the investment, Phoebe."

"No, it's important to you."

I cupped her face between my hands. "You know what else is important? The most important? You."

"Oh," she muttered. "So, you're not mad at me?"

"No. Fuck no. Why would I be mad?"

"Because this whole thing blew up in our faces because of me."

"It's not your fault. Even if it were, it wouldn't matter."

"But last night, you didn't even come to bed."

I blinked, realizing how that must have looked from her perspective. I cleared my throat. "Babe. I was just tossing and turning, and I knew I'd wake you up. That's why I slept in Jeremy's room."

"Ohhh, that makes sense."

"You've changed me in so many ways, Phoebe. Before meeting you, I would have done anything in my power to make sure the deal with Jude went forward. But tonight, I told him that I don't actually care about the deal so much, that I simply want our friendship."

Phoebe looked at me with soft eyes. "Griffin, really?"

"Yeah. And it's all on you, babe. But—" I laughed without humor. "—I have many, many faults, such as completely getting lost in my head when I'm focusing on an issue. It's not something I do consciously. But I will work on it."

Her eyes watered a bit. "Don't worry. I love you with all your faults."

That was music to my ears. I had no idea I actually needed her to say that. I was so into this woman, and she needed to know that right now.

"And I love you, Phoebe. With all I have. I can't promise that I'll do better next time. But no matter what, I don't want you to think I'm pushing you away. Why would you even think that I'm pulling away from you?"

She shrugged, swaying a bit. "I don't know. I guess I'm just used to being blamed for everything."

"I'd never do that. I worship you, Phoebe. Don't you know that?"

She giggled. "You're going to make me swoon. And I already have trouble keeping my balance!"

"Don't worry, I've got you."

"I know you do."

"Promise you'll never worry about this again."

"I'm going to try my very best. How about that?"

"Good enough," I said, then strengthened my grip on her, pulling her flush against me. "What do you say about going home?"

She flashed me a grin, putting her hands on my shoulders. "I thought you'd never suggest that. I've been fighting the urge, but I'm running out of willpower."

"What urge?" I asked.

"To jump your bones… or your cock."

I started to laugh as my cock twitched. She was more than a bit tipsy. She was adorable.

"Let's go to the car," I said.

"Should we say goodbye to Hannah and Chase?"

"Oh, yeah. I had completely forgotten about them," I admitted.

"That's not possible."

"I told you, you have that effect on me, Phoebe."

We went toward the house, but before I even had a chance to knock, the door swung open. Hannah was grinning, and Chase shook his head.

"Have you two been spying on us?" Phoebe asked. If I didn't know before that she was tipsy, now I would have been sure of it.

"Oh, not really," Hannah said. "We just kept an eye on you from the window."

"Babe, you were completely spying," Chase stated.

"Hey, if I was spying, then so were you."

"No, I was simply next to you."

"Uh-huh. Keep telling yourself that, Chase."

"Right," I said. "Well, thank you for looking after her tonight. We're going to go."

"It was our pleasure. I can't wait to see you again tomorrow and meet your parents, Phoebe," Hannah said.

Phoebe leaned in, hugging Hannah. "Thanks a lot for everything."

I was happy that my woman was so at ease around the family.

Gently steering Phoebe toward the car, I opened the door and helped her in by the ass.

Yeah, no question. Phoebe was the woman for me.

CHAPTER 36
GRIFFIN

ONCE WE WERE in the car, she talked my ear off about the marshmallows she had tonight.

I liked that she was such a chatterbox. Even though I'd been dead tired the whole day, I was feeling very refreshed now.

We arrived in a matter of minutes, and she smiled, looking up at the house. "I'm so happy that you live so close to the inn. Means I can visit Hannah often."

"Anytime you want, babe." I got out of the car, and she did at the same time, practically jumping out of it. She swayed, then straightened up.

"Phoebe, you should have waited for me," I said, hurrying toward her.

"I'm good. I'm good. Crap, I'm not. I ate a lot. I'm not even sure why I'm tipsy. Oh," she said, as if she'd just remembered, "I didn't actually eat the rest of the day."

"Why not?" I asked as we went into the house.

"I don't know. I guess I was too nervous."

Fucking hell, I'd made her stress so much that she forgot to eat? That wasn't good. Phoebe never forgot to eat. It was one of her pleasures in life.

As soon as we stepped inside, I plastered her against the

front door, drawing my fingers up and down her cheek. "Phoebe, tell me what I can do so you never stress out like that again."

She smiled, putting both hands around my neck. "I guess you could let me spoil you when you have a tough evening. You know, just kiss you here and there, hang around you."

"I can do that," I said.

"But I'll work on myself so I'm not a scaredy cat all the time."

"You're fucking not. You're one of the strongest people I know. I love you so damn much." I wanted to tell her more things, but I couldn't find the right words at the moment. I needed to kiss and touch her too badly.

I kissed her so hard that I pushed her flat against the door, one hand at the back of her head so she wouldn't get hurt. I would spend my whole life proving to this woman just how important she was to me. And I'd never tire of it. Quite the opposite—it would be my honor.

I tangled our tongues, deepening the kiss. I was so hungry for her, it was as if a physical ache took over my body. I didn't just need a release. I needed *her.* She tasted like marshmallows, and I fucking loved it.

Without giving her any warning, I lifted her over my shoulder.

She shrieked. "Oh my God, what are you doing?"

"I figured this is the fastest way to get you to the bedroom." I walked upstairs with her.

I actually liked this angle. She patted my buttocks with her palms, making me laugh. Then she squeezed them before patting them again, now actually moving to a rhythm.

"What are you doing?" I asked.

"Using them as drums. Hey, they sound cool."

This woman is something else.

When we reached the bedroom, I carefully put her down.

She pouted. "Why did you interrupt me? I was thoroughly enjoying myself."

"I want you, Phoebe. I need you so damn badly." I tilted her chin up, then kissed her lips.

I dragged my mouth down the column of her neck, slowly feeling each of her inhales and exhales. It was exquisite. I'd barely made it to her collarbone when her skin turned sensitive. She had goose bumps on her arms. How could she react so deliciously simply because I was kissing her neck?

I bunched her dress in one fist and then pulled it over her head, feeling her muscles contract beneath my touch. Her entire body was preparing for pleasure—bracing itself. As it should, because I was going to rock her world tonight.

The room was dimly lit. The only source was from the night-light under the bed, but that was more than enough. I wanted to get my own clothes out of the way too. Tonight, I wanted as much skin-on-skin contact as possible. I needed to get lost in her, for our bodies to move and feel as one.

I tugged at the bottom of my shirt. At the same time, she yanked my belt away.

"You want me naked," I stated.

"What gave you that idea?" she murmured in a teasing voice.

While I was quickly undoing the buttons of my shirt, she took her time, pushing my pants under my ass. I stepped out of them immediately.

"Hey, why are you in a hurry?" she teased again while tugging at my boxers.

She gripped my cock in her fist, pushing down the boxers with her other hand. Then I felt the flat of her tongue on my crown. I dropped my head back as a groan tore through my chest, a shock of pleasure coursing through me. It was completely unexpected, and I hadn't braced for it at all. I swung my hips forward, and she immediately took her hand away and slid her mouth down my erection.

"Fuck, Phoebe," I exclaimed.

She looked decadent in the dim light, on her knees, moving one hand up and down between her thighs.

"Sit on the bed, babe."

Licking her lips, she pushed herself up on her haunches and then sat right at the edge. But as I kneeled in front of her, I had another idea. I sat next to her instead and pulled her onto my lap so her back was to me. I could see our reflection in the mirror across the room. She gasped when she noticed it.

I kissed her shoulder blade, smiling against her skin as I trailed my fingers on her inner thighs.

"Spread even wider for me, Phoebe."

She opened her legs, and they dangled on the outside of mine.

"Oh, Griffin," she murmured.

I inched closer to her pussy and pressed two fingers against her opening—just on her folds, without touching her clit. She cried out, dropping her head back.

"No, I want you to watch," I whispered in her ear. A tremor shook her, but she straightened up, keeping her eyes focused on my hand in the mirror. "That's it. Follow my commands, beautiful, and I promise you'll come."

"And if I don't?" she asked in a shy voice.

"I'll prolong this and torture you."

She kept her eyes in place as I started to rub little circles around her clit. Her body jerked, and she pressed her thighs together. On instinct, I stopped moving.

"Keep them wide open for me, babe," I instructed.

She drew in a sharp breath, but instead of opening them, she pressed her knees together.

I still wasn't touching her clit.

She groaned in protest. "Don't stop please," she begged.

Fuck. I could resist many things in this life, but not the sound of Phoebe begging for me.

Still, I waited until she parted her legs before touching her again. This time, when I brushed her clit, she buckled forward, shoulders hunched. Her eyes were fixed on my hand. She was slick now—so slick, in fact, that I could slide inside her and she'd be able to take me.

But I wasn't going to give her my cock yet. Instead, I alternated between circling her clit and sliding one finger inside her. I watched her face and body intently, moving my hand enough to bring her pleasure but not too much. I didn't want to overwhelm her. With my other hand, I kept touching her breasts. Her nipples were already hard.

I took my hand away from between her legs and instead positioned my cock so the length of it rubbed her entrance. Then I moved my hips, slowly rolling them back and forth, as I rested my mouth on her shoulder, groaning against her skin. I felt her slick pussy against the length of my cock. It was even more of a torture than I'd imagined.

"Oh my God, Griffin. Yes. Please, please, please," she chanted. Then she rolled her hips, too, rubbing herself against my cock.

I stilled, letting her take over, moving at the rhythm she wanted. Only the tip of the crown was nudging her clit, but it was enough. She climaxed seconds later, and I watched her transform in the mirror.

Her chest expanded as she threw her shoulders back. She bent her right leg and then straightened it abruptly. Her whole body was surrendering to the sensations. When her breathing regained a normal rhythm, she opened her eyes.

"Look in the mirror," I commanded, and she fixed her gaze on us again. Then I slid inside her.

Now I was the one breaking my own rule. I closed my eyes firmly shut, breathing in deeply through my nose. I needed to center myself for a bit so I didn't immediately lose myself. I wanted to prolong this as much as possible.

"Oh God, Griffin," she murmured.

I sat completely still. Even so, the pleasure was overwhelming for both of us. Then I opened my eyes and rolled my hips. The orgasm had taken a lot from her; she didn't have as much energy as a few minutes ago. Her entire body was soft, but from the way she clenched around my cock, I knew she was even more sensitive than before. She shuddered every time I touched her clit.

I watched, transfixed, as my cock slid in and out of her while I kissed her back and neck. I wanted to devour this woman every way possible and become one with her. I needed my release. But at the same time, I didn't want this to end. I was close, but I didn't want to give in before I knew she was close too.

I pounded her so damn hard that the sounds of our bodies colliding filled the room. And yet I needed more freedom to move. I put my hand on her pelvis and stilled.

"I need you in another position, love."

She gasped and then moaned, "No, please."

"I'll give you my cock right back. Don't worry," I said, sliding out of her.

I pushed her to her feet and then rose too. Still holding her by the hips, I turned us around so she was now facing the wall.

"Just lean over and put your palms on the wall. Stand on your tiptoes."

She'd love this angle. I slid inside her the second she bent forward. She lost her balance for a split second, but I held her firmly.

Then I moved ferociously, thrusting in and out of her while I pressed two fingers against her clit. I was kissing the expanse of her back, feeling every muscle contract. Only when I heard her muffled scream did I realize she was biting her own arm.

"I want to hear you. There's no one here who can overhear us. Scream the walls down."

She dropped her arm, and her guttural cries filled the room. And I was lost to this woman. One second, I was focusing on her pleasure, listening to her release; the next, my body was on fire. I slowed down because I wanted to feel the way her muscles spasmed around me.

I didn't want to rush her with my orgasm. But then I didn't have a choice anymore because it slammed right into me without warning. I cried out right along with Phoebe.

Once we'd both ridden out our climaxes, I led her to the bed. She immediately lay down.

Her head was turned, one cheek pressed to the mattress, the other exposed to me. I kissed it softly without saying a word.

I'd spend my whole life bringing this woman pleasure and happiness, and it still wouldn't be long enough.

CHAPTER 37
PHOEBE

"DO YOU SEE THEM?" Griffin asked me.

I stood on my toes, shifting my weight from one leg to the other, trying to glance above the sea of people.

"No. Not yet," I murmured.

My parents' flight had landed thirty minutes ago. They were going to come out any second now, and I was beyond excited. Griffin was just behind me, one hand on my back, rubbing it up and down slowly. He was carrying a huge bouquet of flowers for Mom. It would make her day.

A few seconds later, I spotted Mom's trademark curly red hair and Dad's black-rimmed glasses.

I waved at them and then broke into a run. Griffin was right behind me. My parents beamed when they saw me. I hadn't told them Griffin was coming. Dad jerked his head back slightly but smiled. Mom fell for him hook, line, and sinker. I could tell that by the way her eyes turned dreamy the second she noticed the flowers.

"Mom, Dad, hi!" I hugged both of them at the same time. I loved a "family sandwich," as we called it. I'd been very huggy as a kid, and nothing had changed once I became an adult.

"And you must be Griffin," Dad said as we stepped farther away from the arrivals area.

"Yes, sir. Nice to meet you."

"I'm Joseph," Dad said, shaking Griffin's hand. "And this is—"

"Marjorie," Mom finished.

"These are for you," Griffin said.

Mom took them from him with a sigh, then looked me up and down before giving me a little nod. "It's very kind of you to come pick us up from the airport. You shouldn't have done it. We know how to come to the city."

"Nonsense. It was no trouble at all," Griffin assured her. "Are you ready to go to the car?"

"Yes," they both said at the same time.

They told us about the flight as we went to the parking lot.

Mom smiled at me. "Your grandparents send you many, many hugs."

I felt a dull ache in my chest. "I promise I'll go see them soon."

"Nana sent you cookies."

Yes, yes, yes! Nana made *the best* cookies.

Griffin took the suitcases from Dad, rolling them all the way to the car and then loading them into the trunk.

"So, tell me again where we're staying," Mom inquired. "I didn't quite get it. We could have stayed at the B&B where we usually go. You didn't have to spend money on us."

"We're not," I replied.

"My sister-in-law owns an inn," Griffin explained, speeding out of the airport. "And she's got some free rooms right now because it's not peak season. It's not a problem for her to have you. She's quite excited about it."

"If she's sure!"

I nodded. "She is."

"Darling, tell us about your job," Dad exclaimed.

For the rest of the drive, I spoke about my assignments and colleagues. Then they asked Griffin about what he did, and he summed it up nicely. My man was extremely busy, especially since he and his brothers were still working on getting the winery business off the ground. Maybe it was a good thing that he'd decided not to move forward with investing in Jude's business after all.

Jude called earlier this morning, telling Griffin that he could still be in the running as an investor. But Griffin told him that he was more than happy with pulling out of it. They were currently planning a boating trip for us all.

As we drove through the gates of the inn, Mom sighed, looking around the property. "This place is amazing."

Duncan's car was in the yard as well, next to Chase's.

Did Hannah tell me yesterday that Duncan, Riley, and Jeremy were stopping by today? It was possible. Last night was a bit of a blur. All I could remember was this amazing man showing up and whisking me to our house, then doing delicious things to me. But everything else was fuzzy at best.

We quickly got out of the car, and Griffin carried the bags inside. I stood back with my parents, taking each of their arms and walking together with them. They could be a bit shy at social occasions.

Mom leaned into me, whispering conspiratorially, "I like Griffin."

"You're easily bought, woman," Dad said, nodding toward the flowers.

She glanced at him. "You like him too."

"Oh, I do. But it has nothing to do with flowers. He makes my little girl happy." Dad smiled wider than I'd ever seen him. "It's good to see you like this, baby girl. We never had the heart to tell you, but we were relieved when you and that asshole broke up."

I was shocked by Dad's admission. He was never so direct and rarely used the word *asshole*.

"Of course, we wished it would have happened in a more civilized manner," he added.

"It's all in the past now." I'd said this before to appease them, but now it was 100 percent true. My heart wasn't heavy anymore. I didn't have a knot in my stomach when thinking about that time. I'd healed. I never thought this day would come, but here it was. I was head over heels in love with Griffin, and the past didn't even matter anymore.

"Uncle Griffin, I'm so happy you're here." Jeremy's voice filtered from the house, and I instantly smiled.

"Is that Griffin's nephew with the Batman room?" Mom asked as we approached the front door.

"Exactly." I loved that Mom remembered that tidbit.

"By the way, he's got your grandparents' vote."

And now I wasn't just happy, I was ecstatic. My grandparents approved of him. I honestly couldn't wait for them to meet him.

We headed straight to the kitchen, where Hannah, Chase, Riley, Duncan, and Jeremy were gathered. Griffin wasn't here. He'd probably gone directly to the bedroom to deposit my parents' bag.

"Hi, I'm Hannah. Welcome to my inn." She held out her hand to each of my parents in turn.

"It's lovely. Thank you so much for having us," Mom said.

"We're very grateful," Dad added.

Hannah beamed. "Let me show you to your room."

"I can show them myself," I chimed in.

"All right." Hannah smiled. "While you get comfortable, I'll prepare breakfast for you."

"There's no need," Mom replied quickly. "We ate at the airport before we left Montana. Do you want something?" she asked me.

"No. I've had breakfast too." Besides, I knew Mom brought Nana's cookies. I wanted to work up an appetite before I dug into them so I fully enjoyed every bite.

I went over to Jeremy, giving him a proper hug. "I didn't know you were going to be here," I told him.

"We just decided this morning," Duncan explained.

"And we're not staying for long," Riley added.

"What are you doing today?" I asked.

"We're going to the fair. My favorite band is playing," Jeremy informed me.

"It's on Niagara Avenue," Riley went on. "Just a mix of vendors selling stuff and entertainment for kids."

"That sounds lovely," Mom said. "Could we go too? We miss San Diego fairs."

"Why not?" I asked.

"Why not what?" Griffin said, appearing in the kitchen.

"Uncle Griffin!" Jeremy exclaimed. "You can come to the fair with us. Phoebe said yes."

I chuckled. The little guy sure knew how to negotiate.

"My parents would like to go too," I added.

"Sure, we're flexible," Griffin said.

"Great! Mom, Dad, come on, I'll show you to your room."

"Do you want to rest before leaving?" Griffin asked.

"No," Mom replied. "The journey wasn't too long. And we're not that old."

Griffin gave me a panicked look, and I laughed. "No one was suggesting that, Mom. Come on, follow me." I went through the narrow corridor leading to the downstairs bedroom.

Mom stopped at the foot of the staircase, looking up longingly.

"I love Queen Anne buildings," she said.

"I know. And this one is gorgeous."

Griffin had put their suitcases by the door.

"This is so spacious," Mom said.

"We only need about ten minutes to freshen up, and then we'll be right out," Dad added.

"I'll wait for you in the kitchen. Are you sure you don't want to snack or anything?" I said.

Dad shook his head. "Not at all."

"Speaking of snacks...," Mom said, hurrying to the suitcase. She opened it, taking a Tupperware box from between the clothes. "Here are the cookies."

I immediately grabbed the box from her. My stomach rumbled. "Will you look at that? I wasn't even hungry. Thanks, Mom."

I opened the lid as soon as I stepped into the corridor, munching on one cookie while standing there in the hallway. I closed my eyes and got transported right back to my childhood. Nana loved to bake in the summer. She typically also made a delicious grapefruit lemonade. No one else I knew loved grapefruit, but she and I did.

With a sigh, I opened my eyes and headed to the kitchen. "I've got cookies for everyone, homemade by my nana."

Everyone reached for the Tupperware as soon as I put it on the table.

"You know what? Let me take a pic, and I'll send it to Nana." Well, to my granddad. My grandma wasn't terribly good with her phone. But Granddad was quite good at using WhatsApp. "All of you smile and hold up a cookie." I said, and they did. "And, Griffin, can you stand a bit taller? Just so, you know..."

"You stand out," Chase teased. "Yeah, good thinking."

"Hey, you know what? I've got an even better idea," Duncan added. "What if he's the only one who holds up a cookie? That should earn him points, right?"

I looked over the phone at the group.

"That is a great idea," Chase said. "Little bro needs to earn all the points he can."

"Come on, everyone hold up a cookie," Griffin said on a laugh.

I snapped a pic and immediately sent it to Granddad.

Phoebe: Thank you for the cookies. Everyone is loving them. Love you. P.S. That's Griffin in the middle.

"These are very good," Jeremy said, immediately grabbing a second one, even though we hadn't even finished the first one.

"I've got the recipe. We can bake together when you come over."

Jeremy looked at me like I'd hung the moon. Oh, kids were adorable like that. I longed for a tiny bundle of joy.

Griffin was looking at me with an expression unlike anything I'd seen before. I wondered what he was thinking about as we all munched on the cookies. Everyone wanted coffee, too, because it went perfectly with treats, so Hannah started the machine.

Griffin came over to me, pushing my hair to one side. "You smell amazing," he murmured.

I blushed and immediately looked at everyone around the table, but they couldn't hear us past the noise of the coffee machine.

"What were you thinking about earlier?" I asked him.

"That you're good with kids. I can't wait for us to have some of our own."

All I wanted was to turn around and kiss this man thoroughly. Maybe I could steal him and take him to one of the rooms upstairs. What were the chances anyone would notice?

That would be 100 percent.

Phoebe, get yourself together.

I didn't even turn around because I'd risk forgetting my good manners and kiss him senseless. But to show my appreciation for his super-romantic statement, I shimmied my hips a bit.

Griffin tightened his grip on my waist.

Oops. Maybe I shouldn't do that. I'd pressed my ass into the zipper of his jeans just a bit. He didn't have a hard-on yet, but I didn't want to push my luck. My man could go from zero to hard in seconds, and that wouldn't do.

I ate another cookie, chatting with the group until my parents came back.

"We're ready," Mom exclaimed.

"Are you coming too?" I asked Hannah and Chase

"No, I need to sort out some things in the attic," Hannah replied.

"And I'm staying to help," Chase said.

They were so sweet together. I was so happy that Chase was supporting Hannah in all her endeavors. Then again, the Sterling men were like that—loyal, supportive, strong.

"Then let's get going," Duncan said with urgency.

"Duncan, I'm sure we're going to find parking spots," Riley said, but she didn't sound convinced. Parking at fairs wasn't for the fainthearted.

"I want to compliment you on this beautiful home again," Mom told Hannah.

"Thank you. It belonged to my grandmother, and I'm very happy that I got to keep it and continue to run it as an inn."

Mom beamed. "You've done a great job."

Hannah lit up. "Thank you."

We all bid her and Chase goodbye before heading to the cars.

The drive to Niagara Street didn't last long, or at least that's how it seemed to me. Time flew by whenever Mom and Dad visited. As we approached the allotted parking lots, I realized we were already late.

"Why are there so many people here? It's only eleven o'clock in the morning," Griffin exclaimed.

"They've got activities for kids, right? People with kids prefer mornings," Mom said.

That made sense.

We went into two lots that were chock-full before finding a spot in the third one.

"I miss San Diego," Mom said after we all stepped out of the car.

It was on the tip of my tongue to suggest that they move back, but I didn't. I needed my parents, but my grandparents needed them even more, and it wasn't fair for me to make them feel guilty.

"You can come visit us anytime you want," Griffin offered as we headed toward the entrance of the fair. Duncan was probably already there because they'd found a parking spot in the previous lot. "You can stay with us or at Hannah's."

I instantly saw Dad's expression change, and I knew that had sealed the deal for him. Griffin was in his good books forever. Dad appreciated generosity just as much as kindness.

At the entrance, we noticed the trio waiting for us. Jeremy waved with both hands, as if he was afraid that we wouldn't see them.

"All right, what's the plan?" Griffin asked.

"The band doesn't start until noon," Jeremy said. Duncan had a stern expression. Riley was clearly fighting laughter. I suspected neither of them was looking forward to listening to the band, but they were doing it for Jeremy's sake. "We can head to one of those shooting venues where you can win a prize while we wait."

"Yes, let's do that," I said. "I haven't done it since I was a kid. I was never any good at it."

"Don't worry, babe. I'm good at it," Griffin said with a devastatingly handsome smile. "I'll win something for you."

"I look forward to that."

He offered me his arm, and I wrapped mine around it, resting my chin on his bicep as we walked. I was smiling from ear to ear. This was a very happy day. I was here with my parents and Griffin and Jeremy, just enjoying life. It really couldn't get more amazing.

We found the shooting range quickly enough Honestly, I hadn't even realized they were still a thing. Granted, it wasn't exactly a shooting range. You just threw hoops at a target, and if they landed on top of it, you earned a point.

"Are all of you playing?" the guy manning the counter asked.

"Oh no, my husband and I are staying out of it," Mom said.

"I'm not playing either," I said, and Riley also shook her head.

"I want to throw," Jeremy declared.

Jeremy, Duncan, and Griffin took their positions, and the vendor explained the rules briefly. They were very simple: each participant had five hoops. If they could throw three on target, they could choose a gift accordingly. If they hit the target on more than three occasions, they could choose a bigger prize.

The ones on the first shelf were so small that I couldn't even tell what they were from where we were standing. The gifts got bigger and bigger on the upper shelves. The ones on top were huge teddy bears. I was secretly crossing my fingers for one of those. I'd probably look ridiculous carrying it around, but I couldn't care less.

It was fun watching the boys play. During the first three rounds, no one threw a hoop even close to the target.

Griffin let out a groan of frustration. I pressed my lips together, biting down the impulse to make fun of him. Nope, I was determined to support my man, even in small things like this.

"I'm sure you'll do better next time," I said.

He winked at me as all three of them decided to keep going. Which was probably how the owner could afford buying all the prizes in the first place. People kept paying for more rounds, hoping to win.

This time, Griffin changed his throwing position. He took a step back and angled his shoulders, bending his knees. He looked like he was preparing to break into a run. Somehow, it worked. He landed one ring and then another one. Duncan and Jeremy watched in awe.

After the third reached the target, I was absolutely ecstatic. I'd already narrowed my eyes, looking at the gifts on the lowest shelf. I still couldn't see anything. Then I focused on Griffin as he was prepping to throw the fourth one. Maybe he'd give me one of those huge teddy bears.

I kept both fingers crossed.

Aaaaand he missed.

I tried to suppress the pang of disappointment. I was still getting a gift, though. Griffin grumbled, but Jeremy was clapping, and so were my parents.

"All right, you're going to have to win something for Jeremy next," Duncan said. "I'm no good."

"Sure," Griffin agreed.

"All right, you're entitled to a prize from this shelf," the vendor said.

He sounded shocked. I wondered how many people actually managed to win anything.

"You can choose an item yourself, or a surprise one." He pointed at the ones that were wrapped in velvet bags. "There are several items inside, a true mixed bag. I thought up the concept myself." He pushed his chest forward, clearly pleased with himself, which made me laugh. But it did sound like a great idea.

"I'll have a mixed bag, then."

Jeremy made a beeline to us as the guy gave us one of the bags.

"Jeremy, this is not your gift," Riley said gently.

"I know, I just want to look. I'm allowed to look, right?"

"Of course you are," I said. I was planning to share my gifts with him anyway.

I immediately opened the bag and took out several items. One small car—Jeremy was ecstatic, so I gave that to him. Next was a silvery bracelet with stars and things. That was cute. The last item was a… *Is that a Ring Pop?*

"Wow, I didn't even know these still existed," I said. "I *so* loved them as a kid."

This one was berry-flavored, according to the package.

"I know, I tracked down a factory that still produces them." The guy was good. He'd pegged the nostalgia vibe perfectly.

"I can never open these things," I said, tearing at the plastic with all my might.

"I'll do it for you," Griffin said.

He took it from me and tugged lightly at the package. It opened easily.

I took out the ring proudly and held my hand out to him. "Put that on me."

The Ring Pop was in the shape of a huge red ruby. I felt like I was a high school girl again.

Griffin looked at me with a twinkle in his eye. "In a second."

He leaned in, giving me a quick peck on the cheek.

Huh? What was that for? Not that I ever minded him kissing me, but his expression was a bit strange. Then he took a large step back, still holding my Ring Pop.

"What is Uncle… Oh!" Jeremy stopped talking as Griffin lowered himself to one knee.

I swooned as my face exploded in a grin.

"Oh goodness," Mom whispered behind me.

"Phoebe, I know this is unusual. But then again, everything about our relationship has been like that. Impulsive. Crazy. Whirlwind."

I stepped a bit closer to him, putting both hands on my belly to try to stop them from shaking.

"I promise I will buy you an actual ring. But today, here with your parents by our side, I would love to ask you to be my wife. Nothing would make me happier than to know you're mine forever. That we're together in this wild ride called life. To face everything together. Always."

Oh my God, how did he come up with this? There was no way he'd thought about this speech before, and yet it was utterly perfect.

"I accept. Of course I accept. I love the ring, by the way."

Griffin chuckled, but it got stuck in his throat. Then he tried to clear it. He blinked slowly. When he opened his eyes again, I noticed they were a bit glassy.

"I love you so damn much, Phoebe," he said while putting on the ring.

"I love you too," I whispered.

He kissed me again chastely. I kissed him right back until I felt the ring slip back down my finger. I gasped, jumping back from the kiss.

"Whoops. I saved it," I said, holding the ring between my forefinger and thumb. I didn't want to risk losing it, and I wasn't going to eat it either. I was going to keep this forever and ever.

"Congratulations, dear," Mom said. She hugged me as Dad shook hands with Griffin.

"Son, this was unexpected."

"Sir, I'm sorry. I promise that I will formally ask you for her hand before I propose with a real ring."

"You have my approval anyway, but asking never hurts."

While Dad hugged me, I heard Jeremy ask Riley under his breath, "Why did Griffin give her a fake ring?"

"Because that's what he wanted. Maybe that's how he planned it," Duncan said.

"Well, that's not a very good plan, then, is it?" Jeremy asked, and we all burst out laughing. "I'm sorry I said that, Uncle Griffin."

Griffin grinned. "No, you're not, buddy. You're just sorry that I heard you. But don't worry, we still love you."

Jeremy's face lit up. "So, Phoebe, you're part of the family now?"

"Yes," Griffin replied instantly.

I was so blissfully happy, I couldn't even put it in words. I wanted to tell Griffin so many things, but we had to wait until we were alone.

Jeremy threw his arms around me, and I hugged him right back. Glancing at Mom, I realized she was barely holding back tears.

"Mom, did you take pictures to send to Nana?" I asked.

"No. I was too surprised."

"Doesn't matter," I said. "She'll be happy anyway."

"All right, then," Dad said.

"Uncle Griffin, are you still going to play and try to win something for me?" Jeremy asked, sounding a bit shy.

"Sure he is," I told him. "Now that he's already won something, luck is on his side."

"Really?" Jeremy asked.

I nodded. Oh yeah. As far as I was concerned, that's how luck worked.

"I'll pay for another round," Duncan told the vendor.

The guy was still looking at us, totally stunned. "This has never happened here. I'm going to buy more of those rings."

"You do that," I said.

"Although, I don't know many blokes who'd have the balls to propose with a fake ring." He'd said that more to himself than to us, but since Griffin and I were right next to him, we heard him loud and clear.

Griffin laughed, putting his mouth to my ear. "Well, that works for us, doesn't it?"

"Oh my God. Yes, it does. Fake ring for a fake start."

Our story really was crazy. I couldn't wait to tell it to our kids and grandkids one day. I'd always listened with rapt attention whenever Nana told me how she fell for my grandfather. Theirs was an epic love story. But so was ours.

"You know," Duncan said, "I owe you an apology. When the whole fake dating thing started, I thought, he can never go through with it. Wyatt would, but not Griffin."

"Thanks for the vote of confidence," Griffin replied with a laugh. I giggled. Somehow, I couldn't see Wyatt pulling off what we did. Then again, I didn't know him very well. But he was like all the Sterlings—determined and stubborn. One thing I was sure of: when he'd fall for someone, he'd fall hard.

"What can I say, I'm rarely wrong."

"Dad, don't distract him," Jeremy said.

As Griffin took his position to throw, Jeremy said loudly, "Phoebe, can you stay next to him to make sure he's lucky?"

Griffin laughed as I grinned, stepping as close as possible to him without being in his way.

"That's right, buddy," Griffin said. "She truly is my lucky charm. And she always will be."

Dear Reader, This is the end of Griffin's story. The series continues with Wyatt's story.

Preorder Midnight Kisses on my website laylahagen.com!

For a list of all books by USA Today Bestselling Author Layla Hagen, please visit laylahagen.com

You can join my READER GROUP on Facebook HERE.

For a list of all books by USA Today Bestselling Author Layla Hagen, please visit laylahagen.com

Printed in Dunstable, United Kingdom

78132663R00178